AROUND THE WORLD IN 50 YEARS

Adventurous Episodes in the Life of James Winchester

Michael Whyatt Brookes

ISBN-10: 1540477215
ISBN-13: 978-1540477217

**GATHER YE ROSEBUDS WHILE YE MAY,
OLD TIME IS STILL A FLYING:
AND THIS SAME FLOWER THAT SMILES
TODAY,
TOMORROW WILL BE DYING**

**'To the virgins to Make Much of Time' by
Robert Herrick 1591 – 1674**

James Winchester wastes some of this time earning a living as a pilot and aviation engineer. The rest he uses well, savouring all the Epicurean delights that come his way. His journey takes him to a series of exotic locations around the world from a Roman amphitheatre in Cyprus to a down-town night club in Hong Kong. It embraces, from the 1950s to the new millennium, a kaleidoscope of exhilarating, romantic and sometimes downright risqué situations. His friends describe him as an amiable gentleman with a touch of raffishness. His enemies use the word 'rake'. Perhaps the truth lies somewhere in between.....

CONTENTS

Page

PROLOGUE - 1954

Professor David Winchester and his wife Lydia had just settled down to watch 'The Good Old Days' on their newly-acquired black and white television when the doorbell rang.

'Oh blast,' said David. 'Who on earth can that be at this time of night?'

'Well I hope it's our son! Had you forgotten that James is on half term holiday from Gresham's this week? He's been round at Jennifer Penfold's showing her his stamp collection.' Jennifer was the only daughter of the Reverend Cyril Penfold - vicar of St Luke's Church in Alderley Edge - and of his wife Penelope.

'Oh yes of course, I'd forgotten,' said David, getting up and moving quickly to the door, not wishing to miss any of the programme.

Lydia heard her husband open the door in the hall and was then surprised to hear the excited tones of the Reverend himself. As the two men entered the room, shepherded in by her husband, she noticed that the vicar's towering pate, normally a symbol of rectitude and sanctity in its gleaming whiteness, was now positively glistening with perspiration.

There were no introductions, since Cyril Penfold was well known to the Winchester family. In any case there was clearly some matter of importance and urgency that overrode normal formalities.

'I'm afraid,' announced David hesitatingly, 'it seems that James has been showing Jennifer rather more than his stamp collection.

'What do mean?' enquired Lydia with a note of alarm in her voice. 'Is he all right?'

'That depends on your point of view,' responded David. 'The fact is that Penelope has just discovered the two of them in bed together.

'Oh My God!' shrieked Lydia, turning to Cyril. 'How did you manage to let them do that? And in the vicarage!'

'We didn't let them do that as you put it,' said the vicar indignantly. 'We said good night to your son James but after we'd closed the door he apparently climbed in through her bedroom window. Penelope discovered him there when she later went up to take Jennifer a cup of Ovaltine. Penelope's furious and wants me to call the police to have him locked up.'

David took control of the situation, inviting Cyril to sit down and pouring all of them a glass of brandy. 'I'm not clear how James managed to climb up the outside wall of the vicarage. It's quite a height.'

'Well,' explained Cyril, now visibly more relaxed with a drink in his hand. 'It seems that they'd pre-positioned a rope tied to the foot of Jennifer's bed and with that thrown out of the window, and with the aid of a drain pipe, he was able to scramble up.'

At this point David was quite impressed by his son's initiative and daring but didn't feel it appropriate to say so. Instead he offered a more pragmatic suggestion.

'You know, Cyril, I can understand the distress you and Penelope feel, and I apologise for my son's behaviour, but I'm sure that on reflection she will not wish to contact the police or indeed tell anyone else. The fact is that Jennifer is seventeen, and therefore over the age of consent, while James is not yet quite sixteen and therefore, legally, a minor. If we add the fact that Jennifer connived in the arrangement and supplied the rope, an outsider might question who had been seducing whom'. David's grasp of grammatical accuracy did not desert him even in times of stress. 'In any case, apart from the culprits themselves only we as parents know anything about the matter and I'm sure you would not wish to have the story spread further.'

Cyril saw the wisdom in this but now voiced his concern about the possibility of his daughter being pregnant. David thought this unlikely. For all his son's faults, lack of savoir faire did not seem to be one of them. Eventually, they all agreed that a good dressing down was the only sanction that could sensibly be applied. Cyril would return, pacify his wife, and send James back home.

'You know, David, I really don't know what we're going to do with him,' said Lydia after a chastened Cyril had left. 'Two years ago we had that embarrassment in church after he'd changed all the hymn numbers. Then he was brought home by the police for driving one of your cars down the High Street. Only three months ago we had to go to Gresham's to hear how he'd started a betting shop in his dormitory. Now he's started deflowering all the maidens of Alderley Edge, starting with the vicar's daughter. This really is the limit. I don't know what will become of him.'

David was not at all assured that James had yet reached any kind of limit but that only added to his own uncertainty about his son's future. What indeed would become of him?...

EPISODE 1 - ON THE ROCKS (1956 - 1959)

Historical Context

To put James Winchester's personal escapades into some kind of historical context, here's a reminder of a few other more important incidents during this period.

__1956__ British and French forces invade Port Said on the Suez Canal.
__1957__ The Russians launch Sputnik I, the workers' uprising in Poland is crushed and Soviet troops reclaim Budapest
__1958__ The European Economic Community (Common Market) becomes effective and General Charles de Gaulle becomes French premier
__1959__ Castro takes over in Cuba

There were of course further examples of James' indiscreet behaviour during his schooling at Gresham's but somehow he managed to survive there, partly through sheer good luck in not being found out and partly through the patience and tolerance of the headmaster who saw something worthwhile in his character beyond a charming manner and a general *joie de vivre*. It has to be said that not everyone shared this view, perhaps least of all the school's local constabulary who were called out several times to incidents in which he seemed to be the common factor. In each situation his alibis were proof against suspicion.

On the other hand, if there were certain aspects to James' character and behaviour that gave rise to concern, there were other parts of his being that engendered admiration, particularly among the more junior boys at the school for whom James in time became something of a cult figure. He could play the trumpet with aplomb, he was a very strong member of the school's boxing team, and he was an accomplished artist. One might have added that he demonstrated considerable leadership qualities except that he frequently led others in what authority perceived to be the wrong direction.

Just before he reached the end of his time at Gresham's, but this time driving legally, he managed to overturn his car while driving too quickly round a bend but the subsequent breath analysis, avidly conducted by the local constabulary, proved negative and he was reluctantly released. Finally, on his very last day he was found to be splashing a little vodka into some of the younger boys'orange squash at the end of term party and was sent to the headmaster's study for what James later referred to as 'a final bollocking'. Thus it was that he left school but not before collecting, to everyone's surprise, three very creditable GCEs at 'A' Level and a place, starting in 1956, at Liverpool University to study aeronautical engineering.

He also pursued his long-standing interest in aviation by joining the University Air Squadron, which seemed a natural corollary to his studies. Perhaps less predictable was his enrolment in the University Rock Climbing Club, except that it gave added vent to his apparently insatiable desire for adventure. On reflection in later life, when looking down into his brief case could easily have induced a sense of vertigo, he couldn't for the life him think why he'd once been a member of a rock climbing club, but then young people often do strange things. In any case where would the world be if every one sat at home knitting woolly teddy bears?

He'd previously done some rambling in North Wales, the Lake District and the Derbyshire Peak District and discovered that he very much enjoyed spending time in mountainous countryside. His fondest early memory was that of a day out with his father in the Peak District. From their home in Alderley Edge they went by steam train to Edale in the Pennines.

The walk itself, from Edale to Chinley via Jacob's Ladder, was only about five miles but since James was eight at the time and since this was his first trip into mountains, it made a considerable impression on him. Following this introduction, he would later go during the summer holidays to the Peak District with a friend and explore the Winnats Pass near Mam Tor.

The Pass had a narrow, steep road that climbed up west of the village of Castleton, flanked on both sides by steeply rising chalk escarpments. At the bottom were the famous Blue John mines, open to the public, but for an impecunious and adventurous schoolboy those further up the Pass were a better option. These mines had been bored horizontally high up on the sides of the hills flanking the road and it was a stiff climb up either side. Once at the mouth of a cave they used to sit down to eat their sandwiches and watch the tiny cars below crawl up the Pass like beetles.

After lunch they would begin the serious business of exploring the caves by crawling and squirming through tiny passages and crevices by the light of bicycle torches and candles. In later years the thought of children doing anything so idiotic filled him with horror. However, these expeditions did provide an outlet for his sense of adventure and gave him a taste for mountains and climbing.

Walking and scrambling up mountains in Derbyshire was infinitely more exciting than apple scrumping in Cheshire orchards, one of the tamer alternatives. It was also infinitely better than gang warfare with air rifles, which had seemed an exciting and worthwhile pursuit until one boy lost an eye, an incident that brought home to James the fact that he was not immune from damage, although of course he was immune from death, which in any case was reserved for old people: well, old people that is apart from a boy at school called Alfred Pritchard, since Alfred had been run over by a coal lorry - but that was an exception that proved the rule.

Years later when he was in the sixth form, the headmaster and the head of English had taken several of the boys to the Lake District for a few days rambling and fell walking, which again served to feed Williams' love of mountains. This time he'd climbed Helvellyn, Skidaw, Scafell Pike and the Langdale Pikes and done some serious hiking; he'd learned a little about survival and map reading, nothing about rock climbing, and a few things about himself. One was that he very much enjoyed the camaraderie of these ventures and another was that it was all right to be cold, wet, tired and hungry provided one had a warm, secure base to get back to and the promise of a hearty meal. Later he was to add a few glasses of wine or beer to this requirement.

Joining the university rock-climbing club seemed a way of meeting at least some of his requirements. It would not apparently meet the need for feminine company, since there was only one girl in the Club and she appeared to be spoken for, but there were other avenues to explore to meet girls. One was to frequent the students' union, which was seething with feminine pulchritude, but there were also endless parties to attend.

A further possibility, which always gained the admiration of the girls, was to gain access to their hall of residence after hours. This involved scaling a high brick wall surmounted by spikes and then dashing across lawns which, according to rumour, were sometimes patrolled by vicious guard dogs. James had never actually encountered any such dogs on his night escapades and wondered if the rumour had been started

4

by a male student to enhance his reputation. To gain access to the building required cooperation from within but this was usually forthcoming, along with a biscuit, a cup of coffee, a kiss and perhaps even a furtive fondle. To James, bearing in mind his occasional full-blooded trysts with Jennifer, this seemed small recompense for the inconvenience endured but hope sprang eternal and the excitement of gaining elicit entry to the building, whilst of course not on a par with gaining entry to one of its inmates, was some compensation.

Excitement was also to be experienced at the Mecca dance hall across the Mersey at Birkenhead, particularly on a Wednesday evening when unattached and often married ladies came unaccompanied. In view of the age of the ladies concerned, often in their thirties, Wednesday was known to the students as 'Grab a Granny Night'. However in James's experience the 'grabbing' usually involved little more than a squeeze on the dance floor and this was hardly satisfactory for a young man of James's sexual precocity. His early adventures with Jennifer had not come to a sudden end with their discovery in flagrante by Penelope Penfold but had continued ever since in a spasmodic fashion dependant on his returns to Alderley from school and on the availability of suitable accommodation. As James on one occasion confided to a friend, but not to Jennifer, 'Faint heart never fucked fair lady'.

Thus it was that James came to rock climbing as a means of satisfying his lust for excitement as well as his liking for mountains and the outdoor life and so he duly turned up at an evening meeting in the students' union building one late November evening. Of course they were a mixed bunch, from the large and brawny to the small and slim but James thought he could detect another classification of his fellow beings, namely that of self-confidence. Some had an air of composure and self-assurance whatever their physical stature, exchanging a word here and there and sharing a comment or two as they circulated before the meeting started. These were clearly old hands who actually had some experience of rock climbing. Others, like he himself, presented rather insular figures looking around anxiously for human contact but knowing no one there or anything about the task in hand.

The meeting was opened by the Chairman, an older student whom James believed he recognized as a chap studying medicine in his fourth year. He was tall, rugged and direct in his manner and fitted perfectly James' concept of a rock climber, although later he came to realise that good rock climbers came in all shapes and sizes.

The Chairman introduced himself as Bob Fletcher, welcomed new recruits to the club in a friendly manner and explained that the purpose of the meeting was to outline forthcoming activities and for the committee, who sat round a table at the front, to field any questions. For the benefit of new members he introduced an elderly man as Hamish McLeod, President of the Club. Hamish was a distinguished looking man, probably in his seventies, and James couldn't imagine that he played much of an active role in the Club. However, with his white hair and moustache and senatorial features he looked every inch a president and probably had a few tales to tell.

Among other matters discussed was the next trip in ten days' time to Langdale in the Lake District and James put the details in his diary, determined to get into his new hobby as soon as possible. The Club had reserved some cottages in the Langdale Valley and a coach would leave the University Victoria Building at the top of Brownlow Hill at 4pm on the Friday afternoon.

Over the following ten days, James bought a few items that he thought he might need but in truth he wasn't exactly sure what to buy. He settled for a rucksack, a pair of stout trousers, a pair of rubber soled boots from the Army and Navy Store, sweaters and gloves. It never occurred to him to seek advice on what to buy, since he'd always had a tendency simply to do what he thought was appropriate, and he had no qualms about what he was getting into since he'd always seemed to cope quite well in the past in different situations. Others might say that he was impetuous and tended to learn the hard way.

So it was that on a wet Friday evening early in December James joined about thirty other Club members in boarding the coach for Langdale, along with rucksacks, a great number of neatly coiled ropes, bags of equipment and numerous crates of beer. James found a seat and had no sooner sat down than Bob Fletcher spotted him and sat down next to him. In the seat in front of them were Hamish McLeod and Charlotte Harrison, the only girl in the Club.

James learned much about the Club from Bob in their journey up to the Lakes, although hearing was sometimes difficult against a background of obscene songs such as 'The Engineer's Dream', 'Ivan Scavinsky Scavar', 'Poor Little Angeline' and 'When Lady Jane became a Tart'; someone even recited the whole of Eskimo Nell. Hamish and Charlotte appeared oblivious to the row, the latter even through a raucous rendering of 'Charlotte the harlot, the cowpunchers' whore'.

Despite James' sometimes unconventional and forthright approach to life, he was not familiar with these songs and was a little surprised at his own reactions to them. He had to admit that they were sometimes genuinely funny and sometimes clever in their use of words. At the same time he felt somewhat uneasy about such a blatantly open use of obscenities, particularly in the presence of a woman. For him women, love and romance were exciting, fulfilling and admirable; they were not something to be mocked and derided. He noticed one particular student who seemed to be taking a prominent part in the singing. He was loud and unkempt and although large and strong in appearance he was already showing signs of a paunch. James's first impression was not favourable.

They finally reached their destination, a series of stone huts on an estate with four beds to each room, but stayed long enough only to claim their beds and drop their bags before heading for a local pub for dinner. Fish and chips seemed to be the order of the day, washed down of course with several pints of real ale. The beer helped later to distract from the discomfort of the hard beds.

There was much talk over breakfast the following day about which climbs would be undertaken and by whom and plans were subsequently formalised in a meeting immediately afterwards. James saw Bob Fletcher talking to someone who then came over to introduce himself.

'Hello James. I'm John Davidson, Club Secretary. Bob tells me you're new and suggests we might climb together today, if that's all right with you? I thought we might try Napes Needle on Great Gable'.

It was fine with James, who'd seen John at the meeting and liked the look of him. He'd no idea what Napes Needle was and so readily agreed. He also liked the idea of climbing with just one other person since it seemed more private and at this very early stage of his rock climbing he was not anxious to reveal his lack of ability to a large audience.

The coach did a tour of various focal points and dropped James and John off at Wasdale car park, a one hour's hike from the Needle. They had plenty of time to talk, initially about life at the University, before they arrived at the subject of rock climbing. As John established that James had not previously climbed Napes Needle, and then that he had not climbed anything comparable, and finally that he hadn't actually done any rock climbing before, he became increasingly concerned.

'I understood from Bob that you had quite a bit of experience but in fact you haven't got any and we're heading for a climb that's classified in the 'severe' category. Do you in fact have any idea of what that means?'

'In rough terms I gather that climbs are classified as 'easy', 'moderate', 'difficult' and 'severe'.

'In rough terms you're correct. How did Bob get the idea that you have previous experience?'

'Well I can only imagine he assumed it. We did speak about mountaineering and I have done a fair amount of that in the past'.

'Well that's very nice for you but it won't help you very much on a 'severe' climb. In future I suggest you make your level of competence absolutely clear. This is a potentially dangerous sport and we need to exercise great care at all times and to be absolutely honest in our approach. I suppose we could go back but the bus won't be returning for several hours and so we'd have to spend much of the time in Wasdale. On the other hand we could try something on Great Gable itself near to the Needle and at least that way you could start to do a little easy climbing and also have a look at the Needle itself'.

James felt duly chastised and was reminded of his final 'bollocking' from his headmaster. The reprimand had been polite, clear, to the point and fully warranted. He'd just had his first lesson in rock climbing without actually getting onto a rock and he wasn't going to forget it.

An hour or so later he had his first view of the Needle and he was impressed. It stood out from Great Gable like a huge phallic symbol and he guessed it to be about 100 feet tall. He could imagine the possibility of climbing up three quarters of it because there was a crack running up steeply from left to right which appeared to offer the possibility of hand holds and ledges for the feet but the last stage, the gland of the structure, looked impossible to James.

'You're looking at one of the most famous rocks in the world,' said John, 'if only because it's often said to be the origin of rock climbing becoming a sport in its own right. It was first climbed by a chap called Haskett Smith in 1886 and it's been popular ever since. As you might imagine, the last pitch is the hardest and that's what makes it severe. Anyway, if we walk a little further on there are one or two climbs we can try this morning'.

They started off on one or two easy and moderate climbs and James found John to be a brilliant instructor. In addition to being an excellent climber, he was calm, patient and very clear in his instructions and yet behind his quiet manner was a forceful individual who would obviously stand no nonsense. He seemed very mature for his age and James not only liked him but felt there was much to be learned from him apart from rock climbing, although he did learn much about climbing.

He learned about knots, particularly the bowline; he learned that in a roped team only one person climbs at any one time; he understood the need for each person in a team to belay on to a rock; he learned how to take in the rope from a climber coming up from below and how to prepare for a climber falling off.

'And another thing,' said John over sandwiches and coffee at lunchtime. 'Don't hug the rock so much. 'Try to keep your body as vertical as you can so that your weight goes into the rock. If you cling with your face next to the rock then the line of your body is parallel to the rock and you're more likely to slip. Also, although you won't always be able to do it, climb with your legs rather than your arms. They're much stronger. That said, you did well this morning. Do you think you'll take to climbing?'

'Well, I've certainly enjoyed this morning and I've learned a great deal. I can't see any reason why I shouldn't carry on. What do you think we should do this afternoon?'

'I've been giving it some thought. Would you like to have a shot at the Needle?'

'Yes I would', said James enthusiastically and with surprise. 'Presumably you think there's a chance I could do it?'

'I would say a slim chance but nevertheless a chance. We're lucky with the weather and the rock's dry otherwise I wouldn't suggest it, but make no mistake; you're going to find it a very difficult challenge. My guess on what I've seen this morning is that you'll manage to get up to the shoulder near the top. After that I think you may find it too difficult but don't worry if you can't manage it. I'll just lower you down.'

James was flattered that John thought him capable enough with so little experience to at least have a go at the climb. For the first time he was also a little nervous about what he'd let himself in for.

John explained that essentially, although there were a number of different approaches up to the shoulder, the whole climb comprised two pitches, the first of about 17 metres up to the shoulder and the second of about 4 metres to the top. They roped themselves together and John set off climbing the Wasdale Crack, which runs diagonally left to right up the main body of the Needle. To James it looked extremely difficult but John seemed to move up with relative ease, pausing occasionally to work out his next move. Before long he reached the top of the Crack, and then climbed up to the shoulder where he belayed on.

'Now your turn," he shouted down. "Just climb slowly and steadily, thinking about each move before you try it and remembering to move only one point at a time'.

From his instruction in the morning James was reminded that this meant moving only one hand or one foot at each stage, so that he had three points of contact with the rock at any one time.

'And don't worry if you fall off,' was his final comment. 'I can hold you quite easily'.

James did not find it easy. John's cool, deliberate and calm ascent contrasted with his own intense, stomach churning and sweaty struggle. There were moments when he didn't think he could possibly make the next move but each time, with John's encouragement, he somehow managed to scramble to the next foot or handhold. He was clumsy and inelegant but also determined. Eventually he was level with John and was allowed to take a break while they took in the magnificent view, although James's pleasure was marred by the thought of what came next and what came next was the top block up to the summit.

As he looked up he told himself that it was only about 13 or 14 feet but he couldn't see much by way of a foothold or a handhold and once on the slab he would be very exposed. It looked almost as smooth as glass. For the first time he also looked down and although they were no more than 60 or 70 feet off the sloping ground below, he suddenly became conscious of the height and of his own vulnerability. John must have sensed his apprehension.

'You all right? Good', he said, without waiting for a response. 'Just watch what I do and try to do the same thing but remember that it doesn't matter if you can't do it. I'll just lower you down to where you are now and then you can think again. Now I don't intend to fall off but, as we practised this morning, you must belay yourself on before I start to climb. So let's see you do that first.'

James found a suitable anchorage point and belayed himself on with a bowline, which John checked. He also ensured that James had the rope round his back and a good stance in order to take the strain in what seemed the unlikely event of John's falling off. Then John started to climb.

Previously James had been impressed by John's smooth and apparently easy style but this time John was much more cautious, spending longer looking ahead before making any kind of move and scrutinising every possible foot and hand hold before committing himself. When he did make a move it was slow and deliberate.

With each move John made James fed the rope out from his right hand so that it pulled round his back and in through his left hand, making sure that he gave John enough rope not to hamper him but not enough for the rope to be too slack. He checked his stance, so that he could take the strain if John slipped and fell, and his belay to ensure that he himself would not be pulled off the face. All seemed well.

After what seemed a long time, but was probably only a few minutes, John was standing on top of Napes Needle. Now it was James' turn. He took his time finding a start and tried to think not only of the next move but one or two beyond that. He made three moves and then found himself completely exposed on the almost vertical slab just above which was the summit but he couldn't see the next move and his right leg, which was taking most of the strain, was starting to shake. He began to feel desperate.

'I can't seem to find the next move," he called up to John, who was looking down at him.

'Well there's no big problem," said John calmly. "I have a firm hold here and so you could let go if you wish and I could lower you down. However, I suggest you give it a go. Now, move your left leg a little further to the left and a little up and feel for a toehold. That's it. Good. Now stretch your left hand up and again over to the left.'

'James followed the instructions and suddenly felt a surge of confidence as he secured his left hand. At least he had two of his four points fixed securely. Still under John's instruction, James moved his right leg to a toehold and the found a grip with his right hand. Suddenly he was up and on the top.

'Bloody good! Congratulations,' said John, shaking him warmly by the hand. 'Considering your inexperience, you really have done remarkably well. Now let's have a short break before we find our way down.'

They stood on the narrow summit and looked around at the magnificent view, John relaxed and very enthusiastic, James impressed but conscious of the drop on all sides and concerned about how he could possibly climb down. He wasn't going to suggest it himself but was relieved when John eventually suggested he would lower James down to the shoulder below the top slab.

'Climbing down is usually harder than climbing up and I think you've done enough for one day.'

James was lowered down to the shoulder but then climbed down to the base of the Needle while John paid out the rope from above. Soon they were hiking back to Wasdale to catch their coach to Langdale.

That evening by common consent the whole group went down to Ambleside for a pub meal. James sat next to Charlotte in the coach and established contact with her, although it was too short a trip for him to find out much about her. She seemed open and chatty and he took an immediate liking to her. He also took a liking to the generous swell of her sweater, offset by a very slim waist and, with a pang of jealousy, wondered about her boyfriend, but not for long since at this point they pulled up in the centre of Ambleside.

As they were about thirty in number they split into small groups and James was happy to find himself in a group of five which included Charlotte, John and Bob Fletcher. He was less pleased to find that the fifth member of the group was the loudmouth on the coach, Billy Brigstock.

In fact, although rather brash, Billy wasn't quite the bore that James had imagined and his behaviour in the presence of a woman was impeccable. They exchanged information about their backgrounds, swapped a few jokes, ate a good pub meal and drank a few pints of beer, or several vodka and tonics in Charlotte's case.

The men also decided to tackle Bowfell Buttress the following day while Charlotte had already signed up with a group to do a climb on Gimmer Crag in Great Langdale. Billy was a second year student studying architecture and had been climbing for a year. John was studying law and was in his fourth year and he and Bob had both been regular climbers since starting at University.

Once the business was settled, they turned again to light hearted banter and James noticed that Charlotte was quite capable of holding her own when it came to bawdy jokes. Perhaps he'd been over sensitive about her wellbeing on the way up from Liverpool in the coach.

On the way back in the coach James sat next to Charlotte. There wasn't time to say much but there seemed to be an affinity between them which he put to the test by inviting her out for a meal in Liverpool the following week. To his delight she accepted and he looked forward to the meeting.

In the morning after breakfast there was a briefing for the whole party at which Hamish McLeod said a few words about safety and issued a warning of a faint possibility of snow showers, adding that under the circumstances no group should attempt any climb classified as 'severe'. The leader of each group then entered his climb and map reference in the log book so that Hamish would know the whereabouts of all members. They packed their lunch and drinks into rucksacks and set off in the coach.

John, Bob, Billy and James were dropped off in the car park of the Old Dungeon Ghyll Hotel and set off walking the two and a half miles up to Bowfell Buttress. On the way James took stock of his companions. Of the three James now knew most about John, the Club Secretary, having spent the day before climbing with him, and was impressed by his calm, methodical and authoritative approach, which no doubt stretched beyond climbing into other areas of his life. The fact that he was studying law seemed compatible with his measured manner and approach but he was also courteous and good humoured.

Bob the Chairman was tall, broad and hearty in manner and James was not surprised to learn that he spent the rest of his spare time as a front row forward for the University rugby team. His rather long, shaggy hair and deep red bristling beard suggested he spent rather less time at the barber's. The enigma was Billy Brigstock.

James' initial dislike of Billy for his loud and uncouth manner on the coach up from Liverpool had been moderated over dinner the previous evening, when he'd been humorous and good natured but generally restrained. Perhaps it was simply that he'd been drinking before getting on the coach and yet James felt unsettled by Billy. There was something in his manner, his personality or his character that he couldn't identify but which troubled him. There was an element in his nature which he didn't trust and yet he couldn't say what it was. He had no evidence to support the suspicion and was probably being completely unfair in his half-baked assessment.

He resolved to put it to the back of his mind and to give Billy the benefit of the doubt. In any case, harbouring unkind thoughts could affect his own behaviour towards Billy and upset the relationship from the start. He resolved to be more positive towards Billy, hoping to evoke a positive response, and it seemed to work. Billy became noticeably more friendly.

During the hike James learned that Bowfell Buttress is a little under 400 feet in height and that they would be climbing it in 4 pitches. Because it was north facing it was often cold and so, particularly in view of the slight possibility of the odd snow shower, they would be attempting an ascent classified as 'difficult' rather than one of the alternative 'severe' routes. James was not disappointed by this decision.

After about an hour the path levelled and they headed up a ridge path and then crossed some scree to reach the Climbers' Traverse. They stayed close to the base of Flat Crags, traversed the base of the Great Slab past Cambridge Crag and there was Bowfell Buttress across a little more scree - and it certainly looked very impressive: a great slab of black rock that soared high up into the sky.

James chose not to think about how they might climb it and in any case would not really have had any idea. Before they got too close to the foot of the climb Bob and John worked out their intended approach to the top with the aid of a climbing guide to the Buttress.

Once satisfied, they walked across to the base of the ascent and gave a summary to James and Billy of what was intended. James noticed that although Billy had more experience than himself, Bob and John treated them both as beginners.

They had three ropes, two of which were used to rope them all together and a third, which Bob was to carry as the leader, was kept in reserve for emergencies. James was behind Bob, then Billy and finally John to bring up the rear. Bob then set off up the first pitch, climbing easily and confidently, using his legs to climb wherever possible rather than his arms, and occasionally stopping, his arms outstretched and his body in a vertical position as he scanned the rock face above him to decide his next move. Then it was James' turn.

What had looked so easy when Bob had done it seemed a great deal more difficult to James. It took him longer and seemed to take a good deal more effort. From time to time he was over reliant on the strength of his arms and consequently when he arrived at a ledge and Bob shouted down to him to stop and belay himself to the rock, he was feeling considerably out of breath.

Then it was Billy's turn and James took up the slack as Billy climbed up to a position below and it was only then that James had chance to take stock of the view, which was magnificent. It was the grandeur of the surrounding mountains and of the valley below that made him catch his breath but strangely he wasn't particularly affected by the drop below him. He was securely anchored to the rock and confident that when it was again his turn to climb, Bob would have no difficulty in holding him if he should slip or lose his grip. He was too inexperienced to appreciate how quickly enjoyment and triumph could turn to disaster in this activity.

The first leg of the climb had gone well and James

was quietly pleased to note that although he wasn't finding it easy, Billy appeared to be struggling more than he was. At least he no longer felt like the weakest link in the chain. He was hot and sweaty and feeling the effects of the hard physical effort but the adrenalin was flowing and he was enjoying the sense of triumph in conquering the climb.

In fact he was so warm and so wrapped up in his feeling of well being that he failed to notice a change in the weather. What had been a mild and sunny morning was now turning colder and the blue sky was giving way to menacing dark grey clouds that were approaching with remarkable rapidity.

Bob and John hadn't failed to notice the changes taking place and Bob shouted down in gruff but measured tones that it looked as though a storm was coming through and that it would be better if they didn't hang around too long. 'Hanging around too long' wasn't something that seemed to James to be fully under his control but he took the message and did his best to climb as quickly as he could.

Billy was also clearly doing his best but was equally obviously finding the climb physically, emotionally and technically very challenging and James began to wonder what they would do if he simply found it too much for his capabilities.

Nevertheless they all finished the second of the four stages of the climb. Bob climbed higher still and James completed the third stage and belayed himself on. He now had only one stage to complete. At this point snow started to fall. The possibility of light snow falls had of course been forecast, which is why Bob had insisted that no one should attempt any climb classified higher than 'difficult', but a 'difficult' climb in dry conditions can quickly become 'severe' in poor weather and the weather was now worse than poor.

As an icy wind picked up, snow swirled around the four climbers, and settled on every ledge, quickly turning to ice. The temperature dropped dramatically and James, who such a short time ago had felt hot and sweaty, was now cold and sweaty, but it was a sweat induced by fear. His earlier feeling of triumph and wellbeing had disappeared as rapidly as the sun and the warmth.

The visibility was now poor. Above he could just make out Bob through the driving snow and cloud and below he could see Billy but not John. Billy was climbing, his stark white face sometimes looking up anxiously at James as though seeking reassurance and checking to see that James was taking in the slack so that he wouldn't fall far if he slipped. James shouted encouragement and tried to advise him on each move, which seemed to help Billy and certainly helped himself. He experienced a new found sense of responsibility which helped to steady his own nerves as well.

It was clearly a huge struggle for Billy but he managed to reach a good stance not too far below James and belayed on, clearly in dire need of a rest. James shouted up to Bob, explaining what was happening, and Bob seemed satisfied with progress, nevertheless asking for an instruction to be passed down to John to get up as quickly as possible. Since Billy was now ready he called down to John, who started to climb. James still couldn't see him but he could make out Billy taking up the slack below. It was then that disaster stuck.

There was a yell, which James at first thought was Billy. Then he saw Billy desperately struggling with the rope he'd been taking in. Billy was pulled out from the rock but his belay held and he managed to stop the rope he was holding. As instructed, he'd passed the rope he was taking in round his back to increase friction but it seemed he hadn't reacted quickly enough in the first instance and a length of rope had passed through his grip before he'd been able to stop it completely. James could only imagine that John had dropped but had no idea how far.

'Are you all right Billy?' he shouted. It was an automatic reaction to the situation but Billy clearly wasn't all right. He'd been growing increasingly nervous over the past half hour and James could only imagine what state he was in now, hanging off the rock and taking John's weight in a friction grip. 'Can you hold him?'

'Yes, but not for too long,' came back a throttle reply. 'He's fallen off and seems to be just hanging there'. James then heard Billy shouting down to John but couldn't hear the reply.

Shortly afterwards Billy shouted up that John had damaged his arm and couldn't climb. Above, Bob was aware of the commotion but had heard James asking for information and so waited for a reply.

'I think we've got a problem,' James shouted up to Bob. 'John has damaged his arm and says he can't climb. Billy is holding him at present but seems to be in some difficulty.'

James felt himself to be in some difficulty. He didn't have an immediate problem but he was gripped by a fear that seized his spine in an icy grip, made his heart pound and dried his throat. His only salvation was that the poor visibility made it impossible for him to see the drop below.

'Tell Billy he's doing a great job but he must keep hold of John. I'm on my way down.'

Bob fixed his spare rope and abseiled down past James to Billy. He belayed the rope holding John, taking the strain off Billy, and then carried on down out of James' sight to see what state John was in. He reappeared shortly afterwards and he and Billy hauled

John up to a ledge just below them.

'James', Bob shouted up. 'I think John's broken his arm and he certainly can't climb and Billy doesn't want to move at present'. James took this to mean that Billy was in a near state of panic. 'We need help and it's down to you I'm afraid. I don't want to leave either of them and in this weather they'll die of exposure if we leave them alone here. I'll do my best to get them at least partially into survival bags and to give them a hot drink and something to eat. You will have to go and get help. I wouldn't ask you to do this if I didn't think you could manage it. There's nothing harder in the final stage than you've done already. You can do it and all our lives depend on your doing it; so don't let us down'.

James was very frightened at this suggestion but could see the logic of it. He looked up to where he had to climb to reach the top, which was in sight. The first pitch was easy since he could use Bob's original rope to the point he'd reached. After that, apart from one move or two, it didn't look any more difficult than he'd already climbed but this time he'd be doing it without a safety rope and in very poor conditions.

The wind had dropped a little and the snow was less dense but it was still very unpleasant. At least he could focus on the rock in front and above him since the visibility was still poor and he couldn't see much beyond his three colleagues below.

'You've got a map and compass. When you reach the top, head for the Dungeon Ghyll Hotel but if you find someone before, so much the better. The Hotel will call out the mountain rescue team. Don't rush the climb but once you're on top go hell for leather. You'll find an easy route down the side of the mountain. Good luck. We're depending on you.'

James undid his belay, took a deep breath to steady his nerves, and made a first move. He was cold and very frightened, the blood thumping in his head and his mouth tasting as foul as the bottom of a baby' pram: all piss and biscuits. 'Oh fuck', he said to himself. 'This is ridiculous'. He'd come on what he'd thought would be an interesting and exciting weekend of ab initio climbing, safely sandwiched between two experienced climbers. Suddenly he was now climbing solo without a safety rope up a climb that was classified as 'difficult' in good weather and 'severe' in weather such as this. In future he'd stick to flying, which was a good deal safer than this bloody nonsense.

He started well despite the snow and ice and began to gain a little confidence, fighting hard to keep calm and to suppress the feeling of sickness that was threatening to overwhelm him. Then he reached a point beyond which progress seemed quite impossible.

Both his feet were well placed on small but distinct ledges and he had two good handholds but it was the next move or two that put him in a mood of despair. The rock ahead seemed smooth and featureless, with no ledges and no handholds. He was stuck. He couldn't climb on and he couldn't return, not only because there was no point in going back but also because climbing down was more difficult than climbing up.

'Shit! What a bastard!' He felt his legs begin to tremble and what energy there was left in his body began to drain away.

'Oh Jesus', he said, but this time he was praying and not blaspheming.

'What's the problem?' came Bob's voice from below. 'Are you stuck?'

James looked down and was surprised to see that the cloud was now less dense and he could see not only his companions but a good deal of the drop below them. He also noticed that the snow had stopped completely and there was virtually no wind any more.

'I just can't see where to go from here. There are no foot or handholds.'

'Don't worry. It's not as bad as it seems. You can't go straight up but if you look over to your right you'll see a little ledge that you can inch along horizontally for a few feet and if you reach up you'll feel some quite reasonable hand holds although you won't be able to see them. Set off now and I'll keep talking you through it.'

He inched onto the slab with just his toes in contact with the rock and reached up. Sure enough his fingers found a few protuberances that he gratefully hooked them round. His position was now absolutely precarious since the slab was slightly convex and he was pressed hard against it, his body arched with the rock pressing into his stomach, just the toes of his boots perched on a rim of rock and his fingers grasping for anything they could find above his head. He slowly progressed sideways, not daring to move an inch until his right hand and his right foot had found some security, however small.

'Now, feel up and slightly to your right with your right boot. There's a good ledge there. Raise yourself up on it and at the same time feel up with your left hand and you'll find a good hold.'

James felt a sudden surge of energy and a renewed determination. With his heart almost literally in his mouth he made the move and experienced an enormous sense of relief when his left hand grasped a really good, solid piece of rock.

'Well done,' shouted up Bob. 'Don't rush it but you've just done the hardest move on the whole climb and there's now nothing left to worry you.'

It still wasn't easy but Bob was right and the worst was over. A few minutes later James had reached the top and had recovered his breath and his nerves, perhaps helped by the fact that the storm had now passed through as quickly as it had arrived. The wind had completely gone, the sun had come out and the temperature had risen. He suddenly felt confident again.

'Is there any chance you and Billy could climb up and the three of us could lift John up in a sling?' he shouted down to Bob.

'I don't want to move John,' came back the shouted reply from below. Be as quick as you can but we're better placed now the weather's improved again. We'll be all right so long as we don't have another storm. When you speak to the mountain rescue team ask them to get an RAF helicopter if they can. Incidentally, well done on the climb. Now get moving.'

James set off as fast as he could, almost at a jog, and the going was easier than he'd imagined. There hadn't been time for much snow to settle and the way down presented no problems. Even so at best it would take him an hour and a half to get to the Dungeon Ghyll Hotel.

On the way he thought about possible reasons for Bob not wanting to take up his suggestion about them all getting up without help and came to the conclusion that John must have suffered more of an injury than an arm fracture. If so, and John couldn't walk even if lifted to the top, then they would still need help and it might as well be sooner rather than later. Bob's request for a helicopter underlined the point.

James should have been tired after the climb but the urgency of the situation and the elation of having survived pumped him full of adrenalin and he hurried along at speed. His main concern was now for John and he must do everything he could to summon help as quickly as possible. He was panting for breath, his chest felt as tight as a drum and his legs were threatening to give way but his own discomfort was irrelevant.

Eventually he struck a road and headed for the Hotel but before reaching it he came to a cottage. The elderly couple who lived there were very helpful and before long he was speaking to the mountain rescue team and telling them he would be at the Hotel if they wanted him. The couple then drove him to the Hotel, which James thought was as good a place as any to keep in contact with events. There was no way in which he could contact Hamish or any of the other climbing groups but anyone contacting the rescue team HQ would be told of his whereabouts. He briefed the Hotel manager in case he had to leave and then waited.

In a remarkably short space of time the rescue team arrived at the hotel and James told them exactly what he knew and where the three could be found. They knew the climb well and didn't need James to show them the way and in any case after his exertions he would not have been able to keep up with them. He was therefore obliged to stay at the Hotel and wait.

About half an hour later he heard a helicopter in the area and went outside to see one pass nearby and head off in the direction of Bowfell. Not very long afterwards it passed over again, this time on its return journey, and James assumed that his three climbing companions were now safely inside.

It was another hour and a half before the mountain rescue team came back to the Hotel and they had Bob and Billy with them. Both were fine but John was not well and had been taken to hospital in Carlisle. Apart from a broken arm, he'd suffered some damage to his back, which is why Bob and been so anxious not to move him. The rescue team took all three of them back to their accommodation near Langdale and they were there to tell the tale when the others came back from their various climbs.

That evening they all spent their last evening in a

large pub in Ambleside. James was tired but felt he needed a few beers before it was time for bed. The good news about John was that he had badly bruised his back but had not broken it. Of course his arm would mend in due course and he would make a full recovery. After the meal James found an armchair to relax in and he was pleased that Charlotte came to sit on the arm.

'So you're a bit of a hero then?' she said with a smile.

'Certainly not,' he replied. 'Bob's the hero: not me. I don't know what we'd have done without him'.

At that point Hamish came over to talk. "John's a very good climber but he was unlucky today. What seemed like a good perch just gave way under his weight. However, ye did a good job today laddie. Bob told me all about it. Let me buy you a drink. What can I get you?'

'Well I've had enough beer but I would like a scotch thank you.'

'Good choice. And how would you like it?'

"On the rocks please'.

On the way back the following morning the pneumatic Charlotte sat next to him on the coach and at one point put her hand on his.

'Are you free come round to my place for dinner one evening this week?'

'I am but I thought you already had a boyfriend.'

'I did, but it was already coming to an end'.

And so James set out on a new adventure. He continued to explore the contours of the Lake District as well as those of Charlotte Goodwin. Her smooth mountain uplands and her wooded valley and secret cavern gave him many hours of interest, excitement and satisfaction but without the fear of Bowfell Buttress.

EPISODE 2 - AUTUMN IN VENICE (1959-1960)

Historical Context

_1959_ *Tibet's Dalai Lama escapes to India, Soviet Premier Nikita Khrushchev tours the United States, and Britain recognizes the independence of Cyprus.*
_1960_ *American U-2 spy plane is shot down over Russia and Adolf Eichmann is captured by Israelis in Argentina*

James' relationship with Charlotte continued throughout his time at Liverpool University, although he did give way to the occasional amorous diversion. He was sometimes accused of seducing innocent females but he didn't accept this interpretation of his various dalliances. As he was heard to explain on one occasion, he sometimes found himself in situations where it was clearly more chivalrous to accept a lady's advances rather than to leave her feeling unwanted. He protested that he did not like to hurt people.

However, his life did not revolve exclusively around romance since, apart from mountaineering, he had his flying to consider as well as the more boring requirements of the Engineering Department for him to attend lectures and complete certain tranches of work. In sum he reached solo standard flying Chipmunk aircraft with the University Air Squadron at RAF Woodvale, became a competent climber, and achieved a 2.2 BSc in Aeronautical Engineering.

Of course this was not a brilliant academic achievement but bearing in mind the time devoted to his other interests, he felt it wasn't bad and he could live with it. His father on the other hand found his son's academic achievement extremely disappointing. After all he himself had been awarded a first in classics at

Cambridge before going on to get an MA and then a PhD. James seemed to be quite good at a range of things but not excellent at any one of them and that could be his downfall. How could he ever achieve distinction in a field without devoting nearly all his efforts to it? Fortunately he knew little of his son's romantic escapades.

James' mother Lydia on the other hand was more charitable. She expressed her view that James' strength lay in the very diversity of his interests. He was a balanced kind of person who would do well in any environment. He was sociable and charming and his outgoing personality meant he would always be popular.

She knew more of his amorous liaisons than her husband but by now had accepted this side of his nature and in any case told herself it was better that he sowed a few wild oats when he was young since he would get over it and be a steadier sort of person later in life.

She herself had had a very constrained upbringing and was quietly regretful that she had not played the field a little before settling down and now it was too late.

For James the biggest disappointment in his life now manifested itself. Instead of waiting to be called up for national service, he had applied for a short service commission as a pilot but he received a letter saying that, since the current intake quota for pilots was complete, his application could not be accepted at the present time.

He had a choice. He could either wait nine months for the next quota or he could apply immediately for a commission as a navigator or as an engineer, although acceptance in any case would be dependant on successful completion of the selection process. He elected to wait for the next pilot quota but was able to apply immediately for selection assessment at the Aircrew Selection Centre, RAF Hornchurch, which he passed.

The question now was what to do before he was called up for training. His father suggested he should stay on at Liverpool to study for a Graduate Certificate of Education in case his plans for the future changed and he wanted to go into teaching. James had no intention of going into teaching and in any case felt the need for a break from academic study.

His mother was concerned that whatever he did it would be best done away from the area since she knew that Jennifer had designs on him and she thought him much too young to be trapped. The Reverend Cyril Penfold and his wife Penelope were not at all sure that James was a suitable prospect for their only daughter and so agreed with Lydia, albeit for very different reasons.

James' eventual decision caused a resigned shake of the head from his father, an encouraging hug from his mother and a relieved sigh from the rectory. He would go to Venice to try his hand at drawing and painting and see if he could sell anything. He calculated that, even if he couldn't, the remains of his father's generous university allowance would be enough to see him through. His mother thought the idea very romantic and hinted that she would see him all right if he ran out of funds.

The best piece of luck was that his father, through his university connections, had been able to find a flat for him that belonged to the Ca' Foscari University of Venice. It was student accommodation and therefore small and basic but it was cheap and it was within a short walking distance of St Mark's Square. So it was that one bright Monday morning early in August he stepped off an aircraft at Venice Marco Polo Airport and began a new episode in his young life.

The first month went well. The flat was adequate, the

weather was beautiful and the general atmosphere and ambiance of Venice exactly to his liking. He found the life and bustle of the old town and the canals invigorating, the colours and architecture of the buildings inspirational, and the plethora of concerts thrilling. He even sold some quick likenesses in his first week, made friends with a fellow Italian artist called Alfonso Martinelli and through Alfonso met Claudia.

Yet James Winchester was not quite as happy as he felt he should have been. It wasn't that he was in distress or facing an emergency or even that he had a clearly identifiable problem. The world was full of people who had genuine cause for complaint but he wasn't one of them and therefore shouldn't feel as he did.

He was feeling a little down because he was frustrated at not to be getting on with his chosen career as pilot. Patience was not one of James' strongest suits but there was nothing more he could at present and needed to snap out of it. He decided the best medicine for his condition was another glass of wine and so ordered a third Australian Shiraz. No doubt the cognoscenti would condemn his choice and draw attention to the superiority of a good claret but in James' view that was probably reason in itself to choose the Shiraz.

Following the dictates of fashion was not his way and perhaps Ernest Hemingway would have agreed with him in this. Sitting drinking in Harry's bar in Venice, alleged to be one of Hemingway's favourite watering places, inevitably led James to think about him. Hemingway was an enigma: a man of action who suffered from a wide range of physical ailments: a man's man who spent most of his time writing: a strong man who drank heavily and finally shot himself.

Far from feeling critical, James was drawn to Hemingway because he felt similar dualities in himself.

As a child he'd been involved in a car crash and been badly injured and yet he'd turned out to be a competent amateur boxer. He was a self-confessed atheist who frequently went into a church 'just to look at the architecture' but often stayed for the service. He enjoyed all things physical but was now earning his keep, well at least some of it, through drawing and painting.

The first month had been like a wonderful holiday and he'd gloried in the novelty of the experience and the many delights of Venice but now, another five months on, he felt the holiday was over and yet he had another six months to fill before reporting for initial officer training He finished his drink and walked back along the canal to the other side of St Mark's Square, close to the Hotel Danieli, where he'd left his easel.

'Grazie Alfonso', he shouted to his new friend and fellow artist sitting nearby. 'Prego, prego', replied Alfonso, who'd been keeping an eye on James' equipment from under his black cap. James settled himself into his seat and looked across the Bacino di San Marco lagoon towards the island of San Georgio Maggiore. The white façade of the church and the belfry of the 'other' campanile looked dazzling in the late afternoon sun. Splinters of steel flickered off the surface of the water. Perhaps he would paint the scene one day. Perhaps he should find the time to paint want he wanted to paint rather than doing silly cartoon likenesses.

He noticed two women looking at his drawings and paintings. They spoke in hushed tones but seemed to be admiring his work; at least their body language suggested approval. One was sturdy, good looking, with a wide and attractive smile, and aged about 45. She wore a chic deep red suit and no hat. Her auburn hair fell in swirls onto her shoulders. The other was tall, elegant, dressed entirely in black, rivetingly beautiful and looked about seventeen. The black accentuated the paleness of her face and the length of the coat her elegance. James was also struck by the thought that she was wearing a winter's coat although the October temperature was about 21 degrees Celsius.

The two women worked their way along his exhibits until they were standing behind him while he continued to work, with apparent indifference, on a sketch of the waterfront, another one he would probably never have time to finish. At first it had unnerved him to work with people looking over his shoulder but now he was used to it. He deftly brushed in the outline of a gondola.

The older woman bent down to look at his painting with him.

'What a beautiful classical style you have. So many artists these days daub paint on the canvas and call it modern art.' She spoke in an accent that could have been eastern European.

'Thank you, I prefer to paint in the classical style although I do like some modern art.'

'So do I,' she replied, 'but so much of it is junk. When so called artists show no skill with the materials and their pictures reveal no insight into the human condition, I wonder why they bother.' She made the statement with some passion, which intrigued James.

'Do you have an interest in art?' he asked her.

'Yes, I do, although I'm not an artist myself. I collect and I have a gallery.'

James felt both a frisson of excitement and a sense of shame at his present circumstances. He wanted to tell her that he was really not a bad artist, that not only could he paint beautiful and arresting landscapes but that he was also quite a budding portrait painter. He cursed himself for not having any examples of his portraits to hand but he wasn't likely to sell any in the street and if people saw them they probably wouldn't want to buy the cartoons.

'Would you draw a cartoon of me please,' she asked. 'The ones I've looked at are very good.'

Disappointment suffused him. The ability to draw a quick likeness was her assessment of his ability. She was not interested in his landscapes and she would never know that he could paint portraits.

He offered a chair to the younger woman and seated the older woman so that her face was in the best light. She had strong, open features, full lips and beautiful teeth. Her luxuriant, auburn hair shone in the sunlight. She should have been happy and yet he detected signs of strain: the faint suggestion of a frown, tenseness around the mouth and a lack of sparkle in the eyes. James worked quickly and surely as the two women chatted about shopping and where to have dinner.

James finished the drawing and showed it to them.

'Wonderful, simply wonderful,' exclaimed the older woman, whom James had now learned was the mother. 'I think you've read my character exactly'.

James was relieved since not everyone appreciated the exaggerations of the cartoon.

'Perhaps you could do mine tomorrow,' suggested the daughter. 'Will you be here tomorrow?' Her black eyes looked enquiringly into his as she spoke directly to him for the first time.

'Yes, I'll be here,' he replied, wanting to add that he'd walk over burning coals to see her again if he had to, but thinking that might sound a little over-dramatic. She was enchanting beyond any words he could find. Her voice was soft and sensual and yet, despite her young years, mature and assured.

'I'll try to be here about ten,' she added, and smiled. Like her mother she had a wonderful smile but seemed to smile less frequently. Her mother squeezed his arm in a conspiratorial way as she said goodbye and thanked him again for the cartoon. He watched them as they walked away with arms linked, discussing some subject of great mutual interest.

He did two more cartoons in the early evening and then folded up his three small canvas chairs, his easel and his paints and pencils and placed everything into two flat wooden cases with handles. These he carried down a side street to a wooden door, through which he gained access to a small carpenter's workshop. The owner was a new acquaintance who let him keep his equipment here. In the corner was a small hand basin in which he washed his hands and face. It was time to eat.

He walked through the streets to the Rialto Bridge and then crossed over into the area of San Polo, where he had his one-roomed apartment. About two hundred yards from his apartment was a small, inexpensive restaurant. He found a small corner table and sipped a glass of Chianti while waiting for his meal. He also thought about his encounter with the mother and daughter.

The mother had seemed warm, expansive and outgoing; the daughter, whilst quietly reflecting some of the sensuality of the mother, was subdued, mysterious and still. If the mother was a stream, bubbling and splashing noisily over rocks, the daughter was a dark pool, whose movement was slower and more measured. He very much hoped they would return in the morning but the hope was tinged with the reality of his situation. He was a young chap rather low on funds and shortly about to launch himself into his chosen career and she was a very young woman, probably about seventeen, and possibly from a wealthy family if her clothes and those of her mother were anything to go by. Reality was suddenly reinforced by the abrupt arrival of Claudia.

Claudia Omarini did not so much enter a room as burst into it, both audibly and visibly.

'Ciao, Giorgio. Ciao, Giovanni. Ciao, Carla. Ciao, James.'

'Ciao, Claudia,' came the reply from those addressed and also from a few who weren't. Claudia was always very popular and made everyone feel they wanted to be known to her. She was dressed in a figure-hugging top with broad red and white horizontal stripes, a mini-skirt, and high heeled black leather boots that ended just below the knee. She was cheerful, bouncy and attractive and James had grown very fond of her in the six months he had known her. He suspected that beneath the flamboyancy was a determined, ambitious and yet vulnerable young woman.

At present she was working three nights a week behind the bar to help support herself at university but she was older than the average student. James had an idea that she'd started her first degree at the age of twenty and that she was now about one year into her masters. He supposed she was about twenty-four.

Claudia bought herself a drink at the bar and came to sit at James's table. James smiled at her.

'I'm surprised you have time to sit and talk with the clients,' he said.

'I always have time to talk to you, James Winchester - you handsome, romantic English artist. And in any case I am not working tonight.'

'Then shouldn't you be studying?'

'Perhaps, but I need to eat. Have you had a meal?'

'No but I'm just about to eat. Why don't you join me and be my guest,' offered James.

'Benissimo. You are very kind. Or do you think you can seduce me with a plate of spaghetti?' She laughed and added with a twinkle in her eye, 'You would have to include at least a bottle of good red wine even to stand a chance.'

'Then you shall have a bottle of good Chianti - but

with no strings attached.'

'Allora, I accept but you do not flatter me Signore Artist. Most Italian men I know would at least want to try. Then I could turn you down.'

'Then I'm just short circuiting the process,' laughed James. Claudia might have suspected that he normally harboured a deep desire for her but she would not have known that this evening he was troubled by the image of a pale faced young lady in black and of their meeting the following morning.

They ate their meal and drank their wine and talked about their lives and their ambitions and afterwards strolled along the Grand Canal. Somehow their hands came together naturally as they absorbed the ambiance of medieval buildings, water taxis, gondolas and ornate lamps casting pearls of light onto the dancing canal. They lived with these images but did not take them for granted. The magic of the city persisted, a magic that even survived the occasional rank smell of a faulty sewer.

Finally he walked her back to her apartment and surprised himself by turning down her offer to go in for a cup of coffee. She paused, shrugged her shoulders and went inside, clearly disappointed at his apparent lack of interest. He was confused and having difficulty understanding his own actions. That night he lay in bed and thought about the day without coming to any particular conclusion, other than that he was completely fascinated by the girl in black. He realised that he did not even know her name.

Dawn crept quietly in through a soft drizzle under a grey umbrella of low cloud. A little later James watched the rain through the window of a small café near his apartment. He had decided to be in his spot near the Hotel Danieli by 9.30, in good time to see the lady in black but no earlier than necessary. He thought about

Claudia and the previous evening.

Claudia had come to mean a great deal to him since he'd first met her such a short time ago. She was warm, intelligent and very attractive, and she had a lively sense of humour. He loved her happy smile and the twinkle in her eye and he felt very relaxed and natural in her company. He also knew she found him attractive and that she did not have any other man.

Why then had he not tried to develop their relationship further? He had never before faced this question squarely. She seemed responsive and very happy to be in his company and had given no indication that she would resist getting closer to him. The answer was suddenly clear to him. He was afraid. She had come to mean so much to him that he was afraid of changing the nature of their relationship in case it should get worse rather than better. He was fearful of taking the plunge. He also had to remind himself that he was on a gap year and that the real business of a career had yet to start.

The answer surprised him because he had never previously met such a problem. He did not consider himself to be a Lethario, although others might, but reluctance to start an affair with a desirable woman had never before resulted in too much hesitation. Yet here he was, prevaricating like a blushing virgin. At least that had been the situation until yesterday. Now there was a new element and one he did not fully understand. He was on the verge of starting a relationship with a lovely woman whom he admired and desired; a relationship that could perhaps even survive the lengthy training in the RAF that lay ahead of him . Yet he was holding back because of a very young woman who had spoken one sentence to him and about whom he knew nothing. It made no sense.

By 9.30 am he had his easel set up and had started

to draw a middle aged woman while her husband looked on with an amused smile. He worked quickly because he wanted the drawing complete before the lady in black arrived, but he need not have worried. She didn't come. By lunchtime he had completed another two drawings and it was clear that she was not coming. He felt a bitter, deep disappointment and not a little surprise. Life had its disappointments but he would have put money on her turning up. Neither she nor her mother looked like people who would fail to keep an appointment. Yet he had been proved wrong and so perhaps he wasn't such a good judge of character.

He spent the afternoon painting a waterscape and a couple of cartoons but his heart was heavy and he finished at 4.30 pm. Alfonso packed his kit away at the same time and together they found a relatively cheap bar down a backstreet and attacked a bottle of wine. Alfonso was about ten years older than James. He had a wife and a couple of children somewhere near the train station at San Lucia but he was always ready to stay for a drink. They talked about business for a little while but James couldn't get the mysterious lady out of his mind and was soon asking Alfonso if he'd noticed her.

'Si,si James. Que bella donna e que figura meravigliosa.'

James was surprised that Alfonsa had noticed her figure since she'd been wearing a heavy black coat. Then he realised that in fact Alfonso had been admiring the mother who'd been wearing a red suit. Dirk laughed and explained the misunderstanding. It was the first time he'd laughed that day and he felt better. They decided they needed a second bottle of wine. Alfonso telephoned his wife, who seemed to be very understanding, and they also ordered a couple of plates of spaghetti. This sort of evening was just what James needed and he made the most of it. It was about 11.30 pm when he arrived back at his apartment and got into bed. He fell asleep to a kaleidoscope of revolving images: paintings, people, water taxis, Claudia, and of course the lady in black.

Few people were about the following morning. A sea mist obscured the views and gave a strangely remote feeling to those who ventured out. James completed cartoons for a young couple on honeymoon who were deliriously happy and completely oblivious of the weather. Their joy was infectious and James went off to lunch in a fairly relaxed frame of mind. Later, as he was walking back to his pitch, he saw Alfonso in an agitated state waving at him and beckoning him to hurry over.

'Amico, amico. Ho visto la signora in colore rosso. Era qui'. Alfonso had seen the lady in the red dress and she had been asking after James. More than that Alfonso had not been able to understand and so the mother had written a note for him to give to James. James hastily took it and read:

'Dear Mr Winchester

We apologise for not coming to see you yesterday but unfortunately my daughter was unwell. We should be very pleased if you would visit us at the hotel Danieli. Perhaps we could meet in the Bar Dandolo at 6 pm this evening. Please telephone room 106 if this is not convenient and we can arrange another day and time.

Ivana Novotny

James felt a chilling frisson of excitement run through him. He sat down and lit a cigarette in order to think. When he did so he realised there wasn't much to think about. The daughter wasn't fully recovered and therefore they wanted him to draw a cartoon in the hotel rather than out on the street.

The Hotel Danieli was probably the best hotel in Venice. Situated a stone's throw from St Mark's Square and the Bridge of Sighs, it had a commanding position overlooking the lagoon. It was made up of three Venetian palazzi dating back to the 14th, 19th and 20th centuries. Inside it was liberally festooned with Murano glass chandeliers, precious rugs, hand-carved marble columns and antique pieces. The fact that his newfound lady friends were staying here augured well for his commission.

The afternoon seemed to drag inexorably. He drew a couple of likenesses and then went for a coffee. At 5.45pm he was walking through the doors of the Hotel Danieli. As he entered the Bar Dandolo he saw them seated at a small table and went over to join them.

'Good Day, Mr Winchester,' said Ivana Novotny, offering him her hand. 'I don't think I introduced you when we met the other day. This is my daughter, Libena. Please sit down, Mr Winchester.'

A waiter was immediately present, and checking that the ladies did not need their glasses replenishing, James ordered a vodka and tonic.

'I was most pleased you were able to come, Mr Winchester', said Madame Novotny in very cultured English 'with only a hint of an eastern European accent, 'and I'm so very sorry that we did not keep our appointment with you yesterday but unfortunately Libena was ill. Now, as you know, we wanted you to draw a likeness of my daughter. However, I have made a few enquiries and now understand that you paint portraits in oil'.

'Yes, I do'.

'You did not have any examples amongst your other works outside'.

James explained why he didn't have any on display but added that he would be more than happy to show them other examples of his work.

'Yes, we would like to see some.'

James was delighted since a portrait in oils would be a good commission. They agreed he would return the following day with one or two examples and after that they spent the next forty-five minutes discussing art in general. He learned little more about them other than that they came from the Czech Republic and that Ivana was a countess. Since there was no mention of a husband and father, James assumed that the Countess was either divorced or widowed.

The daughter said little but seemed to be watching James intently at all times. So much so that occasionally she seemed to lose track of what her mother was saying. From time to time he met her coal black eyes with his but hers seemed to want to linger in contact a little longer than he felt comfortable with. The Countess was charming, practical, worldly and adaptive to the subject in hand. Libena was intense, private and focussed, although quite what she was focussed on was not clear to James.

'Do please bring your wife, or should I say partner, to our next meeting,' Mr Winchester. James realised that his mind had begun to wander and he quickly brought himself back to reality.

'Well, I don't actually have either,' he heard himself say.

'I see,' said the Countess. 'Well, thank you so much for coming Mr Winchester. We look forward to seeing you in reception at 10.00am tomorrow morning. She had already arranged with the manager for a room near reception to be made available so that James would not have too far to move his paintings.

The following day's viewing appeared to go very well from James's point of view. They both expressed considerable liking for his pictures and he was commissioned to paint a portrait of Libena. The arrangement allowed for five sittings each week, which would allow James some time to continue with his routine work but would also ensure rapid progress on the portrait. Since James didn't own a studio, he had arranged to hire one from a colleague. However, he needn't have bothered since the Countess wanted to have the work done in their suit of rooms in the hotel. Dirk wasn't too keen on this idea since it meant leaving a good proportion of his tools at the hotel. It also meant that he couldn't work on the painting in his own time. However, the countess was insistent. She said he could have a key and work on the picture when she and her daughter were both out.

The next afternoon James returned with some equipment and made a few preliminary sketches. The Countess was around the apartment but was careful not to crowd him. Most of the time she read in her bedroom. He then began to establish a relationship with Libena. This was important to James because if the features were going to mean anything, he had to see beyond them. He had to get below the surface in understanding her, but it wasn't easy. She seemed perfectly at ease, in fact so much so that at times she appeared disconnected from the immediate as though experiencing a kind of Zen Buddhist calm. Yet at other times he sensed, but only through her dark eyes, an emotional cauldron.

However on the surface she was polite, affable and quite charming. He learned that her father had died about two years ago and it was fair to assume that he'd left mother and daughter a sizeable fortune judging from their lifestyle. They clearly travelled widely and frequently, and obviously in considerable comfort.

James returned the following afternoon but this time the Countess was out. He took some photographs of Libena and then continued sketching and making notes about colours and tones. In fact, while stunningly attractive, she was remarkably lacking in colour. Her alabaster skin, ultra white teeth and pearl necklace and earrings contrasted with her black hair dark eyes and black dress. Only the deep red of her ample lips offered colour and his gaze flicked between them and her brooding eyes.

'Do you find me attractive she asked?' taking James unawares with the suddenness and directness of the question.

'Well…yes. Yes, I do,' he replied, and immediately felt his response to be inadequate.

'But then I suppose you paint many attractive women,' she continued.

'No, not all that many, and seldom any as attractive as you,' he said, struggling to make up lost ground.

'Does a male painter look at a woman in the same way as a doctor: simply as an object for study?'

'Yes, I suppose I do much of the time. If I didn't analyse the subject, whatever it is, and break it down into its constituent parts I wouldn't be able to paint it. I find all my subjects interesting and some of the women attractive but I can usually separate my personal feelings from my work.'

'What happens when you can't?'

'Then I suppose my work suffers with the distraction.'

'Is your work suffering now?'

'I am finding it difficult to concentrate.'

'Then why don't you stop painting for the day and get us both a drink from the cabinet over there.'

James had seldom encountered anyone apparently so purposeful and direct, and certainly no woman as young and beautiful as Libena. For her age she was remarkably self-assured and poised. Under her instruction he made her favourite cocktail for them both, since she insisted he try it. He did and then they had a second, sitting together on a large settee and discussing art, music, books, and favourite dishes. They were still sitting there when the Countess returned.

James felt embarrassed to be found drinking with Libena when he was being paid a very handsome sum for painting but he needn't have worried. The Countess, who now insisted he call her Ivana, joined them in a drink and was very convivial company. She then invited him for dinner later that evening and in the meantime he went back to his own apartment to shower and change.

The opulence of the Hotel Danieli gave way to the rain, glistening pavements and grey steel waterways of a late October afternoon but, if his vision was monochrome, his thoughts were a blaze of primary colours and his feelings as calm as hot chestnuts popping on a grill. Was Libena simply teasing him or was she genuinely flirting with him? He wasn't sure.

Later that evening they met in the Grand Salone and then went to eat in the Restaurant Terrazza Danieli overlooking the lagoon. Ivana was wearing a three quarter length red dress that accentuated her ample figure, while Libena wore a deep blue, less flamboyant dress, which, together with her black hair, accentuated her pale skin. A diamond choker necklace gave her an expensive and unapproachable aura. Over dinner they discussed art, music and literature and Dirk, whilst not overwhelmed, was impressed by the depth and range of their knowledge.

After dinner they were drinking coffee when Ivana announced suddenly, 'Please excuse me but I must go now. I have another engagement. I have very much enjoyed your company this evening, James'. James rose to his feet while Ivana gave her daughter a peck on the cheek and was gone.

James sat down again but his face must have

registered a little confusion and surprise. Libena looked at him directly and a faint smile flickered around her lips.

'I hope you're not upset that mother's left us?'

'Well, no, I just hadn't expected it that's all.'

'Mother has a boyfriend. He's a French count she met in Monaco last year and has seen quite often since then. He flew in to Venice this afternoon just to see her'.

'Well I'd be surprised if she didn't have a boyfriend,' said Dirk. 'Your mother is a very attractive woman'.

'Mother thinks you're very attractive too, and mother has very good taste,' said Libena without any trace of a smile and then added while looking directly at him with her coal black eyes, 'And I agree with her. In fact you're one of the most attractive men I've ever met.'

The directness of her look and the simple boldness of her expression took James by surprise, and it must have shown.

'I hope I haven't embarrassed you', she said. 'You look a little taken aback'.

'I suppose I was. You hadn't given me that impression until now. I'm not sure what to say'. And that was not an exaggeration. It wasn't often that James was completely lost for words but this time he was.

'You could tell me what you think of me.'

James paused to take a breath, to calm his racing pulse, to assemble his thoughts and to find words to express them adequately. He sipped his wine as a cover and then spoke deliberately and slowly. What he said was important and he wanted to get it right and not simply make a flippant comment.

'When I was a boy my favourite film was 'Ivanhoe' with Robert Taylor and Elizabeth Taylor. She was the most beautiful woman I'd ever seen, with her delicate features, her coal black hair and her alabaster white skin.

Throughout my life that image has remained for me the image of the perfect woman; that is until I saw you for the first time. You immediately reminded me of her but your beauty exceeded hers. You literally took away my breath. Since then I've had a chance to look below the surface and I've become frankly fascinated by your personality, your intelligence, your ideas and by something I can't define. There's something mysterious, even sad about you but I don't know what that something is. I can only tell you that I find you deeply attractive although the words themselves seem inadequate'.

There was a silence and then a look of sadness, almost anguish, crossed Libena's face.

'I'm sorry,' said James, I didn't mean to upset you.

'Please don't apologise. Those are the most beautiful words anyone has ever spoken to me'. Then, pulling herself together, she added, 'Can we go for a walk?'

It was a clear, warm September evening and James noticed that the stars looked particularly sharp and bright as they walked across the Ponte della Paglia, into St Mark's Square and past the Campanile. Libena put her arm through his and held him tightly and James wondered what he'd done to deserve such luck.

They wandered through the back streets and over canals until they reached the Grand Canal, where they had a coffee. Neither needed the stimulus of alcohol. Afterwards they strolled back arm in arm to the Hotel Danieli.

Once in her room she flung her arms round him, kissed him passionately and then whispered in his ear, 'You do realise that I'm not going to let you go tonight, don't you? But please be kind to me. I know it's unusual these days but I've never made love before. Incidentally, mother will not be back until the morning'.

James had made love to a fairly large range of girlfriends but never once before had he experienced a woman like Libena. She was tender, passionate, flirty and completely open in her lovemaking. It may have been the first time for her but she would not have benefited from any previous experience. They were as one and they made love several times that night until a glow to the east signalled a new day, the first day of James's life in his new state of being. He was a man in love. A man who felt his life complete and for whom life now had a new and deeper meaning.

He whistled happily as he showered and dressed and then came back into the bedroom where Libena was still sitting naked on the bed as he'd left her.

'You'd better go now, Darling,' she said, and he kissed her lovingly. She clung to him for a moment and then released him to stare into his eyes. 'Whatever happens in the future,' she said, 'I want you to know that I love you.'

'And I love you too,' he replied, 'but nothing is going to happen to us. We must work out how we can live together'. She did not reply but looked at him wistfully as he smiled, waved and left the bedroom.

Riding a tsunami of vibrant emotions, Dirk flew back to his apartment to prepare for a working day ahead but was really thinking only about the evening when he would see Libena again. Of course he would see her before that since she was bound to visit him at work during the day. In fact she didn't come during the morning and at lunch time he was hesitant to leave his stand in case he missed her and so bought a sandwich and stayed put. Nor was there any sign of her during the afternoon and by five o'clock he was distinctly anxious. He decided to put his tools away and go straight to the hotel.

The tall, lugubrious receptionist looked James up and

down while pondering his question and then replied in immaculate English, as though to better James' inadequate Italian:

'The Countess and her daughter checked out of the hotel this morning, Sir.' James was incredulous.

'But did they leave a message or a forwarding address?'

'No, Sir, they did not leave any messages and I would not be empowered to let you have a forwarding address, even if I had one. I'm afraid there's nothing more I can say, Sir.' The final statement was clearly intended to close the door on any prolongation of the conversation and as if to underline the point he returned to perusing his ledger.

James was stunned and disoriented. He was also in turn confused, angry and deeply hurt. Had she felt nothing at all for him, particularly after last night? Had it all been nothing but a cheap sham on her part? How could she just book out of the hotel without saying anything to him or leaving him with any sort of explanation? Or was there a more sinister explanation? Had they been forced to leave against their will leaving no time for farewell notes? The more questions and possibilities that came to him, the greater was his confusion and distress.

He found the nearest bar and downed a whisky, and then another. Then he headed for Del Cavalieri, overtly to drink wine but subconsciously to seek the friendly warmth of Claudia Omarini. He was lucky since she was not only there but just coming off an early shift. Her eyes lit up when she saw him and she made a willing drinking companion. Later they shared a pizza and eventually he poured out the whole story, indifferent to her feelings through drink and his own suffering. She hid what she felt, embraced him and kissed him on the cheek.

'Well, you poor bambino. That's what happens when you chase after these foreign women. I think you should let me help you take your mind off her'.

'Claudia you're wonderful and I might just let you do that but right now I need some sleep and time to think.' And with that he hugged her warmly and stumbled out and down the street to his apartment, not to think but to fall into a deep sleep.

Several days went by and then a letter from the USA arrived. He opened it to find it was from Ivana:

Dear James

I am writing to explain our sudden departure from Italy and to apologise for the pain that this will inevitably have caused you. Unfortunately I have something even more painful to tell you as well: painful to both of us because I believe you have developed strong feelings for my daughter in recent weeks. However, I will do you the courtesy of being honest and direct.

Libena has terminal cancer and is not expected to live long. When we came to Venice at her request she confided in me that she was still a virgin and that before she died she wanted to experience physical love with a man and she selected you as that man. To you this may seem calculating and cold blooded but I hope you will understand how she felt. Of course she wanted to feel a warmth and affinity for the man she chose and she was indeed genuinely drawn to you as a human being as well as to your obvious physical attractions. Nor, since Libena is a very beautiful young woman, did it seem to us such a poor deal from your point of view. We had overlooked the possibility that you might develop strong feelings for her.

We had not intended to leave so abruptly but on the morning in question Libena became ill and I moved her to a local private hospital for twenty four hours until she had recovered sufficiently to travel to our home here in New York. Later I was very sorry that I had not found time to contact you but at the time her wellbeing was all I could think about.

I am genuinely sorry for the distress we have caused you and for having to convey such unpleasant news. Libena has now taken a turn for the worse and is not expected to live long. I have not included a forwarding address since I'm concerned that it might simply upset her more if you try to contact her. I will write to you again after the inevitable happens.

Good luck with your paintings, which we really do admire, and our best wishes for your future life. I hope you can find it within yourself to forgive us. I am enclosing a cheque for the portrait which you were unable to finish through no fault of your own.

Yours sincerely

Ivana

In fact if James had had an address and flown to New York he would not have had time to see Libena. Two days later he received a second letter from Ivana to say that Libena had died peacefully in her sleep. Libena had been unable to write herself but wanted James to know that she loved him dearly and was deeply sorry that she could not spend the rest of his life with him.

James had encountered the most disturbing problem he'd ever had to face and he found it very hard to deal with. Within a few days he'd decided that he could no longer stay in Italy with the constant reminders of his time with Libena. He was extremely fond of Claudia but her entreaties were not enough to keep him in Italy and so he left to return to England and to start a new chapter in his life but his time in Italy would cast a dark shadow over the rest of his life.

EPISODE 3 -THE AMPHITHEATRE (1960 to 1968)

Historical Context

__1961__ Moscow announces first man in orbit around the Earth, the first, U.S. spaceman rockets 116.5 miles up in 302-mile trip, and East Germany erects the Berlin Wall between East and West Berlin

__1962__ Cuban missile crisis erupts, France and West Germany sign treaty of cooperation ending four centuries of conflict and Martin Luther King delivers "I have a dream" speech

__1963__ President Kennedy is shot and killed in Dallas,

__1967__ Israeli and Arab forces fight The Six Days War and Red China announces explosion of its first hydrogen bomb

James eventually received his RAF joining instructions in the summer of 1960 and duly reported to RAF Kirton-in-Lindsey just north of Lincoln for a twelve week ground course in how to become an officer.

There was much to learn about RAF procedures and much to do in terms of physical activity but for a fit young man it was interesting and it was fun. Even the parades were taken with much good humour and the course Warrant Officer's obscene and sarcastic wit was the cause of much amusement. Advocates of political correctness would have swallowed their blue pencils but this was a little before their humourless and dispiriting influence had cast its grey mantle over life.

Of course it was open to question as to whether the males of Lincoln found it so much fun when a coach load of officer cadets muscled in on their dances every Saturday night. Officer Cadets and Teddy Boys were not natural allies but there were few outbreaks of violence and in any case there seemed to be plenty of spoils to go round.

Occasionally James went home to Alderley Edge where Jennifer continued to make herself available for sensuous encounters and she never failed to please. With maturity she had increased her repertoire of delights and James suspected that he was not the only recipient of her favours. In a way this was something of a relief to him since he did not want to think that she was waiting anxiously for his increasingly rare returns to the fold.

He gained the impression that she was reacting in typical fashion against her rather strict upbringing as a vicar's daughter – and good luck to her. She had now developed a little extra weight but it seemed to suit her, particularly as a good number of the pounds appear to have been added to her bay window and she now sported the most delightful pair of breasts he'd ever seen or indeed touched.

He was particularly struck by this one hazy summer's day when, Cyril and Penelope Penfold having gone out for the day and Jennifer having invited him to her bedroom for a particularly steamy tryst, she subsequently lay naked on her bed illuminated by the glow of a descending sun. Her golden orbs had a Rubenesque magnificence that arrested almost his entire attention, a little of his attention being diverted to the small triangle of hairs nestling between her creamy thighs which the sun also picked out like threads of silk.

It was an image that would live with him for many years. Yet thoughts of Jennifer were always followed by those of a young lady in black whom he would never see again. His short relationship with her in Venice would affect his relationships with other women throughout his life because she had been, and would remain, the love of his life. Other women would come and go but she would remain for ever in his thoughts. In quite a serious way that would become a problem for him in his future relationships.

James' ground training was followed by basic flying training on the Hunting Percival Jet Provost, recently introduced, and then advanced jet training on the de Havilland Vampire, at which stage he was awarded his much coveted pilot's wings. Finally he completed his training at the Lightning Operational Conversion Unit and was posted to 111 Squadron at RAF Wattisham in Norfolk.

He was now not only a fast jet fighter pilot but a pilot on one of the world's most advanced aircraft and he was very happy with life. What could be better? During the day he thundered around the skies at anything up to 1,500 miles an hour and in the evenings and at weekends he partied in the officers' mess or sought out girls in Bury St Edmunds, or Norwich or anywhere else in East Anglia that took his fancy. Moreover his meanderings around the area were now facilitated by the acquisition of a second hand, red, open top MGB. Things couldn't get any better, and yet they did. In 1965 he was posted to RAF Akrotiri in the south of Cyprus not far from Limassol.

Flying, swimming and exploring the island now took up much of his time but he also became interested, much to his own surprise, in amateur dramatics. The year before his arrival an Education Officer had produced a Shakespeare play at the nearby Roman amphitheatre at Curium. The production had been a great success in many respects, not the least of which was that the proceeds had gone to charities in Limassol, which greatly pleased the military hierarchy as a means of cementing relations with the local people on this troubled Island.

This year was to see the production of Antony and Cleopatra and James had been cast as Antony. So it was that we now find him one day at the theatre waiting his turn to rehearse.

It was a wonderful time of day. The afternoon on-shore breeze had given way to a still and mellow early evening as the sun, beginning its immersion on the horizon, sent out its last rays of warmth and painted the stone yellow ochre. James began to strain his eyes to make out the RAF base at Akrotiri across the bay but his attention was distracted, first by the lazy wheel of a griffon vulture overhead and then at his left foot by the fleeting scrabble of a gecko as it sought sanctuary in the scrub. In the distance he could just hear the dull thumping of a village irrigation pump.

'Act II, Scene V please!' The producer's voice called out from the centre of the amphitheatre down to James' right and James watched as members of the cast rose from the rings of tiered stones and made their way down to centre stage and out to the wings. As Antony, James was not yet needed and was glad of the opportunity to rest.

He'd arrived on the Island in September 1965 and expected to return from Cyprus to the UK in 1968. Life was good and he'd stay longer if he could. Starting work at 7 am was something of a bind, particularly if he'd had a late night party or been dancing into the early hours at a Turkish kebab restaurant in Limassol the night before. On the other hand he usually finished on the base at 1 pm each day, unless there was an exercise on, and after that his time was his own. At least that was the theory. In practice much of his spare time now was being taken up by the play.

It was early June, the sticky warmth lapped round him like a hot bath and trickles of sweat ran down the back of his neck and down his chest. The spring flowers had all gone now: cyclamen, anemones, wild chrysanthemum, crocus, orchids and rockrose. But the dry air was still pungently aromatic. Perhaps it was the sage or the carob trees or the wild olives.

He was sitting at the left hand end of the top tier of stone seating. Down to his right Cleopatra, Charmian and Mardian were rehearsing Act II Scene V. To James, Jane was not a typical Cleopatra with her tall, statuesque figure, her strawberry blond hair and her sea blue eyes, but no doubt the make-up artist would work a miracle. Personally he preferred her as she was and wished he knew her better. She was very outgoing, full of life and laughter, and extremely popular with all the men.

The rest of the cast, including roman soldiers, Egyptian attendants and various officials, sat around the amphitheatre reading, smoking or drinking soft drinks. The set was three quarters finished. Electricians were still laying cables, fixing Fresnel lights, and tinkering with dimmer boards. Various props were lying around. The producer was complaining irritably about the need to learn lines, adding 'and for God's sake put some life into it'. In other words all was normal with three weeks to go before the first night. No doubt it would be another stunning success and yet again a sizeable sum of money would be raised for Cyprus charities.

He was distracted by the grating of metal on stone to his left and looked down the sheer side of the amphitheatre to the passageway below. A member of the cast, a roman soldier, was standing quite still, watching a team of people putting up a marquee changing room on a nearby hill. He must have just turned and caught the tip of his sword on the stonework.

Well here at least was one member of the cast who was ready. James couldn't remember having seen him before but he certainly looked the part with his perfect uniform, impressive physique and deep tan. He looked like a Roman soldier from the top of his crested helmet to his sandaled feet. James looked away for a moment but when he looked back the soldier had gone, although he hadn't appeared in the theatre itself.

James was deeply moved by Curium: not just by the amphitheatre, which was so redolent of the ancient world, but also by the whole area of Apollo's Temple further along the escarpment and by the remaining evidence of the catastrophic earthquakes that had hit the area over the centuries.

He'd read that, according to Herodotus, Greek immigrants from Argos in the Peloponnese had founded Curium initially in 1200 BC and that the last of the Kings of Curium had sailed on his quinquereme with the Cyprus fleet to help Alexander the Great at the siege of Tyre. Curium city had finally been abandoned after a series of Arab raids in the 7th Century AD and the episcopal seat transferred to what was then Episkopi village.

In the second half of the nineteenth century, the American Consul, General di Cosnola, had discovered a great treasure at the Temple of Apollo comprising gold and silver ornaments, rings and ear rings, necklaces, vases, marble statuettes. James was fascinated by Curium and by the rich history of the whole island. Ruled at times by the Phoenicians, the Greeks, the Romans, the Turks, the British and others, Cyprus was now in dispute between the Greeks and the Turks and the British sphere of influence was restricted to the Sovereign Base Area and a few other military bases.

As he watched the sun sink below the horizon, other names associated with Cyprus came to mind. A little further west was Aphrodite's Rock where, according to legend, Homer had told of Aphrodite being born from the foam. Further east, King Richard 1st's ship had taken refuge at Limassol in a storm on his way to the 3rd Crusade. There he had married Princess Berengaria of Navarre on 12th May 1191. At Famagusta, according to legend, Othello had lived out his tragedy with

Desdemona before being immortalised by Shakespeare. If ever there was a place of magic on earth that wove history and legend together, this was surely it. He hoped that the island would continue to spin its magical web and yet the current names of EOKA, Grivas and Makarios didn't fire the imagination. Perhaps time would embellish them.

The producer calling him for the next scene brought his reverie to an end and he walked down the steps to the centre of the stage. The scene with Cleopatra didn't go particularly well. According to the producer, he was not showing enough passion for her. Later he sat on the stone steps with Jane while they had a break and a bite to eat. As always in this part of the world, darkness had descended quickly and the electricians had fired up the generator and put on the lights. The generator was hidden behind a small hill and the diesel engine was barely audible.

'Do you fancy a ham sandwich?' asked Jane.

'Yes, thanks,' replied James. 'They look delicious. And I've got a bottle of local wine if you fancy a drop. It's Commandaria.'

'We don't normally drink until we've finished rehearsals,' she said smiling. 'And Walter doesn't approve.'

'I'm not offering it to Walter, and in any case I need a drop. It's not as though I intend to stagger on set. Oh, I can see Walter's point of view. It must be difficult enough to produce the play without having a cast of drunks but one small glass with a sandwich isn't going to make any difference. In any case my performance couldn't be much worse according to what he said just now.'

'He didn't say that. He simply suggested you were a bit cool with me. Do you want to talk about it? Is it something I'm doing?'

James put down his ham sandwich and lit a cigarette, playing for time. He drew in deeply and blew out the smoke in a long thin stream. Of course he knew why he came across as cool towards her. It was because he found her so disturbingly attractive and didn't want her or anyone else to know. And the reason he didn't want them to know was that he didn't think he'd stand a chance with her. She wouldn't look at him twice and in any case she already had someone. That way lay humiliation, not to mention difficulties for future rehearsals.

'No, I'm sorry. It's just me. I can do the Roman imperial stuff but the romantic bit is rather harder.'

'I'm surprised. I saw you last year in that play at Berengaria and I thought you   played the love scenes very convincingly. What was her name? Louise Matthews?'

'Oh, that. Yes, but that was on a much smaller and more conventional stage,' he said, deliberately avoiding the reference to Louise. 'I think there's something about a roman amphitheatre that makes it more difficult to play intimate scenes. Here it's like acting in a goldfish bowl, almost surrounded by the audience; and you can see every one of them'.

Actually he thought he'd hit on a good point here because what he was saying was true. In a conventional theatre the footlights, floods and overheads meant you couldn't really see the audience at all. In Curium the spectators were there all round you, many of them eating from the hampers of food they'd brought. Seeing people gnawing on chicken legs wasn't his main difficulty with the love scenes but it certainly didn't help.

'Oh. Well that's all right then. I thought it might be something to do with me,' she said, and then she smiled at him.

'Hardly,' he said.

For a moment she looked as though she was going to take him up on his use of the word 'hardly'. Instead she took out a cigarette, lit it and lay back on her bag. Down below the Roman soldiers were sharing a joke and a wave of laughter rippled round the auditorium. From their body language it was a joke they found amusing but not one for the ladies. James noticed that only a couple of them had on any sort of uniform, and they were hardly complete.

'Where's the other one?' asked James, as much to himself as to Jane.

'The other what?' asked Jane.

'The other soldier,' replied James.

'There isn't another one. They're all there,' she said.

'No. I saw another one when I was sitting up there waiting for my scene. He was outside the amphitheatre over there, watching the chaps on the hill putting up the marquee. I hadn't seen him before but I noticed him particularly because he looked the part completely. He was totally ready, unlike the rest of us.'

'Well, I thought I knew them all but I suppose Walter could have found another one. I wonder where he is now then.'

'I wonder,' said James, but now that he was more relaxed, having talked himself out of a corner over the love scenes, he was able to pay more attention to Jane. She wasn't wearing anything particularly arresting - just a pair of fawn slacks and a pale blue shirt – but she looked devastatingly attractive, even in the glare of the stage lights. Her hair was lighter and more luminescent, her eyes glowed in the reflected light and a spotlight caught her right breast straining against her shirt. He wanted to reach out and hold its soft roundness in the palm of his hand. Instead he drained his glass and drew heavily on his cigarette.

At that moment he saw Walter climbing up the

stone seating towards them. Walter, a squadron leader over at Akrotiri, was tall, slim, dark and handsome. He was also happily married, faithful to his pretty wife Claudia, and so not a threat to any of the bachelors. He was also a little effete and therefore perhaps would not have constituted a major threat. From James's point of view he was pleasant enough and, more importantly, an excellent producer. As he approached them he was wearing his Gregory Peck half smile.

'Look you two. I've been thinking. There are several scenes we need to rehearse as a matter of urgency and they don't involve you. I want to work on those and pick up some of your scenes next time. Would you mind?'

'No. I don't mind at all,' said James, 'but in view of what you said earlier I'd rather thought I had a few things to put right'.

'No. I think your Antony's coming along very strongly. As I said, the main improvement to make is in the love scenes with Cleopatra here. Show a bit more passion. Look and sound as though you mean it. After all, she's not that bad looking,' Walter added, with a wink at Jane.

'There's nothing wrong with Jane. She's very attractive,' said James. 'It's just me. I'll work on it.' He didn't look at Jane as he spoke.

'I hope you've both finished talking about me', said Jane, who didn't look at all upset at being spoken about.

Their conversation was interrupted by more guffaws from the soldiers, who were apparently appreciating another joke. James was reminded of the missing one.

'Walter. I was just saying to Jane a moment ago that I saw another roman soldier over the back of the theatre a little while ago, and he wasn't one of those down there. But Jane says there aren't any more. Who's the one I saw?'

Walter looked down to the stage. 'No. Jane's right. There're only six and they're all there. I don't know who you saw'.

'Well… I must have been mistaken,' said James. He was incredulous but in view of Walter's categorical statement did not know what to say. He didn't want to accuse Walter of not knowing who was in the play he was producing. He had after all personally recruited every member of the cast; nor could he point to the seventh soldier because he was nowhere in sight.

'I must press on before this lot get bored. I'll see you two at the next rehearsal the day after tomorrow.' With that Walter turned and ran down the steps to the auditorium, calling out to everyone to get ready for the next scene.

'Well, I suppose we might as well go,' said James. 'You don't want to hang around any longer do you?'

'No, let's go,' agreed Jane, gathering up her bits and pieces. 'Do you fancy a drink on the way back?'

'Yes. Good idea. We could go to the bar in Episkopi village.' He was surprised but pleased she had suggested stopping on the way back. He really did fancy a drink but a drink with Jane was the icing on the cake.

James had given Jane a lift in from Limassol, about half an hour away. Episkopi village was five minutes from the Amphitheatre, on the way back. In the light from James' torch they made their way from the amphitheatre to his car and then drove off the gravel track onto the tarmac road. To their right a slender waning moon sent shivers of light down the sea.

The coastal road twisted and dived until they entered the Turkish village. The area was mostly Greek but here and there were Turkish enclaves and Episkopi village was one of them. The bar was immediately by the side of the road but there was little traffic at this time of night. James ordered a Keo beer for himself and for Jane a glass of Aphrodite, a dry white wine.

James sipped his beer gratefully and looked at Jane as she rummaged in her bag for her cigarettes and lighter. The air was sweet with the aroma of mimosa and alive with the trilling of a thousand cicadas. The flame from her lighter glanced off her eyes as she looked up at him. She inhaled deeply and blew the thin jet of blue smoke into the surrounding blackness.

'What are you thinking?' she asked.

'Of you.'

She continued looking at him without responding, clearly waiting for some elaboration. He paused, choosing his words carefully.

'I was thinking how much I'm enjoying acting in this play with you.'

'I'm glad,' she said, 'because I was beginning to think you don't like me too much; that you might think I'm just a dizzy blonde. I know I come across as pretty shallow at times whereas you seem much deeper. Still waters run deep, they say.'

This line of reasoning was a complete surprise to James and he dropped his normal reserve.

'I've always seen you as highly intelligent, very interesting, and strikingly beautiful: a very attractive woman in every sense of the word.'

She leaned across the table, put one hand on his and said, 'Then perhaps you should show your feelings more, or are you afraid of getting hurt?'

'Could be,' he replied, knowing that she had immediately struck on the right answer.

'Well, let me tell you something, James Winchester, that you don't appear to have realised. I was attracted to you the very first time I saw you, and that doesn't often happen to me. It wasn't anything to do with looks, although you're pretty good looking. It was just a very strong feeling that you are a totally genuine, reliable, honest person – and a little bit more.'

'What more?'

'That you're a bit of a devil underneath.'

'Perhaps.'

There was a pause, while they sipped their drinks, smoked and absorbed the significance of the new level their relationship had just reached. James's mind was sparking with thoughts of romance, love and entwined bodies on white sheets.

'Oh shit!' exclaimed Jane. James hadn't heard her curse before and it blew his romantic notions aside. 'I've left my address book up at Curium.'

'Not a problem. We'll just drive back and get it but let's finish our drinks first.'

'All right. Thanks.' She smiled at him and leant across the table to touch his hand. 'I'm so glad we've had this talk. Incidentally, before I forget, that business about the extra Roman soldier's a bit odd isn't it. I mean you did say you might have been mistaken, didn't you?'

'Yes I did, but what else could I say to Walter? He doesn't know who he's signed up? But I'm telling you I wasn't dreaming. There was another soldier there whatever Walter says.' She gave a non-committal shrug, clearly not knowing what to believe.

They finished their drinks and drove up the winding road back to Curium. James waited outside the amphitheatre while Jane went inside to collect her address book. It was a perfectly still evening and he could just hear some of cast speaking their lines. The party putting up the marquee had left now and there was nobody in sight, although it was difficult to see very much in the half-light of the moon and the overspill from the theatre lighting. In between the splashes of light it was as black as Hades.

He lit a cigarette and waited. She had clearly been

delayed speaking to someone but he didn't mind. He felt completely elated after his talk with Jane and filled with anticipation at the new turn their relationship had now taken. He thought he saw her, or at least a movement in the darkness, but then realised it couldn't be her since she had a torch. A moment later her torch came bobbing along the path round the wall of the amphitheatre.

'Are you there, James? ' she called, swivelling the torch around looking for him, and then she spotted the glow of his cigarette and came near.

'It's a lovely evening. Let's look at the sea.'

With the light of the torch they walked around the wall on the outside of the theatre until they were level with the back of the stage and they could see the sea. The play was always staged when there was virtually no moon so that its light would not interfere with stage lights but with three weeks to go before the first night there was a three quarter moon. They looked at its fragmented reflections sparkling across the sea and at the lights of RAF Akrotiri across the bay.

'You know,' she said, 'there are brief moments in life that we never forget and I think this is one of them.'

She reached out and squeezed his hand. They stood like that for a little while and then he put his arm round her waist and drew her towards him, turning into her at the same time. She looked up at him, completely relaxed, and smiled. He kissed her gently on the lips but then, as she opened her mouth in invitation, with increased urgency. She pulled him towards her, pressing the contours of her body into his, and he felt a rising hardness in his loins. Her back was hard against the stone wall as he thrust his limbs against her.

Suddenly she froze. 'I'm sorry', he said and pulled away from her.

'No, it's not you,' she said in a hoarse whisper. 'Someone's watching us.'

He turned round and there, just a little further down the passage, was the seventh Roman soldier. He was standing quite motionless, staring fixedly at them but without any particular expression or emotion. He didn't seem embarrassed, or friendly, or aggressive….or anything. He was just there.

'Can I help you?' asked James, 'or do you just want to stand and watch?' There was no response from the soldier.

'Well who the hell are you anyway?' asked James, stepping forward and feeling it was now time to put an end to this mystery. The response this time was immediate. The soldier leapt forward two paces with electric speed and took up a highly aggressive stance with his short sword raised in front of him. His expression was now fierce and determined.

'James. Be careful,' shouted Jane. 'Whoever he is he looks dangerous. Don't go near him'.

In fact James was not about to go forward any further. He too felt that the situation had suddenly taken an unexpected turn for the worse but wasn't sure what to do next. He couldn't run at him because he himself was unarmed and the soldier looked as though he knew very well how to handle the weapon he was now brandishing in James's direction. He certainly looked highly dangerous. Nor could James turn away because the soldier might be on him in a flash, and in any case he had to stand between him and Jane. With his heart pounding in his chest, his hands trembling and his legs feeling distinctly weak, he stood his ground and waited, wondering what he could do if an attack came. If he could escape the first cut with the blade, he might be able to land a punch. It seemed to be his only hope.

Jane thought otherwise and started shouting for help in a very loud voice. This seemed a highly practical course of action but not one that had occurred to James.

The racket she created also registered with the soldier, who for a moment seemed unsure of what to do. He glanced about him as voices responded from inside the amphitheatre.

'Hang on!

'We're coming!'

'Where are you?'

Suddenly the soldier turned sharply, knocking the bag round his waist against the amphitheatre wall, and disappeared round the corner. At that moment members of the cast appeared, breathless and excited.

'Are you all right?' 'What on earth's going on?' 'What's the problem?'

Jane put her arms round James and hugged him. Then she turned to face everyone and said, 'It's all right. We've just had a very nasty fright from a stranger but he ran off when you came.'

There were many urgent questions from all sides but James fended them off, saying that they had not had a proper look at him in the dim light and in any case perhaps he had not meant any harm. He'd suddenly come round the corner and taken them by surprise and he had looked rather threatening for a time but had then suddenly taken to his heels. He would try to give description of the stranger later but first wanted to speak to Jane in private to compare their perceptions. The truth was he was very confused and did not wish to make an idiot of himself by telling them what he really thought. Jane clearly had the same idea.

Some of the cast were less than satisfied with this and wanted to persist with further questions but Walter put a stop to it.

'Look. It's late. Let's call it a day and I'll speak to James and Jane tomorrow and we'll see if there's any more to be done.' James was thankful to him and waited until he had ushered them all back down the passage towards the amphitheatre. Jane waited for him while he went forward to the spot where they had last seen the soldier. He spotted something on the ground, stooped down and picked it up to examine it.

'What's that?' asked Jane.

'I'll show you later,' said James, taking her arm and leading her back to his car.

They were just getting into the car when Walter appeared.

'I hope you're going to tell me what that was all about. And don't tell me it was nothing. You were making enough noise to wake the dead,' he said to Jane.

'I know. I'm sorry. We'll talk to you in the morning.'

James and Jane drove off, at first in silence, both trying to find words to express their bewilderment, excitement and sense of shock, both hesitant at first to put words to their thoughts.

'Well at least you've seen the seventh soldier. I didn't dream about him. But who the Hell is he? I mean what lunatic dresses up as a roman soldier, lurks around in the shadows and then threatens people with a sword?'

'James. I know you're going to tell me not to be stupid but……..'. She was lost for words.

'Well. Come on. What are you trying to say?'

'I don't know. It's just that he looked…well, he looked so real.'

'I know what you mean. He did. He looked completely authentic and I'm very relieved he ran off. I thought for a moment he really was going to attack me and I'm sure I would have come off second best. He looked like a killer. He gave me a look that made me feel weak at the knees.'

She reached for his hand and squeezed it. 'I thought you were wonderful.'

They reached the outskirts of Limassol and the

lights of the bypass.

'Look,' said James. 'I know we had a drink in Epi village but we've had quite a shock since then and right now I could murder another beer.'

'Me too,' she agreed and so they pulled into one of many bars that never seemed to close.

They sat close together at a table under a wall light at the back of the bar and sipped their drinks.

'I know you're going to think I'm being completely ridiculous but what if he wasn't a lunatic dressed up as a roman soldier.'

'What do you mean? What else could he be?'

'What if he was the real thing?

'Do you mean a ghost? A phantom?'

'Well I told you it would sound silly but I cannot get over the fact that he looked so real in every sense.'

'I'm not laughing,' said James. 'In fact the thought kept crossing my mind but I didn't want to say anything. I had a very strange feeling in his presence, a cold feeling. In one sense he looked very real but in another he seemed completely unreal, as though he was ....well from another world.'

'What did you pick up in the passage? You bent down and picked something up. What was it?'

'Oh, I'd almost forgotten. I don't think it's anything important, certainly nothing to do with him. It looked like a new coin dropped by one of the cast.'

He fumbled in his pocket and eventually produced it and put it on the table. They looked at it but had some difficulty in seeing it clearly.

'Well it certainly does look like a new coin, but not one I've ever seen before. What does that writing say? Can you read it? I can't see it in this light.'

James held it up to the wall light and studied it carefully.

'Oh fuck!' he said, which was very unusual for

James who rarely used four letter words. 'This side has what I think is a roman flag between two eagles and it says LEG IV. The other side says ANT AVG III and then something I can't read. You don't think that ANT is for Antony, do you?'

In fact it was, as thy subsequently discovered when they handed the coin in to the District Museum in Limassol. The Cyprus Museum in Nicosia confirmed that the coin issuer was Antonia and that the coin was a Marc Antony denarius circa 32-31 BC.

James and Jane never did find a satisfactory explanation for that strange evening but for them the overall outcome was very satisfactory. After the final night of the play, the cast had a wonderful party, to which there were no uninvited guests and later James and Jane celebrated their new relationship with a night of unbridled passion. They continued their relationship until James was posted back to the UK in 1968.

EPISODE 4 – A NEAR MISS IN TEHERAN (1968)

Historical Context

1968 *Sen. Robert F. Kennedy is assassinated and Martin Luther King, Jr., civil rights leader, is killed in Memphis*

During 1968 James received warning of a posting from the Lightning Squadron at Akrotiri to a desk job at Strike Command Headquarters at RAF High Wycombe, which didn't please him, although the pill was sugared by promotion to squadron leader.

He was expecting to leave Cyprus sometime in the autumn but for some reason, known only to the Ministry of Defence, his posting was deferred. However, his replacement at Akrotiri arrived on time and so James was surplus to requirement on the squadron and now a squadron leader. The powers-that-be solved the problem by giving him a short term job at Near East Air Force Headquarters (NEAF) based at RAF Episkopi, not much more than a stone's throw from Akrotiri. This pleased James since it meant that he could stay on in Cyprus a little longer.

He was the desk officer for fighters in the Middle East, which sounded grand except that the squadron he'd just left was the only fighter squadron in the Middle East and it didn't need much help from him. Consequently his new boss, Wg Cdr Geoffrey 'Smokey' Midhurst, wondered if he'd mind taking on a bit of liaison work concerning listening posts in the Middle East. At the time a series of CIA radar sites in Turkey, Iran and Iraq were picking up information about Russian military activity and the RAF had some engineering involvement.

'Smokey' Midhurst acquired his soubriquet on account of his ancient briar pipe which he constantly ignited and which emitted clouds of blue smoke. On account of this some officers had attempted to call him 'Old Shag' but Geoffrey had taken exception to this and so, as a token of respect, the name was dropped in favour of 'Smokey'.

Geoffrey Midhurst was a battle scarred old warrior who'd flown, among other aircraft, Lysanders and Wellingtons in the Second War. He'd also flown a Hausa glider during the Rhine crossing. He was laid back, good humoured and looking forward to retirement to his house near Tunbridge Wells where he could tend garden and amble round a golf course. In the short time that he was going to be at NEAF, James thought he was going to enjoy working for 'Smokey'.

During his first week he met many fellow officers and civilians at the Headquarters, settled himself into the officers' mess and made use of the officers' club, a facility for officers of all three services. Although there were not many naval officers, the army was represented by a battalion drawn from different regiments on some sort of rotational basis which he didn't understand - but then he didn't understand too much about the army generally with their corps, divisions, regiments, and battalions.

What he did understand was that strange noises were regularly emitted from the office next to his which was occupied by a young army captain called Justin Weston-Appleby. Further acquaintance revealed that Justin had acquired a practice golf club and was attempting to improve his swing. There was seldom evidence of any additional activity in his office.

The Army seemed to have a rather different approach to life for which James had a sneaking admiration. He well remembered a recent visit to RAF Pergamos, a local base, by a battalion of the Royal Horse Guards and 1st Dragoons, otherwise known as the Blues and Royals, a cavalry regiment of the British Army and part of the Household Cavalry. They were coming to Cyprus to take part in an exercise. Two junior officers had arrived as an advanced party and the Station Commander, having welcomed them and accommodated them, was keen to talk to them about the exercise. However, he was bemused to discover that their priority was to organise polo ponies for the other officers shortly to arrive.

On another occasion, James was at an evening party at Pergamos after the battalion had arrived, when a lieutenant of the Blues and Royals had addressed himself to an RAF flight lieutenant's wife.

'Tell me, my dear, how does one get off the Island if one needs a change?'

'Well, you can either take a boat from Limassol or Famagusta, or an aircraft from Nicosia, depending on where you wish to go',

'Dammit', he said. 'I shall have to go by air. I've left my boat in the UK'. He did not appear to be joking.

For the first couple of weeks James learned what he was supposed to do and met a good many new people. It was in his third week that he came across a file entitled 'Teheran' and idly flicked through it. It contained a brief outline of the RAF involvement in Iran together with a few staffing details, although most of the staffing issues would be the concern of the Secretarial Branch officers.

He recognised the name of one of the officers in Teheran, Sqn Ldr Archie Middleton, an ex-aircrew officer who had joined the Admin Branch. James had met him on the BEA Med-Air flight when he'd first come to Cyprus in 1965. Archie had had to report for briefing to NEAF at Episkopi before taking up his new post in Teheran.

James had left Heathrow by Viscount at midnight and landed at Nice for coffee at 3am. They'd had breakfast in Malta, landed at Benina and Idris during the morning, arrive for lunch at El Adem in Lybia, and finally landed at Nicosia at tea-time. During all this time they'd sat together and chatted and so got to know quite a bit about each other. Now James began to wonder how Archie was getting on and so had a word with 'Smokey'.

'Yes, I recognise the name although he's not really on our net. We've had a few signals from him but, like you, he must be coming to the end of his time there soon. You don't fancy going out there to see him do you? We had an adverse comment last year from the C-in-C because we haven't been for some time'.

James hadn't given the possibility a thought, but the idea of going there was very appealing. He had little to do in his present temporary role, he would enjoy catching up with Archie Middleton, and a brief look at Teheran could be interesting.

'Fine, Sir. I'll set up a visit as soon as possible but what….hmm…what exactly is the purpose of the visit, other than of course to please the C in C.

'Oh come, James. You're on the Headquarters' staff now. You know the sort of thing: 'liaison visit to ensure compatibility of aims, contribution to allied defence posture, communications, progress status, command and control etc'. You're never going to make it to the Ministry of Defence if you can't learn the language.'

James wasn't at all sure he wanted to make it to the MOD and in any case his studying for promotion examinations to date had stressed the need for clarity of expression. Nevertheless he would do his best to adapt to the requirement on this occasion for the sake of a 'jolly' to Teheran.

He encountered his first stumbling block in the General Office, where he learned that an Argosy aircraft from Akrotiri flew out once a month on a Friday and came back on the Monday and so he could go either for a weekend or for a month. Clearly a weekend was too short and there was no way that 'Smokey' would sanction a month.

'However', added the admin sergeant, 'there is another solution, although you might not like it, Sir.'

'What is it?' asked James.

'Well, I could book you out on a Cyprus Airways flight from Nicosia to Beirut but the snag is that you'd have to spend a night there before catching a connection to Teheran'. The connection was a 707 Pan Am flight staging through from New York to Hong Kong.

'For Queen and country', said James, 'I am willing to exert myself'.

One morning three weeks later James made the flight to Beirut and booked into a hotel there. On first impressions, the town had a well-earned reputation as the jewel of the Middle East. It was in fact an important centre for gold and jewelry as well as an attractive tourist spot, with excellent hotels and lovely beaches.

In the afternoon he took a trip in the city by bus and was fortunate enough to fall into conversation with a Lebanese lecturer from the American Academy who kindly showed him around for the rest of the afternoon.

The next day he arrived at Teheran where he was met by the Air Attaché, William Alderson, a sprightly young wing commander who looked as though he'd just stepped out of an advertising brochure. He drove James to his hotel where they had a drink.

'So if you're only here for a week, you'd better come down to the General Office first thing in the morning and we'll fix you up with a few travel warrants.

'Where do you suggest I go?' asked James tentatively, not wanting to show his ignorance about the location of Air Force personnel in the country.

'Well you can't quite get round everywhere in a week. I suggest you deal with the chaps here tomorrow, catch a train to Babel Shar on Tuesday and come back on Wednesday. Then you can fly to Mashed on Thursday and get back here on Friday. That means you can catch your flight back to Beirut on Saturday morning. Enjoy yourself but don't forget to let me have a copy of your report.'

James met a number of officers and airmen in Teheran the following day but the highlight for him was meeting up again with Archie. He wasn't a big man, but he had an obvious charm. With his raffish smile, his debonair manner and his impeccable good manners he'd obviously come from the David Niven School of life.

'Well old bean,' he'd said after welcoming James to his office. ' How's Cyprus been treating you? Haven't made the mistake of getting yourself hitched, have you?'

'Cyprus is wonderful and no, I haven't got myself hitched. But you're a fine one to talk. You're already married.'

'Well, yes, sort of. I mean the memsahib and I have sort of drifted somewhat. She decided to stay in the UK while I came to Iran and now it's not clear if we'll ever get together again. In the meantime there are other distractions here. You might meet one of them later this week. What's your programme?'

'Well, I'm going to Babel Shar on Tuesday and coming back on Wednesday and then Thursday I'm off to Meshed and coming back on Friday and so it doesn't leave much time.'

'Plenty of time, Squire. You've got this evening, Wednesday evening and Friday evening. I'll pick you up this evening at your hotel. How would 7.30 pm suit you? We can eat out'.

James discovered that Teheran under the Shah was a lively place with many good restaurants and interesting entertainment centres, including the Choux Café Nu and the Cleopatra, which had a plentiful supply of nubile females. While sipping a whisky in the latter, he suddenly realised that he recognized some of the girls doing a striptease. He'd seen them before in the nightclub in Hero's Square in Limassol. They were obviously on some kind of Middle East circuit. Later he paid a small fee for a dance with one of them and she confirmed that they covered Cyprus, Iran , the Lebanon and sometimes Iraq.

Mindful of his journey to Babel Shar in the morning, James persuaded Archie to take him back to his hotel before midnight although he had the impression that Archie would have stayed much longer. He clearly knew some of the girls very well and his popularity was evidenced by their reluctance to let him go.

Once back at James's hotel, Archie insisted on having a nightcap while he explained to James what to expect in the week ahead at Babel Shar and at Meshed. He also explained that on the Friday evening there was going to be a party not to be missed. An old friend of his, a BOAC captain, was flying a Comet out from Heathrow with an additional slip crew. The aircraft was carrying on to Hong Kong but the captain and his crew were staying on for three days before returning to London.

Archie said there would be one great party on the Friday evening that was not to be missed. Since James was due back in Teheran at 5pm on the Friday he would be in time for the party, which was due to start at the bar in his hotel. In the meantime, he had a little more travelling to do.

In the morning an Iranian jeep picked him up at his hotel to take him to the railway station to catch a train to Babolsar. At least that is what James had been led to believe. The only snag was that the Iranian Air Force driver had not been instructed on the destination and did not speak English. James had been rather late leaving his hotel and so time was short. He now made desperate attempts to imitate the sound and motion of a train which the driver appeared to understand but James' powers of simulation were clearly restricted since they duly arrived at Teheran bus station. It was too late to catch the only train but to his immense relief and surprise he found there was a bus that went to Babolsar and it was leaving in twenty minutes time.

So it was that, clad in a Harris Tweed jacket and a pair of fawn cavalry twill trousers., he climbed aboard the Babolsar express, along with innumerable Iranians and several baskets of anxious and highly vocal chickens. Sleep seemed a good idea after his evening out with Archie but this was rendered difficult on account of the erratic performance of the driver and the overpowering aroma of garlic that just about everyone on the bus must have been eating for breakfast. It was at times such as this that he regretted his tendency to volunteer for every new experience that came his way but boredom, mild anxiety and nausea were later to be subsumed by the single central emotion of fear.

The landscape began to change as they ground their way up the Alborz Mountains north of Teheran on their journey to the Caspian Sea. Soon they reached the snow line and James was surprised to see people skiing there, although on reflection he shouldn't have been since Iran had a middle and upper class with high levels of income. Eventually they stopped for a fifteen minute break in the middle of nowhere, except for a shed which, since this was a five hour trip, James had no option but to enter. The memory would live in his memory as long as the smell of second hand garlic.

He resumed his seat at the back of the bus but became aware of an altercation at the front between the driver and a male passenger sitting next to him. The driver then shouted and pushed the man out of his seat before turning and gesticulating to someone further down the bus. That someone turned out to be him. The driver was signalling him to come to the front and take the place of the poor unfortunate who'd been ejected. On his way forward he apologized to the man who'd taken a seat further back but a sullen scowl was the only response, which was hardly surprising under the circumstances and given their mutual inability to communicate.

The driver shook his guest warmly by the hand; gestured for James to sit next to him; and then roared off, keen to demonstrate the performance of his elderly vehicle and his own driving prowess. Standing a Lightning fighter on its tail at the end of the runway and rocketing skywards up to 50,000 feet was all very well, but sitting in the suicide seat next to a lunatic driving down a mountain range was quite another.

Any potential relief to be gained from reaching dry roads below the snow line was immediately countered by an increase in speed. Thoughts of garlic and general discomfort were now dispelled as he concentrated on each corner that loomed up, willing the bus to get round each tyre shrieking, rubber burning bend. And just as the bus ceased its violent rocking motion and straightened up briefly after the previous bend, yet another one appeared ahead requiring James' full concentration to urge it round.

Contrary to all that's sensible and logical, the bus finally reached the plain to the north of the mountains and James was able to spare some attention for the surrounding countryside.

He hadn't known quite what to expect but it wasn't what he saw. It seemed somehow Asiatic and then he realised he was looking at rice fields as far as the eye could see. He also had a strange sensation that he'd just stepped back five hundred years in time. There were strange, earth-roofed cottages emitting smoke which climbed lazily into a clear blue sky and wild horses that ran at the sound of this weird animal that emitted clouds of blue smoke and made the most appalling noise.

However, life appeared to advance a few centuries as they rolled into Babolsar and into a rather quaint square near to the sea, where James found himself deposited along with the rest of his travelling companions. He looked around for any European looking person who might have come to meet him but there was none. However there was, to his immense surprise, what appeared to be an ancient London taxi. Drawn to the only thing in sight reminiscent of England, he addressed himself to the elderly Iranian driver with the only expression he could think of which might offer a form of communication.

'Royal Air Force?'

There was an immediate recognition and he thankfully boarded the taxi and was driven sedately to a villa by the side of the Caspian Sea. The villa was the temporary residence of two flight lieutenants while a number of NCOs shared another villa nearby.

A wizened retainer met James at the front door and ushered him to a spacious lounge where he was shortly joined by Flt Lt Brian Edwards, a slim, fair haired and fresh faced young man with a slight stoop, more characteristic of a laboratory boffin than a military man.

'Would you like a cup of tea, Sir'', proffered the bespectacled young man, and so began James' brief sojourn by the Caspian Sea, only a short distance from the Russian border. He didn't see much of the town while he was there and didn't learn a great deal either. It had apparently once been a significant port, it was now more important as a holiday resort and just short of 12,000 souls lived there but he didn't get much of a chance to look round since the flight lieutenants had decided to eat in and the rest of the time James was occupied speaking to the two officers and other RAF personnel.

Over dinner, a quiet affair with just the two officers, James said he'd heard they had very lively parties at Babolsar. In fact it was Archie who'd assured him he would have a pretty hot time and that local girls were invited to help things along. However, the two officers played it down, suggesting that such stories were wildly exaggerated. James came to the conclusion that for them Archie was a known quantity who would appreciate a good time, whereas he himself, an unknown visitor from HQ NEAF, might set rumours running.

He left at lunch time the following day, experienced another white knuckle ride back to Teheran, and spent the evening having a quiet drink in the bar. Archie was apparently dining out with Cobra, an Iranian lady friend.

On the Thursday morning he was driven out to the airport to catch an aircraft for Mashhad, the other side of Iran near the border with Afghanistan. It was a scheduled two hour flight in a DC 6 of Iran Airways. Once again, as far as he could tell, he was the only European on the aircraft. He settled back to read a book as the piston engines turned over crankily one by one, explosively ignited ejecting clouds of black and blue smoke, and then roared into life.

An hour and forty minutes later James put his book away as the captain of the DC 6 throttled back the engines to a whisper and the aircraft started its descent from a clear blue sky towards the towering cumulus clouds below. They sank gently into the white candy floss, which soon changed to a muddy grey as they reduced altitude and the aircraft began to buck and tremble as it encountered rising currents of air.

To an accustomed aviator such as James this was all

perfectly normal but to many of the other passengers the thumping and juddering was an alarming experience, possibly in their minds presaging imminent disaster. People started talking to each other, perhaps in mutual reassurance or perhaps as a distraction from their situation. A couple across the aisle from James held hands.

James' perhaps somewhat smug self-confidence was a little constrained when the captain suddenly opened the throttle, checked the descent, and then started to climb. After a couple of minutes they rose once more above the clouds where they circled for a while before starting a second descent. If this procedure made James curious and slightly uneasy, it spread visible alarm among many of the other passengers, whose movements and facial expressions showed considerable agitation.

James listened carefully and could detect nothing amiss with the engines and in any case descending and then climbing again was not consistent with an engine problem. Nor could he detect anything odd about the handling of the aircraft although such a problem would not necessarily be evident to a passenger. His conclusion was that there was probably either something wrong at the airfield preventing an immediate landing or else the pilot had a navigation problem; in short he didn't quite know where he was.

After half an hour of descending and climbing, the ambience in the aircraft was tense, made worse by the fact that no announcement had been made to the passengers. The pilot made yet another descent but this time continued the trajectory and James gritted his teeth. His knowledge of the geography of the area was admittedly vague but he had an impression that Mashad was on a plain, or at least he was holding on to that hope. Descending blind into a mountainous area was virtual suicide. He gritted his teeth and waited.

The aircraft continued to bump and rock as it sank downwards, the view from the window disturbingly grey and sombre. Suddenly he caught sight of the ground and it confirmed his worst suspicions. They had dropped into a valley, the sides of which towered on either side of the aircraft. The pilot and everyone in the aircraft had had luck on their side. In fact James estimated that they had let down some way west of Mashad since the aircraft was now continuing down the valley in an easterly direction. In due course they arrived at the airport, joined the circuit and made a routine approach and landing.

He was met by three Marconi technicians who were working with the RAF staff and who had come to take him to his hotel. They were amused by the late arrival of the aircraft and explained that the captain was an American employed by Iran Air to fly a daily triangle from Teheran to Mashhad and then to Tabriz before returning to Teheran. On this occasion he'd lost his navigational aids and had elected to descend on the basis that he knew where he was since he made the flight every day. James was pleased to learn this now that he was safely on the ground and not before. The pilot sounded like an accident waiting to happen and travel in Iran was clearly not without interest.

His tight timetable didn't allow James much time to look around the town but he did learn that it was the second most populous city in the country and the capital of Razavi Khorasan Province. It had been a major stopping point on the ancient Silk Road and had long been revered for housing the tomb of Imam of Reza, the eighth Shia Imam. Apparently every year millions of pilgrims visit the Imam Reza shrine and pay their respects to his shrine. He would like to have spent longer there but work called shortly after he'd booked into his hotel and the next day he was back on the same aircraft returning to Teheran, this time fortunately without incident. Sitting on the aircraft under a clear blue sky without much chance of bumping into mountains, he was able to turn his mind to the party later that evening which Archie had assured him would be a real 'crackerjack'.

James arrived at his hotel in Teheran at 5pm, showered and went down to the bar to find Archie, his friend and the rest of the crew. As he opened the swing doors he immediately noted Archie on the other side of the round bar. He appeared to be heavily engaged with an exotic looking lady with very long, black hair and a startling red dress. Archie saw him and waived a welcome, gesticulating that he should work his way round to his side of the bar. He gesticulated because the room was crowded and the noise level very high. It already had the look and feel of a lively party and it was barely 6pm.

Archie introduced him to his lady friend, Ziba, which apparently means 'beautiful', and in her case it seemed entirely appropriate. The rest of the jostling crowd in the bar all seemed to be BOAC employees. Archie's friend Peter Gosling, his crew and the slip crew were all there, but word seemed to have got around the BOAC offices at Teheran Airport and many other staff had also turned up. James downed a large beer, loosened up after his travels and met some of the crew.

The co-pilot was a handsome young chap called Simon Westfield who'd gained his wings in the RAF on a short service commission and then left to join BOAC. He seemed to be in hot pursuit of one of the air stewardesses, Samantha Wilson, a dark-haired beauty with an eye-popping figure. James spoke to them both for a short time and was quickly seduced by her charm and intelligence as well as by her obvious physical attractions but he felt he was in the way of a budding romance and moved on to talk with one of the other stewardesses, this one a blue-eyed blonde. He found her pleasant, friendly and attractive but he did not feel the same radiated warmth that Samantha emanated.

He was wondering whom next to meet when a smiling Archie grabbed him by the arm.

'I saw you chatting to Gillian. What do you make of her?'

'She seemed very pleasant and she's certainly attractive but somehow she's not quite my type and I got the impression that I'm not quite her type either.'

'Just as well, Squire. I've got my eye on that one and Peter said she's looking for a new romance. It could be my lucky day.

'But I've just met your friend, Ziba. What about her?'

'Unfortunately she's been called away on a family matter. Pity that,' he added with a wink. 'Now who've you got your eye on here?'

'Well I don't want to be a spoil sport but I'm looking forward to a pleasant evening without involvement. In any case I leave for Cyprus first thing in the morning. I'll have to be up at first sparrow's fart.'

'Good Lord, I wouldn't have taken you for a party pooper. Perhaps you'll change your mind once we get the party underway. How about that 'hostie' over there? The dark haired one? I'll bet she could raise your spirits, among other things.'

'She's already taken. She seems to be at very close quarters with young Simon the co-pilot.'

'Oh for goodness sake, he's a babe in arms. Get in there with a bit of your Errol Flynn charm and tickle her fancy. In the meantime, we need to get started. First we're off to the Hilton to the crew's suite for a few jars and then we'll hit the town.'

In fact Archie never got round to hitting the town. They all tumbled into taxis for the short ride to the

Hilton and drinks were ordered up to floor six where the party continued. Since Archie was now heavily involved with Gillian, James floated from one group to another but avoided Simon and Samantha who continued to be heavily engrossed in each other's company. It was all pleasant enough until the cry went up that the Chou Café Nous was to be the next destination for everyone – well, everyone that is except for Archie who seemed to have retired to Gillian's bedroom and was not seen again that evening.

'What a poor show,' exclaimed Peter. 'I come all this way to look up an old friend and he buggers off with one of my crew'. Although perhaps not strictly true in any sense, James understood the sentiment.

Fifteen minutes later James was in the Choux Café Nous with one or two others, the rest having apparently moved on the Cleopatra. Before long he found himself sitting on a chaise long with a local beauty paying an exorbitant price for a couple of drinks, well at least exorbitant by Iranian standards if not by London standards. James was not sure if there were other delights on offer but he was content to chat and sip his drink while Jasmine put an arm round him and chatted to him in passable English. As she did so his thoughts returned to Samantha Wilson, who had made more of an impact on him than he cared to admit. Unfortunately she had gone straight to the Cleopatra.

Less than an hour later it was clear that the main event was at the Cleopatra and so they moved on there, to find the rest of the party in high spirits watching a floor show. James ordered a whisky and joined them, choosing to sit on a vacant bench seat next to Samantha. On her other side of course was Simon the handsome co-pilot.

The show was acceptable without being outstanding but the company was very amusing and he found himself talking more and more to Samantha, who increasingly seemed less and less interested in talking to Simon. He discovered that she lived in Guildford and was a member of the Yvonne Arnaud Theatre there and that her other interests included music, painting, skiing and art. They seemed to have much in common and at one point Samantha suggested he might like to visit her at home and join her in a visit to the theatre. The idea seemed very attractive and he was on the point of deciding to take her up on the offer when she suddenly made a more direct and stunning suggestion as she leaned towards him and whispered in his ear.

'I don't want to sound ungrateful to Simon, who's been very attentive, but I'm afraid I'm finding him awfully boring. You wouldn't like to be an angel, would you, and take me back to my hotel?

In fact James would very much like to have taken her back to her hotel and not been an angel but his brain was trying to sound a small alarm through an alcohol induced fog. There was something he had to think about before heading off to paradise with Samantha but what the hell was it? Time! What time was it? He looked at his watch and saw that it was 3.30am but that was all right because he'd finished his work in Iran and all he had to do was fly back….Oh no! That was it! He had to fly back to Beirut and Cyprus but it was now today that he was flying back and his plane from Teheran Airport was at 6 am. Oh shit!

'I'm sorry Samantha,' he blurted out. 'But I must go. I've a plane to catch at 6 am'. With that he said a general farewell to all and sundry and fled from the Cleopatra.

He was lucky enough to catch a taxi straight away. Within ten minutes he was back at this hotel and within another fifteen minutes he'd packed and paid his bill and was getting back into the same taxi. At the airport he was just in time to get through the gate and was shortly afterwards settling down in his seat for the 707 flight back to Beirut. It was only then that he had time to think about what he'd done. He'd just turned down one of the most attractive women he'd ever met, and one who perhaps nearest to his long lost love in Venice. Life could be a sod.

Later he wondered what Samantha must have thought. She'd made him a very clear proposal and he'd reacted by apologising and rushing away. He imagined she wouldn't have expected a reaction like that and it probably had never happened to her before. He resolved to contact the Arnaud Theatre in Guildford once he was back in the UK in the hope of finding her address or telephone number but of course he never did. Life moves on and times change.

He was back in his office at HQ Near East Air Force on the Monday morning when Wing Commander 'Smokey' Midhurst walked in behind a blue cloud of incinerating Balkan Sobranie tobacco.

'Morning James. How did the trip go?'

'Oh fine, Sir. I'm just getting down to writing my report which I'll let you have tomorrow if I can get it typed quickly.'

'Well there's no great rush. This week will do. No problems then?'

James recounted his trip briefly, highlighting his alarming trip by bus over the Alborz Mountains and his equally worrying flight to Mashhad.

'So you had two near misses then. I knew I'd been right to send you and not go myself'. He smiled and winked at James.

Yes, thought James, but it was the near miss on his last night in Teheran that he would most remember and most regret.

EPISODE 5 - A JOLLY IN GIBRALTAR (1968 – 1973)

Historical Context

1968 *Czechoslovakia is invaded by Russians and Warsaw Pact forces to crush liberal regime*
1969 *Richard M. Nixon is inaugurated 37th president of the U.S, and Apollo 11 astronauts—*
Neil Armstrong, Edwin E. Aldrin, Jr., and Michael Collins—take man's first walk on the moon
1970 Rhodesia severs ties with British Crown and US troops invade Cambodia
1971 A military junta led by Major General Idi Amin seizes power in Uganda
1972 Start of the Watergate Scandal and the "Christmas bombing" of North Vietnam
1973 Vietnam War ends and the fourth and biggest Arab-Israeli conflict begins as Egyptian and
Syrian forces attack Israel as Jews mark Yom Kippur

James eventually took up his desk job at RAF High Wycombe, HQ Strike Command. It was bound to happen but that didn't lessen the pain and so he did everything he could to get himself airborne as often as possible but there was one opportunity he seized which he could have well done without.

He was having a quiet drink early one Saturday evening in the Officers' Mess bar when he struck up a conversation with an amiable flight lieutenant called 'Tubby' Weston. 'Tubby' had been to a meeting at RAF Northwood the previous day but was staying at High Wycombe for the weekend to look up a few old friends.

He would be going to see them later that evening but in the meantime had decided to take in a jar or two before heading off to the married quarter patch.

'Tubby' had recently been posted to RAF Kinloss near Inverness with the reformation of 8 Squadron in a maritime role flying Shackletons. With the planned scrapping of HMS Ark Royal, the Royal Navy's last conventional aircraft carrier, the RN was worried that their task groups would lose their airborne early warning capability. This had been achieved by using the Fairey Gannet, fitted with the AN/APS 20 radar.

The solution to this problem was to fit the Gannet's radar to a long-range land based aircraft until a more modern system could be designed. The Nimrod MR1 had recently entered service with the RAF and this had released Shackleton airframes to be fitted with the Gannet radar. As a result, 8 Squadron had reformed at RAF Kinloss on 1 Jan 1972 and its aircraft were equipped with the "new" Shackleton Airborne Early Warning Mk 2.

'Tubby' was one of the Squadron's captains. James was aware in general terms of 8 Squadron's new role and also of the Shackleton's reputation as an airborne fast food outlet. Its galley was particularly renowned for bacon sandwiches, a possible explanation for 'Tubby's' girth.

While James was bemoaning his lot in having to do a desk job, 'Tubby' was envious that James had spent so much time on fighters while he was lumbering around the skies in an aircraft developed from the wartime Lancaster – but at least he was flying.

They agreed to meet up the following day and go to a local pub for lunch, which gave James an opportunity to show off his newly-acquired red MG sports car, and it was over lunch that 'Tubby' suggested that James might like to go up to Kinloss to 'see how the other half lived'.

At first James wasn't too enthusiastic. Getting up to Kinloss might be a bit of a drag and would probably be quite expensive but the more they talked the more James saw the opportunity for 'a jolly' with a work-related benefit. In their new role, Shackletons would provide early warning of enemy attack and that information would be directed to the UK defence system for an appropriate response and that response would usually involve fighters.

As a Strike HQ desk officer for fighters, James had a legitimate reason to make a visit 8 Squadron. The icing on the cake was that Tubby was scheduled to make a training flight to Gibraltar and so they hatched a plan that James would cease work at High Wycombe one Wednesday afternoon and catch the overnight sleeper to Inverness that same evening. 'Tubby' would meet him on the Thursday morning at the station and take him to RAF Kinloss where James would learn more than he already knew about 8 Squadron's airborne early warning role. With the rest of the crew they would take off for Gibraltar in the early hours of Friday morning and fly back up to Scotland on the Monday morning.

The following morning James broached the subject with his boss, Wg Cdr 'Stuffy' Watkinson. 'Stuffy' was an ex-wartime warrior who'd earned an AFC and a DFC flying Hurricanes and Spitfires at home and overseas and had thus gained a well-deserved reputation.

James sometimes had difficulty in relating the swashbuckling young hero of yesteryear with the gaunt, rather serious and generally correct individual for whom he now worked, but that was perhaps at least partly explained by his marriage to the formidable Henrietta. Poor 'Stuffy' and had made a considerable contribution to the defeat of Goering's Air Force only to find himself later ensconced with a female equivalent, in terms both of overbearing presence and of physical stature.

At first 'Stuffy' was wary of James's suggestion and said he couldn't spare him to go off on 'a bloody jolly to Gibraltar'. He asked a range of penetrating questions but James had anticipated the grilling and was well briefed. A compromise was reached with James undertaking to produce a comprehensive report of his visit and recommendations for future contacts.

'Right,' said 'Stuffy', 'so that's that. You fix up the trip a.s.a.p. but with the timescale we've agreed. I don't want you groping some Scottish maiden round the Trossachs when you should be back here. I can't afford to have you away any longer than necessary and your reputation can't afford any more dents at present. I don't personally care if you roger every bit of available crumpet between here and Marble Arch, but please refrain from mixing your hobbies with work and do not bring the RAF into disrepute.

'Stuffy' was referring to a recent mess party to which James had invited a young lady as his guest. While the rest of the party were engaged in a conga line, kicking their legs out in time to the rhythmic beat of Harry Burt's local jazz band, James was in the darkened ante-room across the corridor becoming better acquainted with his guest. All would have been well had not the head of the conga line decided to lead the others out of the dance area, across the corridor, and into the darkness of the ante-room.

'Lights!' shouted those at the front, as they plunged into the blackness and someone further back in the line switched on the lights. It was too late for James and his guest to take evasive action and so they simply froze like animals in the presence of an attacker. Of course many animals are naturally camouflaged and so the tactic can work for them but not so in this case. Their wildly staring eyes would have been enough to draw attention to them but the real attraction was the naked right breast of the lady cradled in James right hand. To their credit those in the conga line kept their rhythm and continued to kick their legs up at the appropriate point as they jogged past the alarmed couple.

The Air Officer for Administration, or AOA as he was generally known, had overall responsibility for discipline. He might not have taken action had it not been for his wife but she was adamant that such behaviour should not go unpunished and so it was that James had found himself on the carpet, literally, in front of Air Cdr Johnson's desk the following Monday morning to receive a 'bollocking'. He was told that he was walking on thin ice but since neither of the parties in question was married, no further action would be taken. Extra marital dalliance in the RAF was looked upon very seriously and would have resulted in a posting at the very least.

Three weeks after his talk with 'Stuffy', James was at Euston Station to catch the overnight sleeper for Inverness, having completed a day's work in the office. He'd been on this trip once before and loved it: dinner with wine followed by a whisky, a good sleep, breakfast and then arrival at Inverness by 9a.m. in the morning. 'Tubby' was there to meet him and they arrived at RAF Kinloss where James attended the morning flying briefing and then spent the rest of the day learning about 8 Squadron and its new role.

He also learned more about the Shackleton itself. The Shackleton had an unfortunate reputation for accidents although some of its contemporaries fared far worse. The Gloster Meteor for example had a total of over 430 fatal losses of aircrew in peacetime flying compared with, as James was to learn in later life, the Shackleton's 156. The aircraft acquired by 8 Squadron had all seen service in the Middle East and had been due to end their days at RAF Catterick providing fire practice for the RAF

Regiment.

The new AEW role meant that they would now be subject to a refurbishment programme but most of the aircraft had yet to done. In the meantime, the crews had christened each with the name of a Magic Roundabout character. James was introduced during the day to the aircraft that would transport him, 'Tubby' and his crew to Gibralter. It was called Zebedee, although Mr Rusty would have been more appropriate judging from its overall condition.

ETD was scheduled for the Friday morning at 3 am but since James was classed as 'supernumerary crew' and therefore not required to perform an active role on the flight, he could spend the evening at a mess party. So it was that a rather tired James joined the rest of the crew to don a flying suit, acquire a headset and attend a flight briefing. Just before 3a.m. the four Griffon engines each spluttered in turn and then roared into life as 'Tubby' went through his pre-flight checks and then taxied round the perimeter track to the end of runway 26 to face a light south westerly breeze.

Take-off was always one aspect of any flight that excited James. It was the roar of the engines on full power, the gathering of speed down the runway and the defeat of gravity that always brought joy to his soul and even the lumbering Shackleton had an effect on him. However, after twenty minutes tiredness began to take its toll and he went aft to the tail where he could lie down and watch lights on the ground pass underneath as they crossed Scotland in a south westerly direction and headed for the Atlantic. He unplugged his headset to cut off the occasional chatter of the crew but kept it on to dull the roar of the engines. Within ten or fifteen minutes he was asleep.

He awoke to a startlingly bright day as the sun climbed into the sky to his right. His head was resting on the Perspex dome and he looked straight down to a blue sea specked with thin dashes of white crests. He looked at his watch and estimated that the trace of land way over to the right was Land's End. They had a long way to go but at a cruising speed of about 240 mph the whole trip would take about eight hours. He plugged in his headset and gathered that food was already being dispensed in the galley and he suddenly realized that he was hungry.

Although there was a normal crew of ten for operational work, this was a training flight with a total complement of fifteen, some of whom like he himself had come along for the ride, and most of them seemed to be hanging around the galley area as far as that was possible in the confined space. 'Tubby' had left his co-pilot up front and was working his way through a bacon sandwich.

'Grab yourself a bacon sarnie,' he yelled above the din of the engines. 'When you've finished you can come up front with me and John can get some breakfast'. John McArthur was the co-pilot, a fresh faced young man who was disappointed not to be on fast jets but nevertheless still keen on flying whatever form it took.

Twenty minutes later James found himself in the right hand seat with the yolk in his hand under instruction to keep a steady heading and maintain a height of 3,000 feet, which wasn't very difficult given the calm conditions. With little else to do other than periodically carry out an instrument check and slightly alter the heading from time to time when the navigator came through, James realised just how easy it would be to fall asleep.

Engaging in idle chatter was kept to a minimum and so James settled back and thought about other things, including the pneumatic Jennifer, whom he still continued to see occasionally. She was really an enduring friend although their friendship still sometimes took the form of a good hard physical encounter. To her sex was a jolly good sport to be enjoyed with one or two really close friends but there was no sign of her getting married.

It was while he was ruminating in this way that 'Tubby' suddenly drew his attention to a ship which was coming up on the nose.

'I have control', he announced, taking the yolk and easing back on the throttle. 'Let's have a closer look at Boris down there.'

'Boris?' queried James

'Yes,' said 'Tubby'. It's a Russian spy vessel thinly disguised as a fishing trawler. 'Just look at the aerial array.' In fact the aerials didn't mean much to James but they clearly seemed over the top for a fishing boat.

'Tubby' quickly brought Zebedee down to 1,000 feet and then went into a tight circle overhead, or least as tight a circle as a Shackleton could manage.

'We'll just let them know that we've spotted them'.

Several of the ship's crew members came out on deck and started waving, which amused James but didn't surprise him. When flying Lightning's he'd sometimes been sent out to intercept a Russian 'Bear' over the North Sea and exchanged waves with the intruder. Probing western defences was something the Russians did on a very regular basis and it was a deadly game in reality but the crews were all human beings who seized light-hearted moments whenever possible.

After a few circles around the trawler they picked up their previous heading and climbed back to 3,000 feet. The Shackleton's maximum altitude was about 20,000 feet but life was more interesting at 3,000 feet with the occasional ship to look at and it still gave the crew time to bail out in the event of an emergency.

Having spent the best part of an hour up front, John

returned to take up his seat and James went back to sit with the navigator, who seemed to be the only crew member who was actually doing much during the flight.

Brian Higgins was an old 'hairy' from wartime days who was beginning to look forward to picking up his pension and paddling on the beach near   his house in Cornwall. He'd been on Lancasters in World War II and been lucky to escape two tours of operational flying. He was solid, reliable and assiduous on his work, constantly checking and rechecking his calculations.

James remembered the occasion in the sixties when a young navigator had made a miscalculation on a transatlantic flight which resulted in his nuclear bomber making an unscheduled landing in South rather than North America. It had been the cause of considerable diplomatic embarrassment. He was sure Brian would not be making a similar error. A man who had successfully navigated his way with pin point accuracy to targets in Germany at night in all weathers was not going to get lost on a clear day trundling down to Gibraltar.

No, the only potential problem on this flight, concluded James, was whether this old rust bucket would hold together for the whole trip there and back. He wasn't much given to morbid thoughts but he had looked up the accident record of Shackletons and it wasn't good. He couldn't remember all of the incidents but several stuck in his mind.

One had crashed into the sea near Berwick on Tweed in 1952, another off Cromarty in the same year, killing all 14 on board, and the following year three had crashed into the sea, one near Cromarty and two more off Argyll.

Another had crashed into the sea off Gozo in 1954 and two more had been lost in 1958, one near Elgin and another in the South China Sea. Another had been lost during an air display at Gibraltar in 1957 and he was aware of at least four more since then. Still, as the old saying has it, if you can't take a joke you shouldn't have joined. However, as things stood, the old crate was churning steadily southward and all was well.

James was looking forward to a weekend in Gibraltar, which he'd never visited before. He understood that it couldn't be compared with Cyprus or even Malta but he was sure it would have something to offer for a weekend. There'd been some talk of going over to Tangier on the Sunday, which sounded interesting.

About twenty minutes out from Gibraltar 'Tubby' asked James if he'd be interested in sitting up front in the jump seat for the landing and of course James was keen to do that. He sat between and just behind the two pilots and so had a good view of events. 'Tubby' had never landed at Gibraltar and so it would be a new experience for him too and not a necessarily easy one.

There were several potential problems to be aware of, the first of which was that the Rock often produced strange or unexpected air currents which, because of the proximity of the runway, could have a serious effect on landing or taking off. The second was that, with a wing span of 120ft, the Shackleton was prone to float down the runway sustained by a cushion of air, which lead to the third potential problem: the sea was at both ends of the runway and down one side, the other side being bordered by the Rock, an even less forgiving option.

Finally, the runway was crossed by a four lane highway known as Winston Churchill Avenue. While this was clearly the responsibility of air traffic control, things that can go wrong usually do go wrong at some point and in any case it gave the pilot something else to think about.

It would be unfair to say that 'Tubby' was concentrating more than usual on the landing, since any pilot who isn't giving any landing his full concentration is an accident waiting to happen, but 'Tubby's' anxiety level was certainly higher than normal. He'd been given clearance for a long approach to runway 27 and since the visibility was excellent they could see it from a great distance. As they made a westerly approach, Spain was to the right and Gibraltar town and the Rock to the left. The runway number 27 stood out as they reduced height to 500 feet on final and James could see the highway crossing the road and the traffic held up waiting to cross.

'Tubby' had judged his landing well and should have touched down just after the piano keys at the near end of the runway but he had difficulty in getting the aircraft to settle down and she just continued floating along with the far end and the sea beyond rapidly approaching.

They were only about twenty feet off the runway when a sudden gust threw the aircraft to one side, well off the centre line and dangerously close to the edge. With a swift but steady action 'Tubby' fed in full throttle, held the nose level until they had gathered speed, and then eased the nose up. Aborting a difficulty landing is a sensible decision and James was impressed but not surprised by 'Tubby's' professionalism. Fifteen minutes later they made a second approach and landed safely. The Shackleton had not yet claimed another victim.

Lunch in the mess was followed by a trip in a land rover up the rock and later by a visit to St Michael's cave within the rock itself. James was surprised by the number of passages and caves within the Rock if perhaps less surprised to discover the gun embrasures placed there over the years. It had after all been a significant British military base since Admiral Sir George Rooke had captured it in 1704.

During the American War of Independence the combined forces of France and Spain had besieged Gibraltar for four and a half years and the body of

Nelson had been brought here after the victory at Trafalgar, although there was some dispute as to whether or not it had arrived in a barrel of rum to preserve it. The Rock had also been a key factor in British victories in the Mediterranean during the Second World War. The evening was spent in the mess with dinner and a few beers but the 3am start to their day and the long flight finally had its effect and most of the crew had an early night.

The following day, Saturday, 'Tubby', James and three other members of the crew did a little diving in Rosia Bay, and then by the Seven Sisters, while some of the more experienced divers in the crew went diving off Europa Reef. In the evening they found a delightful restaurant in Gibraltar town and stayed there until the early hours.

On their last day most of the crew favoured a trip across the water to Tangier, courtesy of the Mons Calpe, an elderly vessel that did the return trip every Sunday. Apart from wanting to have a quick look at the town, James was also attracted by the romantic notion of a 1953 film he'd once seen called 'The Captain's Paradise'. In the film Alec Guinness had played the role of captain of such a ship with a wife in Gibraltar, Celia Johnson, and a lady friend, Yvonne de Carlo, in Morocco, although she lived in a place called Kalique rather than Tangier. Well their day out did not give rise to romantic adventures of that kind but it did involve an interesting shopping session in the casbah, fending off young boys anxious to part with their sisters, and a revolting meal that would long live in James' memory.

So far James had given little attention to the official nature of his trip and he resolved to think out the nature of his report on the return trip. So it was that he settled into his seat in Zebedee the following morning thinking about his report as 'Tubby' went through his start up checks and taxied out to the runway, the four Rolls-Royce Griffon engines grumbling in anticipation of the task ahead.

With full fuel tanks, fifteen crew, suitcases and bags of loot bought in Gibraltar and Tangier, Zebedee was heavy. It was also a hot Monday morning, which meant thinner air and a more sluggish take-off. However, Gibraltar has a 6,000 foot runway, which is enough for most aircraft and so James closed his eyes and started thinking about the shape and content of the report he would write back at High Wycombe. Shorn of the more interesting parts of the visit, he felt he was still lacking in some important detail, despite conversations with crew members over the weekend. He was still thinking about his report when 'Tubby' opened up the 'taps' to full revs, the four Griffon engines roared into life, and the Shackleton started gathering speed down runway 27 into a slight breeze from 250 degrees.

James' attention was arrested by flight engineer Frank Wilson, who came over the intercom with the calm and cryptic comment, 'Water-meths not working on No 1 skipper'. James was of course aware that the injection into the engines of a water-methanol mixture produced an increase in thrust and thrust was just what was needed right now.

'Thank you,' was 'Tubby's' equally cryptic reply, but he continued to maintain full power.

'V1', was Frank's next message, signifying that the aircraft had now reached the point of no return down the runway and that the only remaining options were to take off or to fall into the sea off the end of the runway.

'Water meths failed on 2, 3 and 4', Frank announced.

'Shit,' came back 'Tubby's' response, and there was no further conversation because there was no need for further comment. Everyone knew the situation and the only question in everyone's mind was whether or not they would have sufficient speed to take-off. The alternative was not attractive.

There was no call of V2, the point at which the aircraft reaches normal take-off speed, because Zebedee did not reach normal take-off speed. Instead it simply ran out of runway and the crew waited for an inevitable sink and then impact. But it didn't happen. Instead Zebedee maintained its heading and runway height, about 12 feet off the sea, and the engines continued to roar at full power. No one spoke because there was nothing to say until gradually it became evident that the aircraft, instead of stalling, was slowly gaining speed and then Sgt Bob Sparkes, air electronics, chipped in. 'We nearly got our feet wet there Skipper.' There were a few chuckles of relief but no reply from 'Tubby' who now faced another problem.

Directly ahead lay Spain and, owing to diplomatic problems over Gibraltar, RAF aircraft were not allowed to overfly Spanish territory. 'Tubby' quickly resolved that he was not going to hazard the aircraft and the lives of all on board in an effort to avoid a possible diplomatic incident. However, if he could avoid Spain he would do so.

The aircraft had now reached an indicated air speed of 120 knots and an altitude of 100 ft, which left no scope for error. With a stalling speed of just under 100 knots he could not put the aircraft into a climbing turn to the left, which is what he would like to have done, since a banked turn would have increased the stalling speed. He therefore lowered the nose to increase speed before pulling the nose up a little and banking left, very conscious throughout that each wing of the Shackleton is almost 60 feet long. With considerable relief he held her on her new heading and began a very gentle climb, the air speed indicator now registering 150 knots. All was well and they climbed to their long range altitude of

5,000ft and cruised at 200 knots. Although they'd all had a good breakfast at RAF Gibraltar, a celebration now seemed appropriate and the only way to do that was to open the galley and have a second breakfast. Sausages, egg, bacon and toast were duly dispensed to all.

The rest of the flight was simply going to be a long flight north, up past Spain and France, west of Land's End, over Ronald's Way on the Isle of Man and North West across northern England and so back to Kinloss near Inverness. James settled down for the long haul with a Wilbur Smith novel and a couple of ear plugs.

'Tubby' couldn't say he was busy but at least he had to stay awake, which wasn't easy with nothing much to do or to look at. A periodic check of instruments and holding height and heading was all he had to do. As on the way down, the only person who seemed to have much to do was Brian Higgins the navigator, who spent all his time at his desk plotting and replotting their route, occasionally giving 'Tubby' a new heading to steer and updating their estimated time of arrival at Kinloss.

They were about 30 miles west of Land's End when it happened. The first thing 'Tubby' heard above the roar of the engines was a loud screaming from one of them. His eyes had immediately taken in the rev counters for all four engines and his hand was already on the throttle to take power off number four engine when he heard a loud thump.

'Fire on No 4 Skipper', came the voice of Frank Wilson over the intercom.' We've had an over speed and I think she's blown up'.

An over speeding engine on the Shackleton wasn't unknown and aircraft had previously been lost through the problem. 'Tubby' was well aware of its history but right now he had a serious incident to cope with. The fire extinguisher on the engine had automatically cut in.

'Give me a visual report on what you can see,'

ordered 'Tubby' to Frank and then let me know of any changes'.

'She's still on fire and I think the fire's spreading pretty quickly. The extinguisher doesn't seem to have worked. It looks pretty bad, Skipper. The engine cowling's melted and I can see the engine'.

'Tubby' had little time to think. 'Peter, radio distress procedure. All crew lifejackets on and strap in. I'll give you thirty seconds. Charlie, get ready to drop the Lindholme gear but don't do it until I say so. John, I need you at the controls; she's getting difficult to handle. I'm going to ditch her'.

'Tubby would have preferred to have loitered at altitude, giving the crew time to put on their parachutes and bale out, but he wasn't sure he had the time. With the wing on fire and the engine cowling melting he didn't know how long he had before the wing disintegrated. He selected full flap and went into a controlled descent

'Skipper, some of the wing panels are coming off. I can see the main spar….and we've just lost the engine.' Frank meant that they'd just literally lost number three engine, which had fallen off.

'Tubby' felt the effect on the controls but thought there was additional damage since he was now having considerable difficulty in controlling the aircraft. He suspected that some of the debris from the wing, or perhaps the engine itself, had damaged either the rudder or the tailplane or both.

He and John fought the resistance in the controls while at the same time keeping a sharp eye on the instruments. Control of speed and rate of descent, while maintaining balanced flight, was essential.

'May Wests on everybody, and brace yourselves for impact. John, open the bomb bays. Ready with Lindholme Gear, Charlie.' 'Tubby' was flying the aircraft but also trying to think of everything he could to aid their survival. The Lindholme Gear comprised five cylinder-shaped containers joined together by lengths of floating rope. The centre container housed a nine-man inflatable dinghy with the other containers housing survival equipment such as emergency rations and clothing. The Shackleton carried this gear to drop for others in distress at sea. 'Tubby' thought they might as well use it themselves if possible.

They were now down to about 500 feet and 'Tubby' was relieved to note that the sea looked calm. He checked his speed to a little above stalling speed, allowing for the extra drag of the open bomb bays. At 200ft he ordered Charlie to drop the gear and John to close the bomb bays.

He readjusted his speed and rounded out just above the sea. He had to get his angle of attack just right: too high and the tail plane would hit first causing a very hard impact: too low and the nose would plough into the water. His aim was to stall the aircraft onto the sea as gently as possible.

Then they struck the water with a huge bang. 'Tubby' immediately lost all forward vision as a great wall of water cascaded over the cockpit but he certainly felt the rapid deceleration. Then the screen cleared and they were stationery.

'Top hatch. Everybody out,' he ordered, but the order had already been anticipated and as he spoke bodies were spilling out of the top hatch onto the top of the fuselage. Tubby unstrapped himself, sent John ahead of him, and moved as quickly as he could down the fuselage, making sure that everyone had evacuated. Consequently he was last out.

When he emerged he was pleased to see tow dinghies had already been inflated and one or two crew members were getting into them and holding them against the fuselage. The rest were either standing or lying on the fuselage or wings.

'Is everyone out?' yelled 'Tubby'.

'We're all out Skipper, but I think we have one or two problems,' shouted Chief Tech Walters, who'd just come along for the ride. Three men were lying down, one of them holding his head. As he spoke, 'Tubby' felt a movement of the aircraft.

'We haven't got much time. Get the injured into the life boats and rest of you get into the water and hang on.' It was apparent that the two small lifeboats that the crew had managed to acquire would not accommodate everyone.

Five minutes later, Zebedee sank. By now 'Tubby' had taken stock of the injured and found that mercifully no one had a life threatening injury. One man appeared to have a broken leg, another a rather nasty cut to the head and a third a broken arm, but given the circumstances they'd been lucky. The lifeboats contained medical supplies and so some comfort was quickly given to the injured men. The next problem was to get to the Lindholme Gear that was about a quarter of a mile away. In particular they needed the nine man life boat that 'Tubby' knew would be in the centre of the five containers.

It didn't seem a difficult job but in fact it was an hour before they drew alongside the containers and another half hour before they'd broken open and inflated the dinghy. Minutes later they were all out of the water and examining the available rations and the safety equipment. They switched on the locator beacon.

'Did you manage to get off a signal Peter,' 'Tubby' asked.

'Yes Skipper', replied Peter, an air electronics NCO.

'Then it shouldn't be too long before they find us'.

As a stranger to the Shackleton flying environment,

James had taken an almost passive role throughout the whole incident. He'd done as he was told as quickly as he could and he'd helped one of the injured out of the aircraft and into a dinghy. Now he found himself next to 'Tubby' in one of the dinghies.

'That was a great piece of flying, 'Tubby'. You saved our lives,' he said. Actually he'd been very impressed not just with 'Tubby's' flying but also with his overall leadership skills.

'I'll second that,' said navigator Brian Higgins. 'I didn't think we were going to survive that one'. The he raised his voice for all to hear. 'I think we all owe our lives to the Skipper. Three cheers for the greatest Skipper in the Kipper Fleet'.

There was an enthusiastic roar from all fourteen in the dinghies, including the three injured men, much to 'Tubby's embarrassment. 'Tubby' was generally a fairly quiet, self-effacing person not given to outward displays of emotion and so he wasn't quite sure how to respond.

'Thanks,' he replied somewhat inadequately. 'But it's really thanks to Pop Gladstone.'

'Who's that?' replied a rather puzzled James, although some of the others nodded in recognition of the comment. Pop Gladstone had become a legend among Shackleton crews following his epic flight on 10 January 1964.

'As soon as we blew the engine, I thought of Pop Gladstone because he had exactly the same problem. He was over Culloden Moor at night when it happened and he landed wheels up on the Moor by the light of his burning wing. All crew members got out and walked a short distance to the Culloden Village Hall where they drank a few beers at the local dance before the rescue teams arrived. Because of what he did I knew it could be done. I don't know that I could have done it without his example.'

It wasn't much longer before they spotted a large piston engine aircraft, presumably a Shackleton, slowly traversing the sky, although not coming particularly in their direction. Suddenly it changed direction and headed towards them. One of the crew members had already prepared the flare gun which he fired when it seemed clear that the approaching aircraft would see them. It rocked its wings in recognition as it flew very low overhead.

The crew of the demised Zebedee gave a cheer as the 8 Squadron aircraft flew past them.

'I wonder who's aboard and what she's doing in this neck of the woods. She hasn't had time to get down from Kinloss,' said one of them.

'She was probably down at St Mawgan,' suggested another.

'I hope he doesn't drop his Lindholme Gear,' said 'Tubby' 'or we're going to have more rescue equipment than you can shake a stick at.' It didn't, presumably because the crew could see that they were already well catered for.

Before long a Whirlwind helicopter of 22 Air Sea Rescue Squadron appeared and one of the crew men came down on the winch to see what help was needed. It was decided to airlift the crewmember with the cut head and the one with a broken arm but to leave the man with the broken leg until an air sea rescue launch arrived, which was expected to be in about a further half hour. He didn't seem to be too uncomfortable and it would be easier to hoist him aboard the launch.

Three quarters of an hour later they were in the launch and on their way to RAF St Mawgan near Newquay. A doctor on board tended to the broken leg and all took advantage of a hot drink. The outcome was a great deal better than anyone could have hoped for and sprits were high when they eventually arrived. The mess laid on a party that evening to round off a very interesting day and one that would long remain fresh in James's memory. He would look upon the Kipper fleet with renewed respect in the future and he'd made a friend for life in 'Tubby' Weston. Once back in a flying role he would invite 'Tubby' to experience a little of the fast jet world but right now he had to return to base at High Wycombe. He wasted no time and was back in his office on Wednesday morning, the day he'd been expected back from Kinloss.

'Heard you got your feet wet,' was Wg Cdr 'Stuffy' Watkinson's opening greeting. ' Nice to see you young fellers getting a bit of active service instead of just boring holes in the sky and mincing about in your No 1 uniform to impress the girls. Anway, if you're free at lunchtime I'll buy you a beer but don't forget that report. I'd like it on Monday morning'

'Yes, sir,' said James. 'I've already given it quite a bit of thought.'

'Stuffy' updated James on a couple of matters that had happened in his absence and then left the office. He poked his head back round the door.

'Good to see you back'.

Coming from 'Stuffy' that comment was the height of warmth and camaraderie.

EPISODE 6 – JEOPARDY IN JOS
(1973 – 1980)

Historical Context

__1973__ Britain joins the EEC
__1974__ Richard Nixon resigns as President of the USA over Watergate
__1975__ Pol Pot and Khymer Rouge take over in Cambodia US
__1976__ Israeli commandos attack Uganda's Entebbe Airport and Jimmy Carter is elected US President
__1977__ Nuclear-proliferation pact, curbing spread of nuclear weapons, signed by 15 countries, including U.S. and USSR
__1978__ Rhodesia's Prime Minister Ian D. Smith and three black leaders agree on transfer to black majority rule, and the "Framework for Peace" in Middle East is signed by Egypt's president Anwar Sadat and Israeli premier Menachem Begin
__1979__ Pol Pot regime collapses, the Shah leaves Iran and Ayatollah Khomeini takes over, and the USSR invades Afghanistan
__1980__ US breaks diplomatic ties with Iran and the 8-year Iran-Iraq War begins

After his stint at HQ Strike Command, James was posted in 1973 to RAF Lossiemouth in Scotland to fly Jaguars and after that, from 1976 to 1979, he did another ground tour at RAF Biggin Hill at the RAF Selection Centre. Despite the fact it was a ground tour he enjoyed the work of selecting officers for the RAF. He also liked the fact that while he could easily catch a train from Bromley into London, immediately to the south open countryside with some wonderful pubs, starting with the Grasshopper on the Green and the General

Wolfe in the village of Westerham.

In the summer of 1979 he was selected for the six month Staff College course at RAF Bracknell but towards the end of the course was advised of a hiatus in his career progression. He was being lined up for a particular role but the job would not become vacant for another eight months and so he would have to take a temporary role in the meantime. However, the pill was sweetened with his promotion to wing commander. The Ministry of Defence suggested a number of options for his pro tem job, none of which appealed to James, and then, almost tongue in cheek, the desk officer said there was a temporary appointment in Nigeria if he wanted something quite different.

The British Government had reached an agreement with the Nigerian Government under President Shagari to provide help in establishing a Staff College for the three armed services. This help was provided by a team of RN, Army and RAF officers whose role was to prepare written exercises, run the training, and tutor their own successors. The Staff College was at Jaji, half way between Kaduna and Zaria in the Muslim north of the country, and housing was provided at Kaduna.

So it was that James was in Kaduna one Friday lunch time in 1980 looking forward to the weekend. He usually did but this weekend promised to be particularly interesting. To start with, he was looking forward to a round of golf in the afternoon at the Kaduna Golf Club but first he had to do a little shopping downtown, which he did not particularly enjoy. It wasn't so much the general squalor but the fact that the shops here in northern Nigeria rarely had food of much interest and apples and cheese, which he liked, were never available. Rumour had it that they were banned to promote the local farming but he was never sure about that.

What he was sure about was that he wanted to buy

some lamb and rather than buy frozen New Zealand lamb from a local store, always assuming it was available, he would prefer to buy fresh meat from the market place in the old walled part of the town. The imported lamb came in by ship to Lagos, 600 miles to the south, and was then transported up country by refrigerated trucks, except that it was not unknown for the refrigeration units to break down and for the meat to defrost, only to be refrozen later. First James dropped in to see Lagos Charlie, a local trader, to buy a carved ornament for a friend's birthday, and then he headed down to the market place.

He parked his Volkswagen at the side of the track leading to the market within the mud walls and the lepers surrounded him as usual, clambering for his sponsorship. He selected one who seemed half capable and gave him a coin to protect his car while he was away. It may be 1980 but some parts of the world were a little behind others in health care, and indeed in most other aspects of civilised western life.

He was now accustomed to the violent stench that assaulted his nostrils as he passed through the archway into the old town, as well as to the riot of colour that greeted his eyes and the jabbering Hausa language that filled his ears. Banks of vegetables and fruit were laid out on the ground or on trestle tables, but colour was also provided by the costumes of the people, particularly of the women in their bubas, or loose fitting blouses, and their Kabas, single-piece dresses of varying styles and gloriously bright shades. Harry headed for the meat tables.

Meat to the western eye is identifiable by its texture, colour and cut. However, when an animal has been hacked to pieces, and the pieces are in any case black with flies, identification is more of a problem. James selected a couple of chunks and was depositing them in his bag when a friendly voice interrupted his concentration.

'Good morning, James. Shouldn't you be heading for the golf course about now?' Brigadier Julian Walters, the senior British officer in these parts, was a large, amiable man who lacked the cutting ruthlessness to reach higher rank but who as a consequence was well liked by his fellow officers.

'Oh, hello Sir,' said James, shaking him warmly by the hand. 'I shall be heading there just as soon as I've finished shopping. Are you playing today?'

'I'm afraid not. The memsahib has other plans for me this afternoon. By the way, are you going to Jeremy's drinks do this evening?'

'Yes I am. I think it starts at 6.30pm and so I'll have to get a move on if I'm to play a full round.'

'Excellent. I'll see you there. I won't keep you now but I would like a word with you later.' The Brigadier waved a cheery farewell and set off with his characteristic limp, acquired it was rumoured, during the Korean War.

James finished his shopping and headed for the Kaduna Golf Club, where he met with three friends to make a foursome. It was June and so the course was still a little green but rapidly drying out. In the winter it was lush and wet and in the summer bone dry, with the advantage that the ball seemed to bounce on forever, and the disadvantage that the 'greens' were in fact brown and kept playable with a spray of oil.

James enjoyed the game but kept coming back in his mind to the Brigadier's comment about wanting to say something later to him and wondered what it might be. He detected something guarded in Julian Walters' manner. The job they did was pretty straightforward and hardly secret. It didn't warrant a conspiratorial touch of the nose and a knowing wink.

The drinks party later was at Jeremy Thompson's place. Jeremy was an affable Lieutenant Colonel who was good at his job but also something of a bon 'viveur' who enjoyed a party and was an excellent host. He'd invited about fifty people, including Kate, an American who was not connected to the military but who was doing some research north of Kaduna for her PhD in sociology. James was a little surprised to see Kate since she had in the past earned the displeasure of the Brigadier by having an affair with one of his married officers. James had subsequently had a brief fling with Kate and wondered if she was to be the subject of the Brigadier's discussion.

In fact she wasn't. Later during the party James felt his arm being gently squeezed by the Brigadier, who steered him into the kitchen, which was now otherwise unoccupied.

'I believe your heading for Jankari tomorrow, James. Is that right?

'Yes, Sir. I'm taking a few days leave and should be back by next Friday'.

'Capital! I expect you'll have a very interesting time, particularly as you're going to have distinguished fellow guests. I gather President Shagari and his retinue are also going up there this weekend, although I don't suppose you'll be allowed very close to him. In a way it's to do with that that I wanted to have a brief chat. The Americans are keeping an eye on Shagari and they're sending up a CIA agent to Jankari to cover his stay there. I've offered to let the agent travel in convoy with you for reasons of safety.'

'Well whose safety are we concerned about, Sir?' asked James. 'You surely don't mean that I'm to look after a CIA agent to make sure he doesn't get into trouble?'

'Well, yes, that's exactly what I do mean, James.

You see this agent is a woman and it's obviously not a sensible idea to let a woman wander around this territory unaccompanied. She's young, blond and attractive into the bargain, but come to think of it the biggest danger to her is probably from you', the Brigadier added with a twinkle in his eye.

'Will she be armed?'

'I didn't ask her, but she probably will be.'

'So I, unarmed and with one shooting practice on the range each year to fall back on, will be protecting an armed CIA agent?'

'Yes, it's a strange old world isn't it old chap, and particularly out here. I've told her you'll meet her outside my place at 08.30 hours, which I assume is the sort of ETD you had in mind. Now, why don't I get you another gin and tonic? Oh, while I remember. Her name is Olivia Wilson and she's a New Yorker.'

James wasn't desperately keen to shepherd Olivia Wilson up to Yankari. For one thing he wanted to take the lesser of the two roads linking Kaduna with Jos, which was *en route*, in order to look up some old trains he'd been told he could see at Kafanchan. Not that he was a train buff but he had been told they were worth seeing. For another reason, he wasn't wild about brash American ladies, and a gun-toting female New Yorker pursuing a career as a CIA agent sounded brasher than Oliver Reed on speed.

When he pulled up at the Brigadier's house at 08.25 the following morning, she wasn't there but there was an unfamiliar Peugeot 406 parked outside. As he pulled his 6ft 2in frame out of his beetle, the front door opened and Julian Walters appeared with Olivier Wilson.

'Good morning James,' beamed the Brigadier. 'May I introduce you to Olivia? Dorothy and I thought it would be a good idea to invite Olivia for breakfast.' Looking at the slim, smiling, blond apparition facing him, James considered that it had probably been Julian rather than Dorothy who had conceived 'the good idea'. Dorothy, he noticed, had not come out to say farewell to Olivia.

After a brief introduction, they set off in convoy, with James leading the way, and Kafanchan was the first stop they made since Harry was determined to see the trains. They were indeed worth seeing, but even more interesting was his first real conversation with Olivia. Contrary to his assumption, she was not at all brash and quickly came across as an intelligent, pleasant woman with a ready sense of humour, and she was certainly attractive. Her blonde hair was set off sharply by her red shirt which revealed a slim and shapely figure. She was also wearing long, off white slacks, and a sensible pair of walking shoes. In this territory a woman needed a companion, particularly a woman of her allure.

He liked her steady gaze when they talked and her complete lack of self-consciousness about her attractiveness. She even showed interest in the rusting old railway engines that had been shunted into a siding and left to degrade into the landscape, the ochre rust reflecting the yellow and brown of the dry surroundings. However, it was July and very hot and so they couldn't stand around outside for very long without feeling the intensity of the sun. Neither of their cars had air conditioning but at least there was a steady flow of air on the move.

They continued on the next stage of their journey towards the Jos plateau region, passing through savannah grasslands with an occasional baobab, tamarind or acacia tree. The only habitation was the occasional cluster of huts and sometimes a mud walled enclosure surrounding the hutted dwellings of a richer inhabitant. He thought of his last trip out of Kaduna when he'd driven north through Zaria and towards Kano, stopping at the mud walled encampment of an old scholar who was currently writing a book on the emirs of northern Nigeria.

He was a genial old man with three wives, each occupying a separate dwelling with her children. James knew him well enough to have asked him how often he went to visit each one to which the old man had responded with a pained expression and an explanation that since he was a great man he didn't go to them – they came to him. Such a situation would no doubt have shocked the liberal sensitivities of the Hampstead Heath intelligentsia and yet out here it made a deal of sense. Women had few rights and were very vulnerable. At least this man cared for his women and the large number of children was vital to help cultivate the fields where there was no mechanisation.

At last they arrived at Jos and instead of immediately taking the road out to Bauchi and Yankari, James called in to see Bob, the manager of a local mining company. Bob was a Scotsman who'd spent the last twenty five years here and was always very warm and welcoming. A jovial individual with an ample girth, white hair, and black horn rimmed glasses, he always ready to dispense a whisky or a beer whatever the time of day but on this occasion Olivia and James both opted for coffee. They discussed old times for a while and then Bob added a note of caution about the game reserve at Yankari.

'As you probably know, Shagari and his crowd are there at the moment and I gather they've high jacked almost all the accommodation whether or not it's been booked in advance. I know it's quite a drive back and forth but if you do have a problem get back here and I'll fix up a room for you both.'

This sounded to James a very attractive option but before he'd thought of what to say, Olivia, smiling sweetly, said:

'That's very kind of you Bob, but if we do have to accept your offer could you make it two rooms? James and I only met this morning'.

'Of course', said Bob with just the hint of a smile at James. 'Anyway, if all goes well, please drop in on your way back and both stay the night anyway. I'll have two rooms ready for you.' James thought he detected a slight emphasis on the 'two'.

Shortly afterwards James set off again at a steady pace with Olivia following behind in her Peugeot. The Yankari Game Reserve was busy when they arrived and there was a problem with the accommodation, or at least with Olivia's, in that she didn't have any. She argued with the attendant on the desk and offered the usual 'dash' in the accustomed manner of resolving problems but he did not accept the bribe. Clearly someone was offering more or perhaps leaning on him in a manner he couldn't refuse. No doubt he was in an impossible position with Shagari and retinue turning up unexpectedly and demanding accommodation. Here you wouldn't refuse the local police chief or militia let alone the staff of the President.

Olivia was clearly very frustrated. 'Do you have any idea why I'm here?' she asked James.

'Yes I believe I do know,' he replied.

'I thought you might have an idea because you didn't ask what a single woman is doing travelling around here on her own. And since you know, you'll realise that I have to stay here, room or no room.'

'I suppose you do......' said James, trying to look concerned, '.....or alternatively you could take up Bob's offer and use one of his rooms, although I must admit it would be quite a long way to drive backwards and forwards each day you're here. Incidentally how long do you intend to stay?'

'I have to be here as long as Shagari's here, which we think is about four days. How long are you staying?'

'Well not that long certainly. I thought about a couple of days because I want to take a diversion up to a hydro-electric scheme to see an old acquaintance. Of course you could have my room once I've gone and I could return this way and escort you back to Kaduna. So the accommodation problem is only for the first two nights.'

'I don't suppose there's any possibility of sharing your room is there?' she asked rather sheepishly.

'Well of course there is and I would have suggested it but for your disinclination to share a room at Bob's place.'

'Well circumstances change and I seem to be running out of options.'

The accommodation comprised a rondavel, a round thatched structure which mirrored native dwellings, but there the similarity ended. Inside it was more than adequately furnished with two single beds, wardrobes, a kitchen dining area, and a sitting area, and a bathroom space. It wasn't lavishly furnished but it was certainly comfortable and more than adequate, although the preservation of modesty would not be very easy. They unpacked, shared the drawer and wardrobe space and then pooled their food, which they would be reliant on during their stay there.

By now evening was fast approaching and after the lengthy drive, night time animal watching was not on the agenda. Instead they planned a menu for dinner which centred on preparing a salad and throwing pieces of meat onto a barbecue just outside the hut. James had been well briefed and had brought a bag of charcoal. However the Wikki Warm Spring was nearby, a fresh water spring which looked very inviting after their hot and dusty drive and so they decided on a pre-dinner swim.

Olivia changed into a royal blue single piece costume which contrasted beautifully with her blonde hair and her figure drew his eyeballs like iron filings to a magnet, although of course he pretended not to notice. The water was gin clear and about four to five feet deep and the bottom was covered with pure white sand which set off the clarity of the water.

Swimming and relaxing eventually gave way to a little horseplay, splashing each other or trying to push each other under the water, and soon they were getting on very amicably, the heat and sweat of the day having been washed away. As night fell they were still enjoying the sensuality of floating in the cool stream, occasionally exchanging glances and smiles, enjoying the experience, enjoying that is until James's attention was caught by something in the darkness of the bank behind Olivia.

The two points of light at first confused him but he realised with a frisson of excitement that he was looking at the eyes of an animal, perhaps one that had come down to the river to drink. After all they were in an African game reserve. Without wishing to alarm Olivia, he declared he was hungry and that it was time to prepare dinner and so they left the spring to the animals.

Over dinner Olivia asked James what animals they might expect to see in the Reserve. Although looking at the animals was not her prime reason for being there, she saw no reason not to take advantage of the opportunity, provided she could also fulfil her prime role. James explained that, as far as he could remember, the Reserve was stocked with elephants, baboons, waterbuck, bushbuck, crocodile, hippopotamus, antelope, buffalo and various types of monkey. Even lions were occasionally spotted, and as he said this he thought back to the eyes he'd noticed in the dark.

They'd finished a bottle of wine over dinner and so James opened a second and they continued to talk into the night. He described his work for the Nigerian Armed Forces and she said a little about her work but only in very general terms. They went on to talk about their families and their backgrounds. James had never been married while Olivia was already a divorcee following what appeared to have been a dreadful marriage. They discussed politics in the USA and England, music and literature. It was 2am before they finally decided to call it a day and went to their separate beds, tired, content and in a happy and relaxed state of mind.

They were a little late in rising and had time only for a quick bowl of cereals before joining an organised morning tour by truck around the reserve, or at least part of it. They didn't see any lion but there were hippopotamuses, crocodiles, elephants, and plenty of waterbuck and bushbuck. Olivia was particularly amused by the baboons. All in all the morning was a great success, not only in terms of observing the animals but also in the extent to which they enjoyed each other's company. After only two days, James felt quite an affinity with her. Knowing his own impetuous nature, he gave himself a little pep talk about not taking people at face value and advised caution. Despite his reputation as a man's man, he was essentially a romantic at heart and could be damaged emotionally more readily than he would ever admit to anyone else.

Over lunch in the restaurant Olivia told James that she had to be alone for the afternoon but was at pains to say how much she'd enjoyed the morning and was looking forward to the evening.

This didn't come as a surprise to James who'd been wondering when Olivia, or Ollie as he'd taken to calling her, would start to justify her time there. He couldn't imagine precisely what she was supposed to be doing or how she would set about fulfilling her brief other than that in general terms he knew she had to keep an eye on

Shagari. Somehow she seemed to know what the President was doing and where he was in the Reserve, although he himself had seen no sign of him. However, he had noticed a few 'heavies' around whom he took to be security men.

He had also been aware that Ollie had an interesting looking case that she had occasionally taken outside for 15 or 20 minutes. Perhaps it was a radio and perhaps that was how she was exchanging information with her people. Whatever her instructions, she clearly had a task on for the afternoon.

James didn't really mind since he wanted to do a little bird watching which possibly wouldn't have been of interest to Olivia. Actually it wasn't really of great interest to James either and was something he'd never done in the past but since coming to Nigeria he'd developed a passing interest to the extent that he'd bought a pair of binoculars and a book on the birds of West Africa. He'd read in the brochure that the park was inhabited by a variety of birds, including the huge saddle bill stork, goliath heron, eagle, vultures, kingfishers, bee-eaters and more, and that it was excellent for serious bird-watchers. He thought that they would keep him occupied during the afternoon until Olivia was free again.

He had a mildly interesting afternoon but perhaps thought more about the forthcoming evening with Olivia than he did about the birds he was watching and was surprised at the impression she'd already made on him. He'd had a number of affairs over the years, had enjoyed all of them and had kept in touch with most his lady friends because they'd all been friends as well as lovers. Yet he knew instinctively, even though Olivia was not a lover, and could not even be described as a friend after such a short acquaintance, that there was already a bond between them that was almost as strong as anything else he'd experienced before, always of course with the exception of Libena in Venice.

As they'd arranged to meet in the bar at 6pm, James was there at 5.45pm and Olivia arrived at 5.55pm, another point in her favour. He tended to be irritated by ill-mannered people who were late for meetings and appointments, but she was clearly on the ball and she looked beautiful. In her simple yellow dress she exploded into the room like a ray of sunshine, caught his eye, gave a broad smile and came over to him. As he rose to his feet to greet her and was muttering something about how lovely she looked, she put her arms round him and gave him a very welcoming and unselfconscious kiss.

'Have you been lonely without me?' she laughed.

'Well actually, I spent the morning with a multitude of birds – but none as glamorous as you. What would you like to drink?'

They took their drinks to a corner table.

'Did you manage to do what you had to do this afternoon? asked James.

'Yes, pretty well.' She paused to sip her drink. 'But you didn't answer my question. Were you lonely this morning without me?'

She looked directly at him without smiling and James realised with some surprise that it was intended as a serious question.

'Yes I was and I missed you more than I can say but I have to confess that I don't really understand it. We only met the day before yesterday.'

James hedged his response because he was torn between declaring his true emotion and not wishing to embarrass her with a gushing outpouring that might not be reciprocated and might therefore be embarrassing for both of them.

'I missed you too and to be honest I'm a little

frightened because I haven't felt this way before. I suddenly feel I'm jumping off a cliff.'

James reached out and held her hand, wanting the physical contact but also needing to reassure her. She squeezed his hand in turn and they sat in silence for a few moments.

'I'm afraid I'm going to be rather busy tomorrow but I'm sure you'll understand that I can't explain.

'Yes, I understand,' said James, who was well versed in the need for reticence over security matters. 'I think I'll go off for the day. There's an old acquaintance I could look up not too far from here.'

'I'll get back in time for dinner. Will you be free then?'

'I can't promise but I should be'.

Over dinner that evening James felt a very strong closeness between them. Her looks, the tone of her voice and the occasional touching of hands told him that their relationship had reached a higher level. When they'd finished eating and left the table, her hand sought his immediately and naturally.

'I don't feel like a drink this evening. Can we go back to the hut?'

As soon as they were safely in their rondavel, Olivia put her arms round him and kissed him.

'Do you think there's room in your bed for two?' she asked.

'Well we can certainly try,' replied James. 'I could chop an arm off if it might help,' he laughed.

'Certainly not. I think you might need everything you've got,' she replied, and he did.

They made love initially with a burning passion and then again with a greater degree of tenderness and then again….finally falling asleep in each other's arms in the early hours of the morning. To James it was a night of perfect satisfaction with every warm, fiery, gentle, powerful, lustful and tender emotion brought into play. He didn't know how but he was going to have to rearrange his life to make sure they could stay together. Never again would he find such a perfect partner and he was going to hang on to this one.

'Will you be travelling far today?' she asked him over breakfast.

'Well, not having been there before, I'm not really sure, but I imagine it will about an hour's drive. The chap I'm going to see is called Tom Wilkinson and he's the manager of a hydroelectric scheme in the hills. I met him a couple of months ago in Kaduna and promised to look him up on this trip. He seems to be something of a character, having lived here with his wife for twenty five years. Apparently he was born in Preston, qualified as an engineer at London University, and took a job initially in Bolton, which is a town in Northern England. Of course, if you were free today I wouldn't go, but as you're not I may as well carry on with my original plan.'

'Yes, I agree with you. If you stay around here I'm not going to be able to concentrate on my work. As they say, absence makes the heart grow fonder. I'll be more than ready to see you when you get back this evening and to hear all about your day.

They went back to their accommodation, James threw some fruit and a bottle of water in his car, and Olivia kissed him goodbye. As he drove away he looked back through the rear view mirror and noticed that she was standing transfixed looking after his car.

James had a very enjoyable day with Tom and Mary Wilkinson, an eccentric but kindly and hospitable couple, and afterwards he drove up a mountain to find one of their reservoirs, where he had a leisurely swim before heading of back towards Yankari. It seemed to take much longer going back but then, as he told himself, there was not much point in arriving too early or indeed in risking an accident on the way. Eventually the gates of the Reserve came into view, as did the barricades blocking the entrance and the armed soldiers who were standing around outside.

He approached one of the soldiers to ask what was happening but the soldier seemed to be in a high state of agitation and immediately challenged him with his AK47. James explained that was looking for a friend who had been in the Reserve but the soldier, who was clearly not there in any capacity other than to prevent entry, told him to go away, indicating that he would be shot if he didn't. James's flimsy experience of the lower ranks of the Nigerian military cautioned him not to make a scene and he went back to his car.

Clearly something of significance had happened during the day for the Reserve to have closed and the fact that Shagari had been there set alarm bells ringing in James's mind. What on earth had happened and even more important to him at that moment was what had happened to Olivia? His imagination began to run wild but he told himself to keep calm and to think carefully. There was nothing to be gained here and drawing attention to himself might well have a detrimental effect on his capacity to help Olivia, particularly if he was arrested and locked up for a spell. He would set off back to Kaduna, but call in to see Bob in Jos on the way. Bob normally had his ear to ground and might know something.

In fact Bob did know something but it was tantalizingly little. Someone Bob knew had been out on safari at Yankari and had heard what sounded like gunshots. By the time his truck had got back to the main domestic area, whatever had happened was over, but very soon the place had been swarming with police and soldiers. All visitors had been interrogated and either arrested or sent off. Bob's acquaintance had been lucky and told to leave immediately after questioning. He'd called in on Bob for a beer before heading off south. Apart from that Bob had learned nothing.

'Oh, and by the way,' added Bob, 'the normal radio and television services seem to have been suspended. A voice keeps telling us there are technical problems and that services will be resumed as soon as possible.'

James was wondering what to do next. His inclination was to go back to Yankari and see if he could persuade someone to tell him what had happened to Olivia but he first decided to try to telephone the Brigadier to see if he had any information. The emphasis was on the word 'try' since any attempt to telephone outside Kaduna normally met with failure.

He tried first to telephone Julian Walters in his office at the Nigerian Staff College at Jaji but was unable to get through and so, as a last resort, he phoned his home number and to his surprise immediately got through, although it was Julian' wife, Sarah, who picked up the phone.

'Hello Sarah, it's James here. Is the Brigadier at home?'

'Thank God, James. Where are you? Are you all right?'

'Yes I'm fine but there seems to be some sort of problem at Yankari. I went away for the day and when I got back the place was closed up and heavily guarded. I haven't even got my clothes and case. Do you know what's going on?'

'Yes, James. We haven't got any details but we think there's been an attempted coup by a faction of the Nigerian Army while President Shagari was away at Yankari. You're lucky to catch us in. Julian's ordered everyone to leave their houses and to take refuge on the Kaduna base, which is better protected than the domestic site. We're just back collecting a few things. Here's

Julian now. I'll put him on.'

'Julian here, James. I overheard the last bit and so you know almost as much as I do. There's been an attack on the Nigerian MOD in Lagos and a co-ordinated attack on the Government Building in Abuja. I'm pulling everyone back onto the Kaduna Base. I've spoken to the Base Commander and he's remaining loyal to Shagari and has offered us protection if we need it. Where are you now?

'I'm in Jos with Bob Wilson at the mine, Sir. I think you know him.'

'Yes I do. Have you got that girl Olivia with you? The Americans have been asking after her.'

'No Sir. She stayed at Yankari today and I went out for the day. I haven't seen her since breakfast.'

'Pity, but the Americans will have to look after their own. In any case there's nothing you can do at present. She's probably been held for questioning. Now I would suggest you get back here as fast as you can but I don't have any information on the state of things between Jos and Kaduna. How do things seem in Jos at the moment?'

'Well if anything it seems strangely quiet. Perhaps people are just keeping off the streets. If it's all the same to you, Sir, I'll happy to stay here with Bob for the present. At least you know where I am.' James didn't want to add that staying in Jos meant that we would be nearer to Olivia, although he couldn't see at present what he could do to help her that the CIA couldn't do much better.

'I assume our normal work is suspended for the time being?'

'Yes, it certainly is. At present we can't be sure which side anyone's on or how far the coup has got. Try to call me on the Kaduna base number each day until we know how things stand.'

'Will do, Sir. Good luck.

In fact the following day James could not get through to the Brigadier, or anywhere else. He tried phoning the Yankari Reserve but that was also impossible. By the third day at Bob's he was growing very impatient at the lack of news of the coup but even more so of Olivia. He went out once or twice into Jos and there now seemed to be more people about as though things were getting back to normal. In the afternoon the radio and television services came on again and reported that there had indeed been a fairly widespread but rather disorganized attempted coup which had failed. An attempt had been made on Shagari's life at Yankari but his bodyguard had thwarted the attempt and Shagari was now safely back in Abuja. James was about to try once more to phone the Brigadier when the Brigadier phoned him.

'You've heard the news no doubt. James. The attempted coup failed and things are getting back to normal. We've now moved back into our own houses on the domestic site and we're getting back to normal work the day after tomorrow. I assume you can drive down tomorrow morning?'

'Yes, of course, Sir. Is there any news of Olivia?'

'No, I'm afraid not old chap. Did you get on well with her in your short acquaintance? You do seem to be very concerned about her.'

'Yes, we did get on well. Is there any way we can find out?'

'I've got a call book to Lagos tomorrow. I'll see if my CIA contact has any news. In the meantime get down here as quickly as you can.'

'Of course, Sir. I'll report in to you as soon as I get back.'

Bob thought James needed to be taken out of himself that evening and so suggested a tour round a bar or two in Jos but James was not in the mood for a pub crawl and so politely declined. In any case, the last time he'd spent a night on the town with Bob, he'd found himself climbing a wooden outside staircase and when he'd asked where they were going, was told that they were about to enter the 'jewel of Northern Nigeria', otherwise known as Madame Fulani's bordello.

In fact, although he wouldn't wish to go again, it had been an unexpected and interesting experience. Having climbed the stairs in darkness, they'd opened a wooden door and stepped into a large room reminiscent of an officers' mess anti-room, furnished with leather arm chairs and portrait photographs on the walls. On the far side, in a raised arm chair, a large black woman had been regally ensconced. Bob had introduced James to Madame Fulani, who'd beckoned them to sit on either side of her and then summoned a young woman to bring drinks for the guests. What had followed had been a surprise to James. There was no mention of the principal business of the establishment. Instead Madam Fulani had given him a historical and fascinating dissertation on the emirs of Northern Nigeria.

When she'd finished, James had asked her about the photographs around the walls to which her reply had been, 'Ah yes, these are among my more distinguished guests. Perhaps after your next visit we could have the honour of your photograph on our walls.' Bob had winked at James, a signal that perhaps it was now time to leave.

Interesting as his last visit had been, this evening James simply wanted to stay at Bob's and have a couple of beers, which is precisely what they did. In the morning, James said farewell to Bob and thanked him for his hospitality.

The trip back to Kaduna was relatively uneventful, 'relatively' in that he was stopped at one point by an army patrol but with his military identification card had no difficulty in persuading the officer in charge of his status. In any case there was little sign of tension, which seemed to confirm that the emergency was at an end.

Once back at Kaduna, he headed straight for the Brigadier's house. A maid showed him into the sitting room and Julian Walters came in from the kitchen and shook his hand warmly.

'It's good to see you old chap. Everything all right on the way down?'

'No problem. I was stopped once by a military patrol but not for long. Things seem to be back to normal.'

'Yes, I think they pretty well are, although not for the blighters who planned the coup. I understand most of them have been rounded up. There'll be a series of courts martial but those found guilty will face a firing squad. Now then, let me fix you a drink. What'll you have?'

'A gin and tonic please, Sir,' said James.

'Make that two', said the Brigadier to the maid who disappeared next door and came back very quickly with the drinks. In the meantime Julian and James had settled themselves down in two capacious armchairs.

'Any news of Olivia, Sir?' asked James.

'I'm afraid there is old chap. I was just getting round to that. She was shot and badly wounded. The Americans have flown her back to the States. I'm sorry to be so blunt but there's no way I could wrap it up. She was on the spot when the attempt was made on Shagari's life and she intervened to protect the President. I understand she took out a couple of them before a third one fired at her at point blank range. Both the Americans and the Nigerians are talking about putting her up for a medal. She certainly seems to have been a very brave girl. I hope you didn't get too attached to her because I doubt she'll be coming back to Nigeria.

'No, of course not, Sir. I'd only known her a couple of days as you know.' Deep inside he felt things would not be the same again and he was right. Communication with the outside world was difficult at the best of times and so it was two months before he was able to establish where she was and a further month before he received a reply to his letter. They continued to correspond for a time but then their lives moved on in different directions and he never saw her again.

EPISODE 7 - BOTTOMS UP IN HONG KONG
(1980 – 1983)

Historical Context

__1980__ Ronald Reagan is elected President of the USA, terrorists seize Iran embassy and hostages in London and Mount St. Helens erupts on May 18th in Washington
__1981__ The Thatcher Government in England begins the privatisation of nationalised industries and the Egyptian president, Anwar el-Sadat, is assassinated
__1982__ Britain overcomes Argentina in the Falklands war
__1983__ Terrorist explosion kills 237 US Marines in Beirut

Three months before leaving Nigeria, James had at last received a flying posting on Harriers, as Officer Commanding No 3 Squadron, RAF Gutersloh in Germany. His career seemed to have taken a rather strange course but at last he would now be back to flying. Initially he had to attend No 233 Operational Conversion Unit at RAF Wittering before taking up his post in Germany.

It was now 1981 and good to be back overseas again and better still to have his own squadron; life was good and he intended to enjoy it. The only snag was that the RAF seemed to think that all stable officers were married and that unmarried ones were loose cannons. In fact it had been made clear to James that he could forget being a station commander in the future unless he had a wife by his side, which was not something James could envisage. However, he was determined to make the most of his time in Germany as well as enjoy the flying.

He'd always had a natural aptitude for flying which

now stood him in good stead in flying the Harrier. On account of its vertical and short takeoff and landing capability, the Harrier was a very different kind of aircraft to fly from anything he'd previously handled but he took to it like a duck to water and quickly became one of the best if not the best pilot in the squadron. If he enjoyed his flying, he enjoyed the social life in RAF Germany almost as much and the first year past very quickly.

No one appeared to have paid much attention to matters in the South Atlantic and so the belligerence of Argentina came as something of a surprise when, on 2 April 1982, their forces invaded the Falkland Islands. James would love to have been involved, not from any great desire to go to war for its own sake but, for all his faults, he was a very patriotic person and therefore indignant that another country should see fit to invade United Kingdom territory. He read accounts of competing claims to the islands and concluded that, historically, the UK claim was stronger than Argentina's and that, compared with Argentina's other claim on the grounds of proximity, the wish of the pro-British islanders was much the more persuasive argument.

He was even more envious when he learned that No 1 Harrier Squadron, based at RAF Wittering, would be forming part of the task force, operating from HMS Hermes and he decided to ring his opposite number at Wittering. In fact his colleague was excited at the prospect of what lay ahead but also a little troubled. The crisis had arisen at a time when he was a little short of pilots and he was talking to the MOD about one or two reserves. James saw his opportunity.

'Well, look no further old sport. I'm your man.'

'What! How could you possibly come along? It's no reflection on you personally but you're a wing commander and you're OC 3 Squadron. I'm not sure I could accept another wing commander in the squadron even on a temporary basis and I don't think there's any chance of MOD agreeing to anything so irregular. There's more chance of my maiden aunt taking her clothes off in Raymond's Revue Bar. Anyway, who's going to look after 3 Squadron?'

'Look at it this way. We spend all our days practising for a war but never seem to have any opportunity to put it into practice. Well here is an opportunity and I want to take part. My argument to MOD would be that I could learn an immense amount from this experience in a short time and then take that back to my squadron and pass it on. I would go as a reserve under your command and with no executive authority in your squadron. As far as my squadron is concerned, I've got a very competent deputy who could look after the shop while I'm away.'

'Well, I can see an argument there but I hope you don't expect me to put such a crazy idea up the line.'

'No I don't. That's up to me and all I would ask of you is that you don't argue against it if they ask your opinion.'

'All right but frankly Squire I don't think you've got a cat in hell's chance of getting MOD to agree.'

'Thanks. I'll get back to you to let you know how I'm getting on'.

Having now passed the first hurdle, James set about other aspects of his strategy, the next stage of which was to speak to his deputy, Squadron Leader Freddy Whitehouse. As he expected, Freddie was delighted at the prospect of commanding the squadron for an extended period and saw no problems from his point of view. In any case he was quite used to taking over when James was on leave.

All James had to do now was to persuade MOD. This was the big hurdle and James was not at all sure that his persuasive charm would succeed but here he had a stroke of luck. His old boss from his brief spell in NEAF, 'Smokey' Midhurst, had somehow got himself promoted to Air Commodore and was now flying a desk in MOD on the staff of the Chief of the Air Staff.

'Bloody Hell! You cheeky bastard!' was 'Smokey's initial reaction. 'You haven't changed a bit.'

Behind the invective, James sensed a willingness to listen and he deployed his argument about the need to spread front line operational experience, adding that OC 1 Squadron had a current pilot shortage and that he was sympathetic to the idea. In fact 'sympathetic' was perhaps a little strong but James felt it wasn't too short of the mark. He also added that his No 2 was very capable of managing his own squadron in the meantime and that it would be good experience for him. When he'd finished, there was a pause at the other end.

'Well, I'm not promising anything you blighter, except that I'll get back to you with an answer in due course.'

'In due course' turned out to be three days, which was remarkably speedy for an MOD response, but what was even more surprising was the nature of the response. James had thought his idea intelligent and imaginative, even if rather self-serving, and therefore most unlikely to receive a positive answer from MOD. In fact he was wrong. The response came in the form of a signal appointing him to temporary operational duties in the South Atlantic.

He enjoyed his trip down to the South Atlantic on the SS Atlantic Conveyor, although he would have preferred to have flown one of the six harriers from No 1 Squadron directly down to the Ascension Islands but he was in no position to seek any further favours. He met them there and they all went down together to the South Atlantic where they transferred to HMS Hermes.

Tragically, the SS Atlantic Conveyor was later to be sunk.

Altogether No 1 Squadron flew over 130 ground attack sorties, of which James took part in just two, both of which were ground attacks on Stanley Airfield. It wasn't much in the great scale of things but to him they were very important. Those two sorties were after all the only time when he'd taken part in active combat.

As soon as the Islands had been taken James was on an RAF VC 10 and back to the UK to take over his squadron. He would like to have gone on leave for a week or two but thought it unwise even to think about it, having been away long enough. In fact all was well back at base, as he'd expected and his deputy, Squadron Leader Freddy Whitehouse, went on leave for three weeks.

Having re-established himself on the squadron he began to think about a spot of leave for the following month and struck on the idea of going to Hong Kong. The RAF had what was called an indulgence scheme, whereby one could fill in a yellow form and express a wish to go somewhere on an RAF trooping flight. If there was room for non-duty passengers, the MOD movement section would fill up spaces on a first come first served basis. James filled in the form, gave a wide range of possible dates and promptly forgot about it.

He was therefore surprised, when he picked up the phone one rainy Wednesday morning, to hear a flight lieutenant Movements officer asking if he still wanted to go to Hong Kong because there was a seat on Friday if he wanted it. He wanted it and having squared matters with the Station Commander and discussed it with his deputy he confirmed with MOD that he would go.

He discovered that trooping to Hong Kong was subject to a contract with British Airways through which the MOD bought spaces on aircraft which meant he would fly from Heathrow to Kai Tak, an old RAF base also used by civilian aircraft. So it was that he found himself strapped into a BA Tri-Star on the Friday evening with a twelve hour flight ahead of him. He quite liked the occasional long civilian flight, provided he had enough leg room. There was nothing to do but read, eat, watch the occasional film, and of course take the odd 'bevy'.

In fact on this occasion there was something else to do because he found himself sitting next to an Army major and was quickly engaged in conversation. Major John Castleton was heading for retirement soon but in his time had obviously led an interesting life in various parts of the world when the British reach had been much greater. In fact he'd spent the greater part of his career overseas, much of it in the Middle East at places such as RAF Habbaniya, 55 miles west of Baghdad. As a fluent Arabic speaker he'd been employed on intelligence duties monitoring Russian activity in the region. For his final tour MOD had succumbed to his request and given him his current role as administrator at the British forces HQ Hong Kong.

During the course of their periodic conversations, John Castleton asked James about his accommodation arrangements, which, in view of the lack of time, were non-existent. James had thought he would simply book into a hotel once there.

'Well you could do old chap, but you'd probably get into the Officers' Mess and it would be a better and cheaper option. The hotels tend to be quite pricy. I suggest you find a place for the first night and then ring the President of the Mess Committee to see if they'll take you in there. I expect they will. He's a very pleasant chap, a fishhead in fact. Commander Bill Watson. I'll write his number out for you'. John was a bright, trim little man with speech as clipped as his moustache. He wrote out the telephone number and then settled down for another snooze as the aircraft captain announced they were now overhead Delhi. James looked down from 38,000 feet and saw a maze of lights in night time Delhi. James had never been to Delhi, or indeed India, and the capital looked very pretty from his vantage point, but he imaged it was rather less so at close quarters. Nevertheless he looked forward to visiting the country at some point.

James had heard from friends about Kai Tak airport and its landing pattern and was looking forward to it. He wasn't disappointed. The runway had been constructed on reclaimed land from the harbour and, having been extended several times, was now 11,120 feet long. Since one end was in the direction of 134 degrees and the other 314 degrees, the runway was referred to as 13/31. At the northern end, buildings rose up to six stories just across the road and the other three sides of the runway were surrounded by water.

As James looked out of the window, it was clear to him that they would land in a direction of 130 degrees but first the aircraft made a descent in a north easterly direction and suddenly they were over Kowloon Harbour at less than one thousand feet. Having looked up the landing procedure in the UK, James knew that ahead was a small hill and on top of it an orange and white checker board, which was the guide to pilots to turn sharp right for the final approach.

James was waiting for the turn but was interested to see how long the course was held and how low they were. Finally the aircraft made a very sharp right turn and James was able to look almost straight down the wing to Kowloon, which he estimated was now no more than 500 feet below and they were necessarily continuing to lose height rapidly. They were undergoing what pilots called the Checkerboard or Hong Kong turn and passengers referred to as the Kai Tak heart attack.

As a fighter pilot, James was accustomed to much more violent manoeuvres but he had a professional interest in the procedure. At about 200 feet the wings were suddenly levelled before the pilot made a further adjustment to find the runway centre line. Then they were down and the engines roared reassuringly as the pilot applied reverse thrust. Even more reassuringly they then fell to a whisper, indicating that the pilot was satisfied they were not about to fall off the end of the runway. James was impressed and thought he wouldn't mind having a shot at that himself.

'That's the fourth landing I've made here and I didn't enjoy it any more than the first one. I'm rather pleased I won't be doing it again,' was John Castleton's reaction to the event.

'Well, we're down now,' was all James could think to say, 'but thank you for your company and for the advice about the mess. I'll give Bill Watson a ring in the morning.'

Once in the town he quickly found a hotel for the evening and in the morning rang the President of the Mess Committee, whose immediate response was to offer accommodation. He arrived at the Prince of Wales building at the harbour side before lunch and decided on a gin and tonic at the bar. There was one other person at the bar: a slim man with slicked back black hair, a pencil moustache and a sallow complexion.

James introduced himself and learned that the solitary drinker was Flight Lieutenant Peter Wilkinson, an RAF policeman of the Special Investigation Branch.

'Are you here on business, Sir?' enquired Peter Wilkinson, with a sidelong glance and a muted tone as though conducting an investigation.

'No, I'm here on a jolly. And you?' replied James.

'Well, I have a little business to clear up. It

shouldn't take more than three or four days and then I hope to have a bit of free time before going back to the UK.'

James knew better than to ask him about his 'little business' but on the second gin and tonic Peter disclosed the reason for his presence.

'After all,' he said, 'a court martial is not a secret or confidential matter. I've been investigating a case for the last sixth months and the court martial starts on Monday morning. I've spent a lot of time here recently gathering evidence but I think we've got enough now.'

'Who's the centre of attraction?' ventured James. 'And what's the charge?' suddenly showing a genuine interest in the affair.

'Well the accused is one Squadron Leader Walter Burrows and the charges are falsification of documents and theft. He worked at RAF Sek Kong, managing some of the contracts with the Chinese. After a month in the job his successor found anomalies in some of the accounts and the station commander called us in to investigate. Investigating on the base itself has been easy enough but dealing with the Chinese at their end of the contracts has been a different matter. Witnesses have not been easy to find but eventually I found a couple who are willing to talk. I just hope they turn up on Monday.'

At this point a third person arrived in the bar and the two exchanged greetings with him. He introduced himself as Edward Richardson, an army officer, but was not much more forthcoming on his background. Blond and blue eyed with a ready smile and a sense of humour to match, he had a general disposition that appealed to James and so when Peter suggested they went for dinner in the mess, and Edward declined saying he was waiting for a friend, James elected to stay with Edward in the bar. In any case James was intrigued by Edward's reticence and wanted to know more.

On his second drink, Edward happened to mention Hereford and from one or two other comments made, James gathered he was a member of the SAS Regiment. There was nothing secret in itself about that but it explained Edwards's reticence to say too much about his work and in any case he, like James, was in Hong Kong on a jolly and not in an official capacity. They were shortly joined by Edward's friend Alex Brown, another lieutenant colonel, who had just flown in from Borneo where he'd been fighting terrorists. He too was here for a little rest and recuperation and to meet his old friend and colleague. Alex was of medium height but that was the beginning and end of his mediocrity. In appearance he was quite good looking with dark, thick set looks and eyes that held their gaze just a little too long for comfort as though he were examining and assessing the object of his attention. He was of course very smartly dressed, ostensibly affable and outgoing and courteous in manner but he moved in a considered, measured way with economy of effort like a panther conserving its energy for the next hunt. 'Steely' and 'muscular' appeared to describe both his manner and his physical appearance. In his presence on a dark night James, normally confident in his ability to look after himself, would not like to have been mistaken for the enemy.

They discussed what they had in mind to do while in Hong Kong. James wanted to travel up north of Kowloon into the New Territories to Fanling where an old friend had retired from the RAF and taken over as Commandant of the Police Cadet Training School. He also wanted to take the hydrofoil across the estuary of the Pearl River to Macao, a Portuguese principality and of course to explore Hong Kong Island itself and to take the funicular up to the top of Cape Victoria with its spectacular view of Hong Kong Harbour. He'd heard that a bus ride round the coast to Port Stanley market was worth the trip and the Jumbo Floating Restaurant at Aberdeen was also on his list. Edward and Alex on the other hand seemed more concerned to savour the delights of Hong Kong city itself, starting immediately. They invited James to set about the city with them and he accepted, thinking it might be fun for the evening. In retrospect, 'fun' didn't quite seem to describe the evening.

They started out on Hong Kong Island by having a small beer in each of three elegant hotels: the Harbour Grand, the Mandarin and the Four Seasons. Then they caught the Star Ferry across to Kowloon for a beer at the Peninsula. After that they went down the scale to more familiar and less expensive places before deciding it was time to soak up the liquid with a meal. Edward and Alex seemed to know their way around and before long they'd found a restaurant they were looking for. A particularly interesting feature was that some tables were in discrete alcoves, curtained off from the rest of the restaurant and they chose one of these for a little privacy.

Edward and Alex had much to catch up on and James was fascinated to hear about their adventures in various parts of the world. For their part, they were very keen to learn of James' life as a fighter pilot, which was very different from their own. The Chinese food was excellent and they'd now switched to a mellow red wine from the Boschendal vineyard in South Africa. It was turning out to be a most enjoyable evening.

They'd almost finished the last course when the curtains to their alcove parted and an oriental man entered, ensured that the curtains were closed behind him, reached into his pocket and produced a very unpleasant looking commando knife.

'Please do not speak or make a noise and put your wallets onto the table,' said the stranger in very clear English. 'If you do not, I will kill you'.

He was standing between Alex and Edward but James was at the back of the semi-circular table and therefore slightly further away from the threatening knife.

'Well, we'd better do as he says,' said Edward and so all three shifted themselves slightly and reached into their back pockets to retrieve their wallets. At least that was how it struck James and the stranger as James dutifully pulled his wallet out of his pocket. Edward and Alex also reached into their back pockets but wallet retrieval was not on their agenda.

Afterwards James reflected what happened next because at the time the sequence of events seemed to pass very quickly. Edward's hand shot out and grabbed the wrist with the knife and at the same time his other hand came down in a karate chop on the man's upper arm. At the same time Alex delivered a punch to the man's throat followed immediately by another to his nose. James was aware of a sickening crack as the unfortunate thief's chin caught the table on his fall to the floor.

There was a high level of noise from the restaurant beyond the curtain and it appeared that no one had heard the disturbance. Alex dabbed a little blood from his knuckles and Edward left to find a waiter and report the incident. James looked at the man on the floor and wondered if he was still alive. He wasn't moving and seemed to have taken on a rather unpleasant colour but when he felt his pulse, he detected signs of life.

'I think he's still alive', said James.

'Oh, really,' replied Alex somewhat dispassionately, having now returned to his glass of wine. 'Then I hope he's learned a lesson, although I'm really pleased he's still with us. It would undoubtedly cause a bit of hoo-ha if he joined the feathered choir.'

Looking at the inert body, James thought that he

might still yet join the feathered choir, and he too reached for his wine. Putting on after-burn and rocketing up to forty or even fifty thousand feet in a fast jet was almost routine for him but being so close to an attempted armed robbery was quite another thing. James had long thought he was quite capable of looking after himself, particularly with his boxing experience, but in the presence of Edward and Alex he realised he was very much third or fourth league. These men did this sort of thing for a living.

The restaurant manager appeared. He was a sweaty little man in a state of great agitation. James imagined he was concerned about the reputation of his restaurant. While this was undoubtedly true, James learned later that he feared the man might be a member of the Triad and he did not wish to be on the wrong side of that particular group of gangsters.

The manager took one look at the man and immediately relaxed, having recognized the body as that belonging to a seedy little thief who was known in the area. He would have to tighten up his security if that sort of person was gaining access but at least he didn't have the Triad to worry about. Having established the identity of the thief, he then went off to telephone the police and an ambulance, although the latter was very much an afterthought.

The thief was still unconscious when the ambulance took him away but by this time James' attention was centred on the police who spent some time asking questions of all the witnesses they could identify, including some of the other dinners, and then drove James, Edward and Alex to a police station to make statements. This all took some time and so it was about midnight when they were finally released, at which point it was decided that a drink would be in order.

There followed visits to several seedy

establishments adorned by heavily mascaraed ladies who left no doubt that the bars' incomes were not restricted to drinks. However, the trio had had enough excitement for one evening and in addition the event had had a rather sobering effect on the party, not so much in its own right but for the thought that there could be further repercussions.

The police had put in their minds the thought they might be deemed to have used excessive force on their assailant. Had they acted purely in self-defence or had they taken the offensive unnecessarily?

'People who spend their time in ideological think bubbles unsullied by the realities of life often seem to lack a proper perspective,' was Alex's view on the matter. 'Personally I think the little shit got what he deserved,' he added, to which the others heartily agreed.

The next day James decided to catch the hydrofoil across the Pearl River estuary to Macao, an old Portuguese principality. There was more than a touch of faded glory about the town and it was very Portuguese as he'd expected. What he hadn't realised was that Macao comprised not simply a piece of land on the Chinese mainland, but also a string of islands, the most distant of which accommodated Fernando's Hideaway, a renowned Portuguese restaurant where he had lunch. It was a full day and so he returned to the mess in the evening after dinner had finished but he wasn't hungry and so went to the bar where he found Peter Wilkinson alone and somewhat morose.

Peter had just finished a beer and so James bought them both each another. It wasn't long before the reason for Peter's state of dejection became clear. The judge advocate for the court martial planned for Monday had arrived in the morning and, after sifting through the evidence against the accused, had found it inadequate, which tended to reflect rather badly on Peter's contribution.

The Judge Advocate had suggested that either more evidence be found or the court martial be cancelled. In the meantime he had given Peter three days in which to come up with something more. As Peter explained to James, the problem was that witnesses were too frightened to come forward. Normally Peter would not have discussed the matter with anyone but his situation seemed hopeless and in any case he'd had a few beers before James had arrived.

'The annoying thing is that I'm absolutely certain the arrogant little bastard is guilty, but knowing it and proving it are two different matters'.

'If there's one witness who could make all the difference, who would that be?' asked James.

'Well that would be Liang Tam who works in accounts at RAF Sek Kong - or rather he used to work there. He's a civilian accountant who worked for Walter Burrows but when Burrows was posted back to the UK, Tam suddenly handed in his notice. He gave the reason that he'd found a better job in Hong Kong but I think it most likely that he was involved in Burrow's scam and could see no reason to stay on once Burrows had gone.

He might also have feared being caught. Once Burrow's replacement had taken over it didn't take him long to find a discrepancy in the accounts. It was all to do with the payment, or overpayment of services provided for the base by local firms. My links with the Hong Kong police suggest that some of the firms are owned by the Tongs.'

'What are the chances that Tam would attend the Court Martial as a witness? Pretty slim I would imagine?' added James.

'Well would you? He'd be admitting to his own guilt and at the same time putting his own life in danger from the Tongs. I don't imagine they'd think twice about cutting his throat and dumping him out to sea.'

'But could he not be charged in a civilian court with the same charges that Burrows faces?'

'Yes he could but I doubt we could prove a case against him either. We'd need corroboration from the firms and we're not going to get that. I can see from the documentation I've unearthed that they've covered their tracks very carefully. The whole court martial is beginning to look like a lost cause and I'm partially to blame. I was so convinced that Burrows was guilty and so concerned to get him into court that I let my heart rule my head to some extent. I did think that once I confronted Burrows with the evidence I did have, that he'd come clean and make a confession. Instead he decided to bluff it out, and I must say he's turned out to be a pretty cool customer.'

They sat and drank their beers in silence for a time.

'What do you think will happen to Burrows in the future? If he isn't found guilty of anything, or there isn't even a trial, what will be the effect of this matter on his future career?'

'Well, I'm not sure,' said Peter, 'but I can't imagine he'll progress very far. I imagine he'd soldier on for a year or two and then quietly leave.'

'Would that be such a bad outcome?' asked James.

'It'd be a bloody frustrating one. I've worked for months on this case and I'm sure he's guilty. It sticks in my gullet to think he might get away with it. And he's such a smarmy bastard'.

'I can understand that but perhaps you'll just have to fall back on Churchill's maxim'.

'Which is?'

'Success in life consists of progressing from one failure to another without losing enthusiasm.'

'Well thanks a bundle. I really feel much better now.'

'Well here's another thought, 'If you bust a gut trying to achieve your objectives but still fail, then change your objectives.''

'So what do you think my new objective should be then?' asked Peter with more than a hint of sarcasm.

'In the immediate future, to forget all about the court martial and head off down town with me this instant'.

'Well that might not be such a bad idea. I'm not achieving much sitting here that's for sure,' said Peter, standing up and throwing down the remains of his pint. 'Let's go.'

They caught the Star Ferry across to Kowloon, had a beer in an indifferent bar and then sought out a restaurant. James was not over-fussy about his food but he was not enamoured of those restaurants that displayed live creatures outside ready for death and consumption. He recalled a saying that the Chinese will eat anything with legs except for a table and anything with wings except for an aircraft and the cages outside some of the restaurants seemed to bear that out. Even worse were the butchers' shops which were more like pet shops without any regard for animal care.

They passed a shop with live snakes outside in a tank and another with a raccoon, which was pacing up and down his cage with a look of acute apprehension and settled on a place on Canton Road that simply had a fish tank outside.

They had a very satisfactory meal and another beer before deciding to move on to the Bottoms Up Club in Hankow Road just near the corner with Peking Road. This was a girlie bar made famous in the 1974 James Bond film, 'The Man with the Golden Gun'.

James had heard of the place but this was his first visit and he wasn't sure what to expect. In fact he was pleasantly surprised by the general tenor of the club, which was subdued and rather plush. There were several round bars and at the centre of each a girl wearing only a small thong who was serving the drinks. There appeared to be girls from various continents but they chose a bar served by a Chinese girl, as they were after all in the Far East, sat down on two of the stools surrounding the bar, and ordered their drinks.

They were the only two at that particular bar and so the girl had time to speak to them. She introduced herself as Nuan and explained that it meant 'affectionate', which James was happy to concede might well be true. She asked them what they were doing there and then told them that she'd spent her whole life so far in Hong Kong but was hoping one day to go to America and to that end was now studying accountancy. James found her an interesting and appealing girl and managed to maintain eye contact with her, at least most of the time, despite her naked breasts.

They were thus engaged in small talk when Nuan's expression suddenly changed to one of concern as she looked over James' shoulder. He turned round and noticed a couple of heavy Chinese men who had just come in.

'Do you know them?' he asked.

'Yes', she replied but remained tight lipped and concerned.

She looked relieved when they went to another bar further down the room. James was about to continue the small talk when a cultured female English voice broke into his thoughts from behind.

'Is everything all right gentlemen?'

James turned round to see an attractive looking woman in her thirties in a chic black dress. She smiled warmly

'May I introduce myself? My name's Jane Williams and I'm the owner.

She shook hands with James and Peter.

'Everything is very fine', said James, and Nuan here is looking after us extremely well'.

'I'm pleased to hear it but not surprised'.

James and Peter learned that Jane, originally from Kent and subsequently a dancer at the Windmill, had owned the Bottom's Up Club for a number of years. She learned that they were in the military but not much more. A couple of Europeans arrived at the bar and while Nuan was serving them, James took the opportunity to question Jane about the two Chinese who had clearly disturbed Nuan.

'They're not people I would encourage to come here', she said, 'but I can't always pick and choose who comes through the door. They haven't actually done anything wrong but the staff don't like them because they think they belong to the Triads and they could put me out of business if they had mind to do so. Anyway enjoy your stay and keep out of trouble."

'Thanks, we will,' said Peter. 'We're just looking for a quiet drink'.

'So you don't like my girls then?' asked Jane with a knowing look and a smile.

'I think they're gorgeous', replied James', 'and none more so than the proprietor of the establishment'.

'Thank you kind sir, but both they and I are off limits,' and with that she left them to Nuan and their drinks.

'An interesting woman,' remarked James. 'I wonder how she's come to own and run a girlie bar in Hong Kong. Perhaps it was through some contact at the Windmill'.

They finished their drinks and were about to leave when Peter suddenly grabbed James's arm.

'That's him. That's Liang Tam. What the hell's he doing here? He didn't just come in from outside. He came in through that door where I imagine the offices are. I wonder if he works here'.

They watched him greet a few people here and there and then have a brief conversation with Jane Williams, and from their body language it looked as though he was part of organization,

'She must have employed him after he left Sek Kong. Perhaps he's doing the accounts here,' suggested James. 'This could be your last chance to persuade him to attend the court martial as a witness. You could suggest that he might lose his job here if he doesn't.'

'Well he'll almost certainly lose his job here if he does', said Peter. 'On the other hand, we're really after Walter Burrows. I wonder if the prosecution would play down Tam's part in the swindle if he agreed to act as a witness: perhaps along the lines that he was acting under duress; or that he wasn't sure about the detail. It might be worth a try.'

'Is there enough in it for him?' asked James.

'Well at the moment he's not only unemployable in any government department in Hong Kong but he's also wanted for questioning. The process could clear his name and he could even be employed again at Kai Tak in a less sensitive role. I remember a similar case in Cyprus in the 60s where a local employed in the Supply Section was suspected of having a hand in a NAAFI robbery. He was in a car apparently following a van with the stolen goods but we couldn't tie him in to the theft. He was reemployed in the Education Section where he couldn't do much damage and he apparently did quite well because he was very bright. The same could apply to our friend here. Anyway I could have a word with him.'

Peter put down his drink and walked over to talk to Liang Tam just as he finished talking to Jane and was about to go out through the internal door.

James saw a look of shock on Tam's face as Peter spoke to him and then an expression of distinct fear. He glanced around the room as though looking for someone. When he didn't appear to see whoever he was looking for he seemed to adopt a more aggressive posture and was clearly declining Peter's offer with some force but Peter remained persistent and in turn seemed to be threatening Tam.

It didn't take Jane long to realise she had a problem and quickly moved across the room to intercept the two. James walked over the join them, having some thought of pouring oil on troubled waters if necessary and was just in time to hear Jane speaking to Peter.

'If you have a problem with a member of my staff, would you please address the matter to me and I'll deal with it. Tam, go back to work and I'll speak to you shortly. Now Peter, what's it about?' Tam left though the door from which he'd entered.

'Tam's wanted for questioning in connection with a fraud at RAF Sek Kong. He might be implicit in the theft of large sums of money when he worked on the base. His previous boss there is currently facing a court martial and it's thought they may have been in it together. At the least we need him as a witness.'

'Then you should have spoken to me first. I thought there was something fishy about him and he still hasn't produced the references he said he would let me have. Between you and me I've begun to wonder if he's connected in some way to the Triads. We've had a couple of them in here this evening and I saw Tam talking to them. Did you see them?'

'Well, I saw a couple of thick set men who looked likely candidates, one in a charcoal grey suit and the other in a blue suit. Was it them?'

'Yes, and don't look now but they've just come back in. Perhaps Tam has just contacted them. There could be trouble.'

The two men came over to Peter and they weren't smiling. The one in the grey suit stood in front of Peter, looked him directly in the eye and spoke, ignoring Jane and James.

'Come outside please. We want to speak to you'.

'Who are you and want do you want? responded Peter.

'We will ask the questions and you will do as we ask', said the grey suit.

James stiffened and made it clear he was with Peter. Jane interrupted and addressed the grey suit.

'These gentlemen are friends of mine and they are choosing not to leave at the present time. If you have any business with them it will have to wait. I would ask you not to cause trouble on my premises'.

James was impressed with her forthright approach and wondered how the two would react. He didn't have to wait long. The blue suit smiled at her, seized one of Peter's wrists and twisted his arm up his back.

'There will be no trouble. We're just leaving', said the grey suit, and clearly he meant they were just leaving with Peter. At this point James felt obliged to interfere.

'I'm sorry gentlemen,' he said as calmly as he could, which wasn't easy. 'As you've just heard, we are guests of the owner and we're not leaving at present. Please take your hands off my friend.'

It was now the turn of the blue suit to intervene, which he did by grabbing James's shirt front and tie in his fist and pulling James to within an inch of his very ugly face and his hideous breath. James was drawing back his own fist to aim into the blue suit's ribs when a chirpy voice cut through the air.

'Good evening chaps. You having a little fun without us?' It was Alex. Occupied with the altercation, none in the group had been aware of Alex and Edward quietly entering the room.

Alex stepped forward and placed a hand on blue suit's throat. Beyond that James was not sure quite what Alex did but the effect was dramatic. Blue suit let out a strangled cry and then collapsed on the floor as though in a swoon. Grey suit let go of Peter and looked menacingly at Alex but he also took in the fact that he was now facing Alex, Edward and James, not to mention Peter who was looking distinctly aggressive.

'Why don't you take your friend out of here before there's any further damage?' suggested Alex. 'Here, let's give your friend a hand'. And with that he helped grey suit to manhandle his colleague to his feet.

'You haven't heard the last of this,' growled grey suit, to which no doubt blue suit would have added his quota had he been able to speak, and the pair struggled out of the door.

'Peter and James expressed their thanks to Alex and Edward for their timely intervention but James was concerned about Jane's position.

'I'm dreadfully sorry about that. Will there be any repercussions for you? Getting on the wrong side of the Triad doesn't sound like a good idea.'

'Well, I can't say I'm pleased but I do have contacts above their level and I think I can clear it with them. What I'm going to do with Tam I'm not so sure. I'll have to give that some serious thought. In the meantime, I suggest all you gentlemen get out of harm's way before those two goons come back with reinforcements'. They took her advice, bade her farewell and left by taxi.

The court martial was dropped, Peter was able to convince his superiors that he'd done all he could, to the point of antagonizing the Triads, and he went back to the UK with his reputation untarnished. James, Edward and Alex stayed on to finish their Hong Kong break without further incident and Squadron Leader Burrows left the

RAF twelve months later after it became clear to him that he did not have much of a future in the Service.

EPISODE 8 – NORTH AMERICAN NIGHTMARE
(1983 – 1986)

Historical Context

__1983__ A South Korean Boeing 747 jetliner bound for Seoul apparently strays into Soviet airspace and is shot down by a Soviet SU-15 fighter, and the U.S. and Caribbean allies invade Grenada.
__1984__ Three hundred slain as Indian Army occupies Sikh Golden Temple in Amritsar
__1985__ The Indian Prime Minister Indira Gandhi is assassinated by two Sikh bodyguards. The Provisional Irish Republican Army (PIRA) attempts to assassinate Prime Minister Margaret Thatcher and the British Cabinet in the Brighton hotel bombing. President Reagan re-elected in landslide with 59% of vote (Nov. 7).
__1986__ Mikhail Gorbachev becomes General Secretary of the Soviet Communist Party and Ronald Reagan, 73, takes oath for second term as 40th president

In 1983 James was posted from Germany to the Central Staffs of the Ministry of Defence in Whitehall. He was very sad to leave his squadron but it had to come to an end at some time. Now he was wondering about his future. He'd been immensely proud to serve in the Royal Air Force and, although he'd had little working experience outside it, was prepared to argue it was the finest organisation on earth. It was sharp, efficient, and wonderfully effective and staffed by some of the finest people you could wish to meet anywhere. His life had been exciting, meaningful and full of fun. Unfortunately the MOD failed to reflect these same qualities.

It wasn't so much the people he knew there since most seemed charming, intelligent and hardworking. The

Central Staffs were an amalgam of Army, Navy and Air Force people, supplemented by a smattering of high level politicians and large number of civil servants, although 'supplemented' seemed an inappropriate word. He often felt that the civil servants carried far too much power in their own right. Of course they were ostensibly there to carry out the wishes of their political masters but their political masters were few in number and so the tail often seemed to be wagging the dog.

The problem was compounded by the fact that the MOD was often the last stop in people's careers before they took retirement and so keeping out of trouble by maintaining a low profile was important; so too was making an impression by dropping information into an appropriate pond at the right time.

In other words personal strategies and tactics seemed often to override the requirements of the job. Life became a whirlpool of letters, reports and papers of various descriptions, most carrying artificial deadlines because some high ranking civil servant or military officer said so, so that the paperwork became an end in itself.

To make matters worse, most members of staff seemed to have fairly narrow interests and few had an overall grasp of the defence picture. It wasn't so much their individual faults as a failure of the system to promote a proper examination of the interrelationships of strategic and tactical requirements.

In Air Force terms, the people who really knew best were at station and command level but their voices became fainter the further up the ladder one climbed. Strategic planning was a fragmented process conducted largely through pieces of paper in people's in trays and usually not given enough consideration because of unnecessarily short deadlines.

Among his more lateral thoughts was that the most

useful function of the MOD was to provide a peak for people's careers. Perhaps it was a necessary part of the military and civil service career structure. If so, before their retirement why not send a large proportion of the senior officers, and particularly civil servants, on a three year sabbatical, to Cyprus for example, where they could enjoy themselves immensely and not interfere with the running of the armed forces. Fewer senior people would mean faster decision making and fewer reports. It could also mean better decision making since only the best would be screened to have important functional roles. What a pipe dream!

At a personal level James felt dissatisfied and neutered by this foreign culture. He'd come from commanding a front line squadron where his effectiveness was almost tangible. Here he was an overpaid clerk and he didn't think he could accept that for much longer. Life was too short and he had a good deal of living to do before hanging up his boots. However, there were perks and he was about to experience one. He would regard it as the dénouement of his career in the RAF before starting a new life in Civvie Street.

One of James's responsibilities was to organize the Defence Staff Talks between the UK and other NATO nations on an at home and away basis. Thus talks would be held in Paris with the French and the next time in London: similarly with the Germans in Bonn, the Canadians in Ottawa and so on. He was the secretary and his boss, an air marshal, was the chairman.

Other members of the team would be selected depending on the agenda. The next set of talks would be in the Pentagon, Washington, but in addition the Air Marshal had been invited to open the RAF Day of the Canadian International Air Show at Ottawa on the shores of Lake Ontario. They would combine the two functions on the one visit to North America.

So it was that towards the end of August, James and Air Marshal Leonard Parkinson set out from RAF High Wycombe in the Air Marshal's staff car driven by Sgt McArthur. Their destination was RAF Brize Norton from where a scheduled RAF VC10 flight would take them to Washington.

The Station Commander met them on arrival and escorted them to the VIP lounge where a number of other important passengers had gathered together with a few station officers to host them. James was carrying a locked brief case containing secret papers relating to the staff talks and he kept this in his grip at all times. In his pocket he had an MOD letter stating that the brief case was not to be opened by anyone other than himself.

Seven and a half hours later they descended on JFK airport and shortly afterwards were shepherded quickly through passport control and customs and into the open concourse where they were met by Air-Vice Marshal Jock Winter, the Washington air attaché. James was shaking hands with Jock Winter when he noticed, over the Air-Vice Marshal's shoulder, a man with horn rimmed glasses and a black trilby who appeared to be taking a photograph of them. He saw James looking at him and turned away.

As they sat in Jock Wilson's Jaguar on the way to his house, James reflected on the incident and decided that he was probably mistaken and that the man was taking a photograph of someone else. After all, they were all in civilian clothes and the visit was classified information.

Later that afternoon, on the lawns of the Air Attaché's house, they attended a cocktail party which he'd organised in recognition of the Air Marshal's visit. It was a welcome relief to be walking about in bright sunshine after seven and a half hours in an aircraft seat but it was very hot and James felt he was in danger of drinking rather too much. A large number of wives and lady friends had been invited and of course for James they really made the occasion with their wonderfully chic and colourful dresses and hats.

One woman in particular caught his attention. She had raven black hair, deep blue eyes and a figure that fired an electric spark down his spine. She looked South American but was apparently a congresswoman from New York. They took an immediate liking to each other and spent the rest of the time together at the cocktail party. James would like to have invited her out to dinner but had already been invited to dine with his boss, the Air Attaché and the latter's wife. However he did make a date for the following evening.

The following day, the first day of the three day talks in the Pentagon, went uneventfully and James made his excuses for leaving the rest of the team for the evening. He met his new friend, Janice Waterman, at the Lincoln Memorial and then they went to one of her favourite restaurants that specialised in lobster brought down from Maine.

James was amused by the number and variety of instruments on the table which were apparently necessary for the dissection of a lobster. After a light starter, he was dressed with a serviette round his neck and a finger bowl was placed in front of him to complete preparation for the operation.

Of course James had had lobster thermidor in the UK and, on one occasion, a lobster Victoriana at the Lobster Pot restaurant in west Wales, not far from RAF Brawdy, but this was going to be different. There were no additives or accompanying vegetables: simply a large boiled lobster. Janice had advised him on the size of lobster to order and he'd decided on a two and a half pounder. On the plate it looked very large but in

161

comparison with those hanging from the ceiling, it was small.

The lobster and the animated conversation with Janice meant that James did not initially take in his surroundings and particularly other diners in the restaurant, until he was half way through his dish. At the table next to theirs was a young couple, possibly honeymooners, who looked adoringly at each other most of the time. To their right an elderly couple were working their way methodically and slowly through their meal, rarely speaking to each other. Perhaps they were simply comfortable in each other's presence and perhaps the longevity of their relationship had engendered an emotional communication that made speech almost unnecessary. Or perhaps they were simply bored with each other. James couldn't decide.

It wasn't until his eyes had wandered to the far corner of the restaurant that he noticed a man on his own reading a book and occasionally putting a fork to his mouth. In all except one respect there was nothing particularly special about him. He was smartly dressed in a grey suit, aged about forty five and appeared to be of a fairly stocky build.

As he was sitting down, it was impossible to judge his height. What struck James were his horned rimmed spectacles. Yesterday at the airport he'd thought a man wearing horned rimmed glasses had pointed a camera in his direction and now here was a similar looking man with the same type of glasses. Perhaps they were coming back into fashion.

'Is something troubling you? You seem to be miles away,' remarked Janice.

'I'm terribly sorry. How very rude of me,' he replied but feeling obliged to give an explanation, he told her about the man at the airport and about the man in the corner of the restaurant.

'Well, do you think it's the same man?' she asked.

'I doubt it. It would be quite a coincidence, wouldn't it, and apart from the horned rimmed glasses I can't say I definitely recognize him as the same man.'

They let the matter drop and enjoyed the rest of the meal together. It was when they were having coffee and chocolate that he noticed the man in the horned rimmed glasses stand up to leave. A waiter brought him his coat and a black trilby hat.

'The hat', exclaimed James. 'Don't look round but he's wearing the same hat, and now I see him with it on I'm coming to the conclusion that it must be him. That's quite a coincidence'.

'What do you want to do about it?' asked Janice.

'I'm not sure I want to do anything at present. I can hardly go to the police and say I think I saw a man at the airport taking a photograph of me and I think I saw the same man in a restaurant the following evening'.

'No but you could go over and ask him if it is him and if he was taking a photograph of you and why. I mean he could be a member of the press'.

'Yes, he could, although why the press would be interested in me I can't imagine, or it could still be just a coincidence, in which case approaching him wouldn't matter, but what if it's neither of these two things. What if he's spying on me for some other reason? Perhaps alerting him to the fact that I've spotted him wouldn't be such a good idea.'

'Well listen, Sonny Boy. You're dealing with a New York congresswoman here. I'm not without some influence you know. I'll bet I could get a tail to watch your back while you're here and to look out for him as well'.

'Oh Good Lord, no! That's very thoughtful of you but I don't think we should be over dramatic about it. I'm sure there's more likely to be a simple explanation.

163

I'll just keep my eyes open.'

Janice seemed somewhat sceptical of the wisdom of this idea but let the moment pass with a shrug and by now the black trilby and horned rimmed glasses had left the restaurant and they let the subject drop. The nightcap which Janice suggested at her apartment turned out to be a romantic and gloriously passionate trip to the stars and it wasn't until two in the morning that he left by taxi for his hotel. He saw Janice once more before he and AVM Parkinson left Washington to fly up to Toronto but they promised to keep in touch.

In Toronto they booked into the Skyline Hotel where all the pilots, crews and organisers of the Canadian International Air Show were staying. The event was on for three days, starting with the first day the following morning. The RAF Day, which the AVM would open, was the second day. The Air Show was to be held on the shores of Lake Ontario and the AVM had been asked to make a speech to inaugurate the second day.

The plan was that he should address the crowd of many thousands with his back to the Lake so that just as he finished his final sentence the Canadian Forces Snowbirds display team should arrive from across the Lake at very low altitude and then pull up over his head streaming red, white and blue smoke. It was a great idea but the AVM was clearly a little apprehensive about the arrangement, not helped by the fact that the speech was to be broadcast live across Canada on television.

Thus the first afternoon was spent not in looking around the city, as James would have liked, but in listening to the AVM's rehearsal of his speech and offering advice while the AVM paced up and down his hotel room with this script in hand.

They discussed what to do if his speech started a little late or if he took more time than in rehearsal because one could be sure that, barring a major occurrence, the Snowbirds would be flashing towards them right on time and once they were overhead the AVM would be wasting his time trying to finish his speech if he hadn't already done so. They decided that James would sit on the front row with a programme in hand. When he judged that the aircraft would arrive in ten seconds, he would wave the programme and the AVM would wind up his speech.

That done, they made their way to the bar and en route James left his brief case with the hotel manager who put it into the hotel safe. No doubt the security services would have found fault with this arrangement but James thought it a better option than leaving it in the wardrobe in his room.

It was the eve of the Air Show and the bar was crowded. Moreover, as James learned at reception, many of the visiting display teams had organised parties in their rooms over the four day period and so there was clearly going to be a great deal of action, and not all of it during the day. James had a drink, made sure the AVM was being well hosted by the local military, and then circulated a little.

His job was to smooth the way for the AVM and to help anticipate any problems but he had to be careful not to crowd him too much. By the time they had dinner the AVM had met the Canadian Forces Snowbirds Team and so they went into the dining room as quite a large group, and he continued to stay with the same group after the meal. Before getting too involved himself, James went back to his room to telephone Janice.

She was pleased he'd found time to phone but was anxious to know if he'd seen any black trilby hats or horned rimmed glasses in Canada. He laughed and told her quite honestly that he hadn't given it any further thought but she clearly took the matter more seriously than he did and told him to be vigilant. He promised he would and then went back to the bar and promptly forgot all about the matter, although he hadn't forgotten about Janice who'd made a significant impression on him.

When he got back to the bar he was alarmed to find no sign of the AVM and reception couldn't advise where he might be. However, they did have a list of all the parties on that evening but there were quite a few and the idea of trawling round all of them was a daunting prospect. Knowing the AVM's predilections, he asked which was likely to be the liveliest and the result was unhesitatingly, the U2 party.

Armed with the room number he caught the lift up to the seventh floor where the noise attracted him to an area of several open doors. Through one of them he found AVM Parkinson drinking a whisky and chatting to a couple of U2 pilots as though he'd known them all his life.

'Oh Christ here's my minder', was his comment to his new found friends as he caught sight of James. 'You'd better have a drink,' he added to James and poured a whisky for him from a bottle he'd clearly purloined as his private property.

James felt he could relax a little now. The AVM was settled in and they had little to do the following day except to meet a few people and watch the air display. James chose not to mention the man in the black trilby hat and horned-rimmed glasses without further evidence. In any case he had now concluded that the two encounters had simply been a coincidence.

The following day they were picked up from the helicopter pad behind the hotel and flown to the display area on the shores of Lake Ontario where James and the AVM met some of the officials and spent a couple of hours looking at the static display. Lunch followed and then the aerial display, which was spectacular. In the evening James and AVM Parkinson had dinner in the rotating restaurant on top of the Toronto CN Tower, after which the AVM declared he'd had enough for one day and James found himself alone in the hotel bar, where he'd decided to take a nightcap.

He was sitting on a bar stool reading a local paper and sipping a glass of Californian red wine, when the arrival of two young women distracted his attention from the state of the Canadian lumber industry. They spoke with a foreign accent which he couldn't quite place but sounded eastern European. He tried to concentrate on the newspaper article but found trees a poor substitute for two very attractive young women, one blonde and the other brunette. However, he didn't have to struggle for much longer with the article when one of them addressed him.

'Excuse me, Sir, but are you connected in any way with the Air Show?' asked the blonde one, with a very disarming smile.

'Well, loosely,' replied James. 'Why do you ask?'

'Well, we've just flown in today and we have a couple of days off and thought we'd like to go tomorrow.

'I'm sure the hotel reception can help you. Most of the air show crews and management seem to be staying here. They'll have all the information you need.'

'Thank you, Sir. We'll ask at reception. Do you mind if I ask if you're a visitor? You sound English.'

''Yes', I am English and 'yes' I am a visitor. I'm here on invitation.'

'Are you a pilot?' asked the blonde.

'Well, yes I am although I'm not here to fly, but how about you two? What do you do?'

'Oh, we're air hostesses. We're with Austrian Airlines'.

James had clearly fallen on his feet and he was not

about to let the opportunity slip and in any case the two girls seemed very eager to chat. First he accompanied them to reception where they were able to buy tickets and then they returned to the bar but this time sat to one side in easy chairs around a coffee table.

James explained that he couldn't be with them at the Air Show the following day because of his commitments and that he wasn't too sure about the evening without speaking to the AVM. However, the third day of the Air Show could be a possibility. He would let them know in the morning or leave a message at reception if he missed them at breakfast.

He didn't see them at breakfast and so left a message before accompanying the AVM in the helicopter trip to the Air Show. Despite his exalted position and his experience, AVM Parkinson was clearly nervous about the speech and so James, while trying to appear oblivious to the AVM's trepidation, did his best to calm things down, which was not easy given the noise in the aircraft.

Once on the ground there was no further time for reflection as they were hurried to their seats with five minutes to spare before the AVM was summoned forward to make his address. Of course it went well and James was on the point of waving his programme towards the end as the Snowbirds came low and fast across the water, when AVM Parkinson finished his address anyway. Within two seconds of his final words, the aircraft pulled up behind him trailing red, white and blue smoke and the Air Show was underway.

It was a magnificent day; the weather was perfect and the various displays quite wonderful. Despite his own experience, James had never lost his enthusiasm for watching others fly. For him, however, and probably for a large number of other people too, the highlight of the day was the Avro Vulcan display.

As a boy brought up in Alderley Edge near Manchester he'd been more than aware of the Vulcan being built in the A V Roe factory at Chadderton north of Manchester. Later he'd seen one of its first flights at the factory's airfield at Woodford Airfield south of Manchester, about five miles from where he lived. He'd seen the Vulcan many times since but it never failed to make his spine tingle and now he was about to see it again.

As the announcer called two minutes, James detected a trail of black smoke on the horizon where Lake Ontario met the clear blue sky. Head on the Vulcan had a slim profile but its fast and silent approach was in itself menacing. Then quite suddenly it stood on its tail, revealing its sinister bat like shape but, unlike the almost silent bat, the aircraft climbed with a thunderous roar like Thor, the God of war himself, in terrible mood. The crowd gasped in disbelief, many of them covering their ears, but James smiled with pride. The Brits could still teach their North American friends a thing or two. The rest of the display was of a very high standard but there was nothing to quite match the Vulcan.

James didn't see his Austrian lady friends at the Show but they were in the bar before dinner. They'd had a good day but had now planned to hire a car the following day to drive up to Niagara and wondered if James would like to go with them. James was very struck with the idea. He'd never seen the Falls and to do so in the company of two such lovely females was an opportunity he would not like to miss. On the other hand he wasn't sure how the AVM would react to his taking the day off.

James had arranged to meet the AVM in the bar but was so engrossed in talking to the girls that he didn't notice his arrival until he felt a tap on the back and a brisk voicing saying, 'Well aren't you going to introduce me to your friends?'

'Oh, good evening, Sir. Yes of course. This is Elka,' said James, introducing his blonde friend first, and this is Lina. Ladies, this is Air Vice Marshal Parkinson.'

The ladies fluttered their eye lashes and the AVM gave them an appreciative and very warm smile as he shook their hands. 'I'll bet he's quite a ladies' man on the quiet,' thought James to himself.

'We've invited James to come with us tomorrow,' said Lina. 'If you can spare him. We're going to Niagara Falls'.

'You lucky blighter,' said the AVM. 'As it happens, Tim Watson, our Air Attaché in Ottawa, is down for the show and he's suggested we join him and his wife for the day and then for dinner in the evening. Of course you were invited too, but as you've got a better offer you can bugger off. I shan't need a nanny. I'll square things with Tim.'

'Fine, thank you Sir,' replied James, completely unfazed by the AVM's tone which he tended to adopt when all was going well. When he was formal and serious things were not so good and on the odd occasion when the AVM had called him 'mate' as in 'look here, Mate' he knew he was about to get a bollocking. The AVM's style was unusual for a senior officer and not to everyone's liking but James had developed a considerable respect for him and knew him to be a good deal brighter than many of his status.

So it was that James, Elke and Lina set out on the two and a half hour drive to Niagara Falls. The car was booked for Elke and Lina to drive and so Lina drove with James next to her and Elke in the back. They talked much about flying and seemed very interested in James's flying experience but didn't ask any questions about sensitive defence matters to which James would in any case have been very careful not to reply. His security clearance at MOD was to a very high level and he was very much aware of his position. They also talked about music and about art, which had remained a passion of James' throughout his time in the RAF.

The time passed very quickly and after what had seemed a surprisingly short spell they arrived on the Canadian side of Niagara Falls, and they were not disappointed at their first view. The extent and height of the falls and the sheer weight and rumble of the water could not fail to excite and impress and they gazed at the view for at least half an hour. It was then time for lunch and they decided to eat at the Skylon Tower revolving restaurant which provided an ever changing panorama from altitude.

Over lunch they talked about England, which they'd visited many times, about the theatre and about music and painting. James had visited Austria quite often during his time in Germany and had always found it very attractive in terms of is scenery, both in the countryside and in the towns. He'd remembered that the Sound of Music had been largely filmed there and the girls were very familiar with the film and its songs.

'I went to Innsbruck just after the filming there', said Elke, 'and the town was still alive with memorabilia from the film'.

James hesitated to say anything and it was Lina who quickly interrupted her.

'I think you mean Salzburg'.

'Yes, of course, isn't that what I said? Yes of course it was Salzburg.'

It was a wonderful occasion, eating lunch, sipping wine and having such amazing views sliding past the windows and the two ladies were the icing on the cake. They also seemed to enjoy his company very much and so by the time lunch had finished they were very good friends – and perhaps a little more. The little more was an undercurrent of sensuality that had not found overt expression but which James felt by instinct. They both seemed to emanate a warmth and sensuality that caused him to wonder about the evening.

However, they had not yet finished their experience of Niagara Falls since they'd decided over lunch to take the Maid of the Mist tour in the afternoon. This was a boat tour that took passengers close up to Falls. It was a worthwhile experience and the three of them were in a happy state of mind for the return trip to Toronto. On the way Elke and Lina asked him to join them for a meal in the Chinese quarter in the early evening.

Back at the hotel he tried to contact the AVM but he'd left a message at reception to say that he'd been invited out for the day and did not expect to be back until late; all was well and he'd see James in the morning. In fact the following day was a free day since they were not due to catch a flight back to Washington until the day after when they would connect with an RAF VC 10 flight back to RAF Brize Norton.

James had an hour to relax before preparing for the evening and then at 6.30 pm he met Elke and Lina in the hotel lobby and they caught a taxi down to Chinatown, centred on the intersection of Dundas Street and Spadina Avenue. With many to choose from, they chose a particularly attractive restaurant and ordered a range of dishes, or rather James did since the girls were not as familiar as he was with Asian cuisine.

It was a relaxing meal with good food and wine and a lively conversation which ranged around music, both classical and popular, art and politics but never touched on military matters. The girls had long since established that James was single but now pressed him on why he'd remained unmarried. He gave a variety of reasons but never touched on the most important one, concerning a lady he'd met in Venice and couldn't forget.

Elke and Lina then moved on to sex and wanted to know not only about current lady friends but much more about what sort of things he enjoyed. They were very broadminded and appeared to be making it clear that they would not be averse to a romantic encounter. It was beginning to look to James as though this could be a perfect end to his North American trip but he wasn't sure which of the two he could end up with. They seemed to be equally engaging and he was confused, although his confusion did not seem to be having a negative effect on his libido, which was now rising to meet any challenge ahead.

Both were smartly and rather demurely dressed, Elke in a black evening dress which contrasted sharply with her blonde hair, and Lina in a blue two piece suite that set off her jet black hair, but it was clear that both had very enticing figures. Just as important to James, both were highly intelligent and well educated and both had a good sense of humour. They insisted on sharing the bill and once out of the restaurant they linked arms with James sandwiched between them.

It was still quite early when they returned to the hotel and James suggested a bottle of champagne to mark their last evening together, to which they readily agreed. They suggested going up to their room and ordering the champagne from reception and once they were in the room the champagne was only a short time in being delivered.

In fact the room turned out to be suite, comprising a double *en suite* bedroom, a good sized living room and a balcony with an extensive view and it was on the latter that they gently sipped a glass of champagne and chatted. In fact they each drank two glasses and, the bottle being empty, the girls decided it was their turn to order a second bottle. While they waited for its arrival they both went off for a shower and when they returned they were wearing dressing gowns.

'Why don't you take a shower as well?' suggested Lina. 'You'll find a spare dressing gown behind the door in the bathroom'.

By now James was beginning to sense that they had plans for him but decided to go with the flow. After all, he didn't want to be accused of cowardice in the face of battle and this could be an interesting skirmish. Not that he felt a particular need for another shower, having had one on return from Niagara but if it helped their plan along he would cooperate.

When he came out of the bathroom, they were both lying on the bed sipping the second bottle of champagne. They put down their glasses and made room for him between them and then poured him a glass. It wasn't long before they all put down their glasses having finished the second bottle and James reclined between the two ladies with a great sense of wellbeing…..and that was all he remembered as he drifted off to sleep.

When he woke up nothing seemed to have changed, except that he had a headache.

'I'm awfully sorry. I seem to have dozed off.'

'Don't apologise', said Elke. 'You've been a star. But before you go, would you just help us for a moment.' She rose from the bed, put on her dressing gown, and produced a box from a drawer.

'While we're in Toronto we want to do some shopping. There's so much more choice here than back in Austria. We've each drawn out money in cash and we have the receipts but the total doesn't seem to be right.'

She opened the box and put what seemed a large pile of Canadian dollar bills on the table together with a couple of receipts. James was a little perplexed that they should need his help for what seemed a simple enough matter but he was tired and just wanted to leave as soon as possible and so he sat down and counted out the money. There should have been 700 dollars according to the receipts but there were only 675 and so the girls were correct in that there was a discrepancy, until Lina remembered that she'd taken some out the previous evening and had forgotten to replace it. James kissed them both goodnight and they agreed to meet briefly in the morning to say goodbye. James returned to his room, checked that the AVM was back in his room and was in bed and asleep in fifteen minutes, having first taken a pill for his headache.

An hour later he was awakened by the telephone.

'Hello, James Winchester here,' he said, unsure whether it was the AVM or the Austrian ladies. It was neither.

'Good evening Wing Commander,' said a heavily accented male voice. 'I apologise for troubling you at this hour but I need to see you as a matter of urgency. It's a very important matter and one to our mutual advantage.'

'Please give me some idea of what this is about,' replied James who was curious but not happy about being disturbed from his sleep. 'You do realise I was asleep in bed?'

'I assure you I would not be speaking to you if it wasn't important'.

'Who are you?'

'My name is Hans Fessler'.

'So what's the problem?'

'I have in my possession evidence that you have been divulging secret evidence to unauthorised people'.

'No you haven't because it isn't true'.

'I think you should see the evidence before I forward it to your Ministry of Defence in London'.

'Where are you?'

'I shall be waiting for you in the hotel lobby'.

James put the phone down. He clearly had to meet the mystery caller and see what evidence he was talking about. Whatever this was about it clearly concerned Elke and Lina since he'd hardly spoken to anyone else. He was equally clear in his own mind that he had had not divulged anything of a sensitive nature to the girls during their short acquaintance. Nevertheless this looked like a honey trap of some kind.

He dressed hurriedly and went down in the lift to the lobby - and there was the mystery caller. He had no difficulty in recognising him since he was wearing a black trilby and horned rimmed glasses. James went over to him and he was not in a courteous frame of mind.

'I've seen you before. You were at the airport in Washington. You were also in a restaurant in Washington. Why are you following me and what is this all about? If I don't get a satisfactory answer I shall call the police'.

'I think that would be very unwise Wing Commander. You see I have diplomatic immunity but you would have some serious questions to answer. Why don't we just sit down and discuss this matter in a reasonable manner? Would you prefer to talk in your room or mine?'

'Neither,' said James. 'We can talk in there', he said, pointing to a room off the main lobby.

There was a small table with chairs in a corner of the room and they sat down facing each other.

'As I said on the telephone, my name is Hans Fessler. I work at the embassy of the East German Democratic Republic in Washington'.

The mention of the GDR set alarm bells ringing in James's mind. The mere fact of sitting at a table with a representative of the Russian puppet regime was bad enough, but to know in addition that some kind of threat was being held over him by this person was of deep concern to him. Whatever his faults, James was a staunch supporter of the democratic western world against the unpleasant forces of a totalitarian regime and the whole of his professional life centred on that belief.

'What is it you want to tell me?' asked James, anxious to keep this meeting as brief as possible but concerned to know what the man had to say.

'Certain photographs have come into my possession which clearly require an explanation'. With that he drew an envelope from his briefcase and took out several photographs. With no further comment he handed them over to James.

The photographs were of an intimate nature, apparently showing him having sex with Elke and Lina. Their room had clearly been prepared with cameras and, presumably, microphones. Two of the pictures showed him handling a wad of banknotes. He had fallen victim to a honey trap which was a technique frequently used by the communist states. It was also obviously clear to him that he'd been drugged.

'So I was drugged so that you could take compromising photographs.

'Well I suppose that's one interpretation,' said Hans Fessler, 'but another is that you were not only having sex but also passing on classified information in exchange for sex and money and that is the interpretation the we prefer to put on it and which I'm sure will be of great interest to your Ministry of Defence'.

James' mind was racing. He could see where this was leading and of course was not going to be sucked into the trap but more than that he wanted to get back at this man. Pictures of him having sex could be a little embarrassing but convincing MOD that he'd been passing over classified information on the basis of the pictures was another matter. He didn't think he would have any difficulty in persuading his own people of his innocence. If anything he was rather surprised at the crudity of the trap.

'So what is it you want?' he asked.

'Very little. You have a brief case I believe with papers relating to the military talks you attended in Washington. You let me have the brief case for half and hour and you can have the photographs in exchange'

'And if I don't agree?

'The Ministry of Defence will find copies of the photographs together with snippets of information leading them to conclude that you have been selling information to people behind the Iron Curtain, to use Mr Churchill's expression.

'And if I do agree?'

'Then the photographs will be destroyed, and you will hear no more of the matter'.

Yes, until the next time you want some information, thought James.

'But the leakage of the information might be traced back to me,' said James.

'No, that will not happen. We are always very careful to protect out sources'.

That's probably true, thought James, since they would want to use me again in the future.

James looked pensive.

'How did you manage to persuade two air hostesses of Austrian Airlines to work for you?'

'Well, they actually work for Interflug, which as I'm sure you know is the East German state airline. They do a little work for us from time to time.'

'Charming', said James.

'Shall I come up to your room with you?' asked Hans Fessler, now concerned to press on with proceedings.

'No', said James. 'I'll bring the case to your room.

What is your room number?'

'346. Shall I see you there in ten minutes?'

'I'll be there in half an hour. I want to make a note of all the papers and the number of pages of each.'

'How little faith you have, Wing Commander. Half an hour then.'

James went straight up to his room, although, as in Washington, he'd put the case in the hotel safe. He then telephoned the British Embassy in Ottawa and briefly explained his situation. They told him to wait in his room and they would send someone to speak with Hans Fessler immediately.

James waited as he was told, wondering what was happening. About an hour later he received a phone call and went down to the lobby to meet a representative of the Canadian Security Intelligence Service together with a member of the Consulate-General in Toronto. They had spoken to Hans Fessler who, although he did have diplomatic immunity in the USA, did not have that protection in Canada and they had consequently taken him away for questioning. They had also recovered the photographs and so any copies would be of no value in any subsequent attempt to bribe James.

'Taking everything into account, you seem to have had quite a busy day, Wing Commander', said Charles Brown of the Consulate-General, and James didn't miss the touch of irony in his voice. 'We will of course have to make full report, one copy of which will be sent to your Ministry of Defence. I'm afraid it will have to include the photographs as evidence.'

James met the AVM for breakfast and explained the events of the previous evening.

'Good God. You randy sod', exclaimed the AVM. 'I imagine that might put a bit of a dent in your career, although you did subsequently take absolutely the right action. I'll do what I can to play down the girlie bits of

179

the story and emphasise the last part'.

'Well actually, Sir, I'm going to apply for early release and relinquish my commission'.

'There's no need for that. You have an excellent record and you'll soon get over this matter. I was going to recommend you for promotion and probably still will do. I'm just telling you to watch your step in future. It's not your honesty that I'm questioning. It's your judgement.'

James listened and then explained that his decision to retire had been quite a long time in gestation and had nothing whatsoever to do with the previous evening's events. He fell asleep on the Atlantic crossing thinking about the new life that lay ahead of him. He had already laid his plans.

EPISODE 9 – COME FLY WITH ME (1986 – 2000)

Historical Context

1986 *Major nuclear accident at Soviet Union's Chernobyl power station and Space shuttle Challenger explodes after launch at Cape Canaveral, Fla., killing all seven aboard*
1987 *Richard Branson and Per Lindstrand make the first transatlantic hot-air balloon flight.*
1988 *Terrorists kill nine tourists on Aegean cruise and Pan-Am 747 explodes from terrorist bomb and crashes in Lockerbie, Scotland, killing all 259 aboard and 11 on ground*
1988– 2000 *Thousands killed in Tiananmen Square; Tim Berners-Lee invents the World Wide Web; Mikhail S. Gorbachev named Soviet President; after 28 years Berlin Wall is open to West; Western Alliance ends Cold War; Margaret Thatcher resigns as British Prime Minister (Nov. 22) and John Major succeeds; cease-fire ends Persian Gulf War; Soviet Union breaks up; Maastricht Treaty takes effect, creating European Union; thousands dead in Rwanda massacre; Channel Tunnel Opens; Hong Kong returns to Chinese rule; Good Friday Accord is reached in Northern Ireland; Europeans agree on single currency, the euro; war erupts in Kosovo; and Concorde crash kills 113 near Paris*

While working at the MOD James had been active in planning his retirement in aviation. His skills lay in aviation and in aeronautical engineering and he wished to remain in those fields. On the flying side his skills were current but he needed civil qualifications as a flying instructor. On the engineering side, he had an aeronautical engineering degree but was not currently in practice. Consequently he started, while still at MOD, by getting himself qualified as a flying instructor so that when he retired in 1986 he was able to get a job immediately as an instructor in a large flying training school near Oxford. The salary wasn't good but he had his RAF pension, his lump sum gratuity and the money he'd been able to save while in the RAF. In addition, he'd bought a house many years ago and let it, and so he had a stake in the property market.

Working in the flying training school enabled him to get some practical experience in light aircraft engineering to supplement his studies so that in a couple of years he had qualified to maintain aircraft. It was only now that he could pursue his real ambition, which was to own his own business. What he had in mind was to own a facility which would provide flying training and also service aircraft and provide routine maintenance and repair but he could not find exactly what he was looking for at a price he could afford. Then he had a stroke of luck, or at least that was how it seemed at the time. He met Sophie.

One day late in 1987 he was manning the desk in the office when he noticed a new open top Jaguar arrive driven by a chic blonde lady. She swept into the office and announced that she wanted to learn to fly. Her husband, much older than she was, had always been against it but he'd died and now she was a widow with independent, and apparently not insignificant means, she intended to pursue her ambition. James sat down with her over a cup of coffee and explained what was involved in terms of the practical and theoretical training and examinations and pointed out the need for an annual physical examination. The aspect of least interest to her was the cost.

In fact the school appointed James as her instructor and subsequently pupil and trainer established a strong rapport. Sophie was not only very keen on flying but she had a natural aptitude for it and she was also avid to learn from James's experience. Consequently she made rapid progress towards her private pilot's licence, aided by the fact that time and money did not seem to present an obstacle to her. She passed her five written papers before she went solo, had no difficulty with her cross country test and was champing at the bit for her final general handling test, which of course she passed.

Throughout the training she and James established a good rapport and become very friendly without their relationship developing into an affair. In any case Sophie was already in a relationship and so the question didn't arise. However, they did socialise a little away from the flying training school, initially going for a drink after a training session but later sometimes by staying on for a meal. They talked about their past and about their ambitions and of course James told Sophie about his intention to start a business once he could afford it.

In the spring of 1988 Sophie was awarded her PPL and she and James went for an evening out in Oxford to celebrate. Over meal with a bottle of champagne she had two surprises for him. The first was that she and her partner had split up. She'd never said much about him but James had met him a couple of times and thought they'd got on well together. The second surprise was a much bigger shock.

Sophie had developed a real passion for flying and now wanted to push her interest much further. She'd discussed James's ambition with him many times and shown a keen interest in his plans. What he didn't know was that she'd been carrying out her own research into the feasibility of what he was trying to achieve. Now she put her cards on the table. She wanted to go into partnership with him on an equal basis.

James was immediately attracted to the idea

because it would allow him to achieve his ambition and he told her so. However, he did ask for several days in which to make up his mind. It would be a very important decision and he had to get it right. At first glance she would be getting the better part of the deal. She was offering to meet half the capital outlay and so financially the deal seemed fair. However, he was also bringing to the table a lifetime's experience in flying and engineering and so he felt that on that basis she should be the junior partner.

Sophie countered by saying that she had a master's degree in business administration and was a qualified accountant, two vitally important areas in which James had little knowledge and no experience. James, who'd previously learned that Sophie had business experience but had not quite grasped the level of her knowledge and expertise, saw the logic of her argument and they eventually shook hands on the deal.

The first priority was to find suitable premises without which the whole idea was a non- starter, and it didn't prove to be easy. However, six months later they found what they thought would suit them well and it was for sale at a good price. A warehousing firm at Norwich Airport had gone into liquidation and their accommodation was up for a sale at a price that was well within the budget set by James and Sophie. Essentially it comprised an aircraft hanger within the airport boundary and a mobile office structure inside the hangar. There was also a grassed area outside providing a possible opportunity for further building.

James explained to Sophie, who didn't know East Anglia very well and Norwich not at all, that it wasn't a bad area in terms of light aviation. During the war there had been a large number of RAF and US bases in East Anglia. Many were now inoperable and some had been turned back into agricultural land, but a number had survived in one form or another as accommodation for light aircraft and gliding clubs. In any case a good training school and servicing facility should be able to attract business from outside the area.

Before long they had employed a solicitor, searches had been conducted, they had drawn up a legal document between them, and they had purchased the property. They then registered the business, and set about obtaining the necessary certificates from the Civil Aviation Authority and equipping the hangar to meet their requirements. They bought additional temporary accommodation as a classroom, aircraft servicing equipment and tools, and a Cessna 172. With their combined knowledge and experience they did not encounter any insurmountable problems but the whole process was clearly going to take time and money.

For the first year James kept a contract with the flying training school in Oxford in order to ensure an income flow, although this also of course prolonged the setting up period, and the Cessna enabled him to transit quickly between Oxford and Norwich. During this year Sophie was very active setting up administrative and financial systems and working up the publicity through aviation magazines and local papers. They were finally able to open in the autumn of 1989.

They had an excellent opening ceremony with good television, radio and press coverage but of even greater importance they already had bookings for aircraft servicing and a number of applicants anxious to start flying training. The also got married two days later although they had to defer any thought of a honeymoon.

Getting married had not been on James's agenda but he and Sophie had developed a good relationship over the previous year and getting married had seemed the natural thing to do, and on reflection that was part of the problem. Getting married was just a shoe in and not the great earth shattering and exciting event it should have been.

At first all went very smoothly. They worked well together, the business quickly went from strength to strength and their relationship was all right but it became obvious to both of them that it was really the business that was keeping them together rather than their personal relationship. James blamed himself on the grounds that he was not the marrying kind and should not have taken on a commitment for which he was so ill suited but in truth the problem was down to both of them.

Sophie was an intelligent woman, which was important to James, but despite the fact that she was fifty two she still seemed to think she was a teenager. She often dressed as a youngster, she loved most pop music, and a disco in Norwich was her idea of a good night out. In terms of modern popular music, James had not developed an interest much beyond the Beatles.

Taking everything into account, he and Sophie were not a good match but, despite all their problems, James had hoped that somehow their marriage could be salvaged but one day late in 2000 it had suddenly become clear to James that that was now out of the question.

He wasn't desperately sad about his situation but disappointed that he had in a sense failed and he wasn't used to failure. After all, they'd set out with such high hopes for the future on their wedding day eleven years ago and now their relationship was finished and it seemed to have ended so abruptly. Over the years they'd argued quite frequently but always seemed to survive the disputes, or so he'd thought until last week when he'd picked up her mobile telephone out of curiosity. It was out of curiosity because he was dissatisfied with his own and wanted to have a look at Sophie's which she'd seemed so pleased with.

If he'd had any serious suspicions about her and wanted to check her mobile he'd have waited for a more convenient opportunity. He wouldn't have started an examination of her messages when she was only in the next room and likely to come back at any moment.

She must have had the sound turned off because an incoming message had suddenly appeared without its usual rendering of 'Heartbreak Hotel'. Sophie always had been a fan of Elvis. It was from someone he didn't know called Mark who was briefly extolling Sophie's virtues and looking forward to their next assignation. James's first inclination was to challenge Sophie immediately but he resisted the temptation when he remembered one or two other incidents in the recent past.

On one occasion when he was in her car, she'd jumped in clutching items of shopping and several birthday cards. He'd idly flicked through the cards and found one covered in hearts expressing everlasting love. When he'd asked who that was for, she'd immediately said that she must have picked it up by mistake.

On another occasion he'd tried to contact her when she was away from home but she wasn't where she said she would be. Again she'd been quick to respond with a plausible explanation. This time he would not accept a brush off but do a little research and so, much against his instincts, he'd gone through her chest of drawers and other personal areas in the house.

Within half an hour he had amassed a quantity of evidence comprising letters, photographs, emails and receipts. He had then been to see a solicitor who'd explained that in his view there was ample evidence to seek a divorce on the grounds of adultery, or irretrievable breakdown of the marriage, or both.

That evening he'd asked Sophie to sit down with a gin and tonic and had then handed her a file with all the evidence. She went white and then sobbed but within twenty four hours was saying that she did not intend to give up the lover, and so the following morning James had filed a divorce partition. Temporarily they continued to live in the same house but Sophie would be moving out into a flat shortly. Apparently the boyfriend was married but would also be seeking a divorce. That remained to be seen. He doubted that he would follow through reliably, but that was now her problem.

James was looking through his office window and could see his Jaguar in the car park and decided it was almost time to go home. He suddenly experienced a wave of sadness, not so much at the thought of losing Sophie, because after all they really hadn't got on well for a long time and he'd eventually had to recognise how self-centred and selfish she could be, but he was sad at the sense of waste. They'd spent eleven years of their lives together and built up an excellent business in which she had played a strong part and he acknowledged that without her impetus he may never have started the business in the first place.

Over the years, the business had flourished and, since taking on a couple of mechanics and a pilot as well as buying two more aircraft, he'd also recently started a European wide service for delivering small items required at short notice. These were mainly high value precision engineering components but he would consider anything. James was now very concerned, not only about losing Sophie's skills but also about how they would share the business assets without wrecking the business which both of them had worked so hard to progress.

He locked up his office, said goodnight to George and Brian, his two mechanics, and set off in his car to drive round the ring road to Newmarket Road, where he had a large detached house. Sophie had continued to work in the business, which had not been easy for either of them, but would be going off on Tuesday for a week with her boyfriend, Mark Johnson.

James could manage without any extra help until tomorrow lunchtime, Saturday, when the firm closed for the weekend. For the following week he'd hired a temp to cover his basic administrative needs. The ring road was busy, even for a Friday evening, and so he was later than expected arriving home, although it didn't matter since they now had their own eating arrangements and he was going out to meet a couple of friends for an aperitif and a meal at a new French restaurant down near the cathedral.

Sophie had packed for leaving in the morning but was also ready to go out for the evening with Mark. Mark lived in Newmarket and James had never met him.

'I shan't be back until late,' Sophie announced, 'and I may not see you in the morning because I'm leaving at about 7am.'

'All right,' said James, not seeing any need to develop the conversation.

However, Sophie clearly hadn't quite finished. 'Did you manage to arrange for a temp for next week?'

'Yes'.

'Good. She can at least answer the phone and do some typing while I'm away'.

'I'll make sure she does, but there are a few other things I want her to do as well. The last time we had a temp in, she was actually quite capable.'

'In case there's an emergency of any kind, I've left my contact details on a piece of paper here'.

'Thank you,' said James, not bothering to look at the paper. He wasn't really interested if she went to the moon or not.

Saturday morning was quiet in the office and so he helped George and Brian in the hangar, which he often did. Frequently it was necessary because they had too much work on but in any case he enjoyed putting on a pair of overalls and getting back to the tools. However, he did receive a request to fly some avionic bits and pieces up to Carlisle Airport on Tuesday. He quite liked the idea since so much of his flying these days was brief test flying after rectification or servicing. This time he could get in a fairly long flight, which was more fun.

He checked the forecast with the Met Office and it looked excellent and so he looked forward to flying in accordance with visual flight rules rather than instrument flight rules, which largely meant that he was responsible for not bumping into things provided he kept out of restricted airspace and for requesting permission if he wished to transit briefly through a restricted area.

Over the weekend he noted that Sophie was staying in London from Saturday until Tuesday morning and then flying from Heathrow to Barcelona, returning on Saturday. Four nights in Barcelona in late June sounded very pleasant and he suddenly felt a little envious but he didn't have a lady friend and wouldn't have wanted to spend time there on his own. Perhaps he would get used once again to going on holiday on his own.

He liked the house when Sophie was away and looked forward to the time when she moved out. She was buying an apartment in Bury St Edmunds and then intended to have some work done on it but expected to be able to live in it in three months' time. Their relationship had gone beyond the shouting stage and settled onto a level of cold indifference but he would much rather she wasn't there at all and she probably felt much the same.

On Sunday morning he did a little gardening and on Sunday afternoon gave some thought to planning his trip to Carlisle on Tuesday. He booked a room in a hotel there and hired a car, to be available at the airport. Flight navigation had been transformed by the arrival of GPS but he still liked to plot his course in advance, although he wouldn't be doing that in detail until early on Tuesday morning when he had the met conditions to hand.

However, he did decide on his route, which would take him east from Norwich, through the edge of the RAF Marham military air traffic zone (MATZ), north of Fenland airfield to the Cottesmore MATZ and the North West to Syerston, Mansfield, Sheffield and Huddersfield. From there he would cross the Pennines, keeping under the Manchester TMA or terminal manoeuvring area, and fly up to Morcambe. Then he could head due north up over the Lake District to Carlisle. He looked forward to what promised to be a very pleasant flight.

Monday brought the new temp who was in fact very capable and able to do much more than James had dared hope. This was fortunate since Monday also brought a rushed job which almost terminated any thought of flying on Tuesday but he, George and Brian worked extremely hard and solved the problem by early evening and so James was able to lock up the premises with a clear conscience.

He didn't feel like cooking and so on his way home at 7.30pm called in at a restaurant on Prince of Wales Road. Over dinner he fired off a few emails from his iPad tablet and by the end of the meal felt he was very much on top of his work. He had a glass of wine with his meal, drove home and then walked to a local pub for a beer before turning in for the night.

James was up at 6am and having a breakfast of cereals and toast as the sun rose into a clear blue sky. He turned on his computer and picked up the latest weather from the Met Office: a few scattered clouds at 5,000ft, a south westerly wind of 7 knots, and a temperature of 20 degrees at 3000ft. It looked very good indeed and with this information he completed his navigation log, calculating his heading and time to each way point on the trip. Overall it would take about 3 ½ to 4 hours and so he decided to leave Norwich at about 8.30 am in order to arrive in good time for lunch. At 8am he was pulling his PA 28 aircraft out of the hangar before walking round it to do a visual exterior check.

Once in the aircraft he adjusted his seat, put on his harness and then proceeded with the rest of the check list: parking brake on; radios off; instruments legible, serviceable, readings within limits; flying controls full and free movement, correct sense; and so on......through to starting the engine, checking further instruments, radio check and then asking for taxi clearance from the control tower, having stated his intention to make a VFR flight to Carlisle. He was cleared to Holding Point Alpha 2, Runway 27 left hand, and once there carried out his engine run up checks and pre-take off checks.

His final air traffic request was to seek permission from air traffic to enter the runway and take off.

'Norwich Tower. This is G-BZQC. Ready for departure.

'G-BZQC is cleared for take-off'.

Despite all his years of powered flying and gliding, he still found something exciting in slipping off the brake, opening the throttle a little and moving forward onto the runway. He turned onto the centre line, paused for a moment and then smoothly opened up the throttle to maximum revs. The aircraft surged forward, quickly gathering speed, and since there was only a slight wind from the south west, holding it on the centre line was not a problem.

At 70 knots he eased the yolk back and the Cherokee responded, rising gently into the air. He climbed straight ahead at 80 knots flying due west but instead of banking left at 500 feet and continuing in the circuit, he called up Norwich control and declared that he was leaving the circuit and continuing on his present heading, climbing to 3000ft.

Once settled at his cruising height, he said farewell to Norwich control and established contact with Marham, requesting permission to transit through their zone. Before long he'd passed King's Lynn to his right and was flying over the Fens with the Wash visible over his starboard wing. As promised by the Met Office, the weather was perfect and he sat back to enjoy the flight, every 15 minutes carrying out his FREDA checks: fuel, radios, engine, direction and altitude.

Eventually he reached the Pennines but encountered no difficulty there. Had the weather been poor he would have taken a more southerly route, avoiding the mountains altogether but with such perfect visibility there was no risk involved provided he kept out of controlled airspace which in this case meant flying under the controlled zones but keeping an adequate safety clearance over the mountains. Before long he was over the peaks, had established contact with Warton radar and had Morcambe and the sea on the nose.

The flight over the Lake District was glorious. He headed directly north over Windermere, with Coniston to his left and then towards the southern tip of Ullswater with Helvellyn rising majestically to his left. He remembered climbing the mountain many years ago on an outing from his school. Ahead he could see the mountains shelving more gradually down towards Carlisle and soon he spotted the town itself. The airfield was about 5 miles NNE of Carlisle town. He changed frequency to Carlisle on 123.30 and gave them an initial call.

'Carlisle approach. This is G-BZQC, a PA 28 3,000 feet 10 miles south of Carlisle inbound for landing'.

'G-BZQC join right hand downwind runway 25.

QFE 1015', came the reply.

James adjusted the setting on his altimeter to take the new pressure setting into account, and was about to reply to Carlisle when the engine suddenly coughed a couple of times and stopped.

'Oh, shit,' was James's initial response but his training and experience immediately came into play as he continued to fly the aircraft by easing the nose down to achieve a glide at 80 knots. He tried several times to restart the engine but having failed to do that he resigned himself to a forced landing and started looking for a suitable field. Normally he would have turned down wind in order to give himself more choice of fields but with the mountains below and behind him the only way was straight ahead. Carlisle repeated their last message, assuming it had not been received, but James ignored it for the moment.

He scanned the terrain carefully, looking for a field of sufficient length and without hazards such as electricity cables, high fences, telegraph poles, buildings and other obstructions. He clearly would not be able to glide to Carlisle airfield which was 5 miles NNE of the town. One slight piece of good fortune was that the wind had swung round from south west to west and so he'd be looking for a final approach from right to left in order to land directly into wind. He spotted what looked like a suitable field and decided it was well within reach of his gliding range, allowing for a left hand turn of 90 degrees in order to make his final approach. At this point he radioed his problem:

'Mayday! Mayday! Mayday! This is G-BZQC, a PA 28. Engine failure. Making a forced landing 10 miles south east of Penrith. Passing 2,000 feet. Heading 360'.

Carlisle responded, noting his details. They would be alerting the emergency services immediately but there was nothing more they could do. It was now entirely down to James to save himself and his aircraft if possible. Carlisle would say no more, knowing he would now need all his concentration to make the best possible landing.

He was on what would normally be base leg and would routinely have put down two stages of flap but as things stood he was unwilling to give away height until he was sure he could get into the field. He was now judging his height and position with regard to his turning point and rate of descent. At 500 feet he turned onto his final approach and studied the field ahead. It looked quite long enough and the surface looked firm. Nor could he see any poles, trees, fences, walls or buildings.

He felt relieved and able to put down two stages of flap, followed shortly by the third and final stage, at all times ensuring that he kept his speed at a steady 80 knots. He'd already checked his harness and now undid his door catch. If the doorframe was buckled in a hard landing and he was incapacitated he didn't want the emergency services to face difficulty in getting him out. He also checked that he'd turned off the fuel cock and he now turned off the electrics, having no further use for them.

It remained only to put the aircraft down gently in the field. This would be an anxious time for most pilots, and James was not without some concern, but he did have the advantage of years of gliding when every take off had to be followed sooner or later by a one-shot landing. Everything looked well as he descended through 350 feet and surveyed the field ahead but the one unknown at this point was the state of the field in terms of its surface covering and firmness. It was grass and it looked fine but he would soon know for sure.

As he came closer to the ground the impression of speed increased. He rounded out his descent and held the aircraft as long as possible just off the ground, trying to bleed off his speed and touch down on the main wheels as lightly as possible. Then he touched down and was relieved to feel the aircraft rolling normally, suggesting a good, hard surface. He gently applied the footbrakes and came to a halt. He was down.

On the descent, he'd noticed a road alongside the field and he now saw a gateway onto the road but he was not tempted to taxi up to it. He didn't know what dips or hollows the grass might be concealing and it would be a pity to damage the aircraft after making such a good forced landing. He let the engine idle for thirty seconds, applied the handbrake and carried out the rest of the shut down procedures before climbing out of the aircraft, taking his flight bag and small case with him; he also remembered to pick the spare part he was delivering. If he smoked he would have lit up now but that was a habit of the past. A pint of good beer would do the trick though. First, however, he had to think about the emergency services he'd alerted.

He walked to the gate which led to a small public road, took out his mobile telephone and called Carlisle Airport to let them know that he was down safely and that, while their was no longer an emergency, he would welcome some form of transport. He promised to call them back as soon as he was aware of his exact location. He had a memory from his last look at the GPS that he was somewhere between Carlisle and Penrith. He thought about going back to the aircraft, switching the electrics back on, and checking the GPS for an exact location but he decided against doing this. The fault could have been electrical and he did not wish to risk exacerbating the problem, and it wasn't as though he was in Kurdistan or the middle of the Sahara. He would soon find out where he was.

As it happened, the first vehicle to arrive was a police car with lights flashing and siren screaming. It screeched to a halt and a young constable leapt out, looked at James's flight bag and asked if he had anything to do with a light aircraft reported to be in trouble in the area. A middle aged officer, adopting a more leisurely exit from the car, joined them. James gave a brief resume of the incident but the constable, clearly an aviation enthusiast, had a number of questions purely out of personal interest. The elder officer occupied himself in making a few relevant notes, after which the three of them returned to the aircraft.

'Would you mind giving me a hand?' asked James. 'Just in case the breeze stiffens a little, I would like to turn her into wind.' No sooner had they done this than a fire engine arrived. The fire team proved to be quite helpful in providing rope and metal rods and in helping James to stake the aircraft to the ground.

'What are your plans for the aircraft, Sir?' enquired PC John Barnstaple, the older policeman.

'Well, at this moment I'm not quite sure,' admitted James. 'I need to establish what's wrong with it and whether or not I can fix it here. If I can, then I might be able to take off again and fly to Carlisle airfield as planned. That will also depend on the length and condition of this field, but it looks long enough and firm enough. If not, then I face the prospect of having to have it recovered by road. I think the next thing I need to do is to find a hotel in Carlisle and then hire a car. After that I shall drive to the airport and make my number with them. Incidentally, you don't happen to know who owns the field do you?'

PC Barnstaple was pretty sure that the field belonged to Mrs Jane Carter but he would check and confirm that later. In the meantime perhaps James would accept a lift into Carlisle where the Crown Hotel had much to recommend it. He could also suggest a car hire firm in town.

If one had to fall out of the sky, thought James as he sat in the back of the police car, then the outcome hadn't been too bad so far. He was also ruminating on the possible cause of the problem. A mechanical problem seemed unlikely, which left fuel and electrics. Of the two, he thought perhaps a fuel problem was the most likely. However, further thought was interrupted by PC Graham White, who was anxious to know more about flying in general.

Once in Carlisle James booked himself into the hotel recommended by PC Barnstaple, hired a car and arranged to drive over to the airport to report on his incident. He also contacted the Civil Aviation Authority at Gatwick to report his intentions. He was about to leave for the Carlisle airport when he received a call from Jane Carter, who was indeed the owner of the field in which he'd landed. It seems that Officer Barnstaple had told her where to find him.

He immediately liked the sound of her voice, which was measured, warm and inviting. She assured him that there was no problem from her point of view and that he was welcome to leave his aircraft there for as long as it took to repair it. He thanked her and said he would probably be over in the morning to examine his aircraft. He then drove over to Carlisle airport to discuss the situation. He would have to submit a report which he would copy to the CAA.

Having dealt with the administrative procedures, he went over to the small engineering firm to whom he was delivering the spare part and there he met Brian Oldfield, owner and chief executive of Oldfield Aviation. Brian was a rotund, jovial man given to laughing heartily. He was clearly amused by James's forced landing and asked rather cheekily who he got to do his servicing. Nevertheless he was well-intentioned and helpful and very willingly leant James a range of tools to repair the aircraft, on the assumption that James had some idea of possible causes. On that subject he offered his own views, which more or less accorded with those of James.

Thus armed James returned to his hotel for a shower, a beer and a good meal. After dinner he phoned Jane Carter to confirm that he would drive over to see her at 9.30am and then make an attempt to identify the fault on the aircraft and to effect a repair. She gave him instructions on how to find her house and asked him if there was anything else he needed. Again he sensed a warm and helpful person.

He considered watching a little television but instead, having had a fairly full day, he turned in to bed at 10pm to read a book on his Kindle: 'Blue Horizon' by Wilbur Smith, one of his favourite authors. He enjoyed the writings of Wilbur Smith for his swashbuckling adventure stories and the authenticity of the supporting detail.

He left the hotel at 9am the following morning and headed for Jane Carter's place, which was only about 20 minutes from his hotel. He found her house without too much difficulty, or rather he found her gates and drive but the house itself was not visible from the road. The gates were open and he drove down a long drive through extensive lawns and flower beds towards a large Edwardian house. As he parked the car in front of a stone staircase, the front door opened and a very attractive, dark haired woman appeared. She waited for him as he climbed the staircase and then introduced herself as Jane Carter. He noted her firm, warm handshake and her wide smile.

'Please come in, Mr Winchester,' she said, ushering him into an extensive vestibule and then into a very large drawing room. 'Would you like a coffee or tea?'

'Coffee please, Mrs Carter,' he replied. 'But please call me James'.

'Well that's easy. James was my late husband's name.'

Charles sat down in a comfortable arm chair while Jane disappeared briefly to prepare the coffee. The room was tastefully and elegantly furnished in tans and beiges and the furniture was largely regency. The paintings on the walls were mainly pastoral scenes but there was a striking portrait of Jane Carter, probably painted about ten years previously. Among a number of photographs he spotted a few of a tall, distinguished looking man whom he took to be Jane's late husband.

Jane returned with the coffee, served him and then sat down. 'I'm very interested to know what happened to you. Please tell me all about it. It's sounds very exciting.'

James briefly sketched in his background and reason for his flight before giving her a little more detail about the incident itself.

'You make it all sound so very matter of fact but really you must have been quite frightened,' she said when he'd finished his account.

'Well I imagine my pulse rate did go up somewhat,' he said. 'But you know it's a well-known phenomenon that it's generally after an event like that that the concern sets in. At the time I was wrapped up in carrying out the emergency procedures. Anyway, I don't think one should exaggerate the danger. Every pilot practices an engine failure emergency from time to time and if I was going to have an engine failure I couldn't have picked a better place to have one, with plenty of large fields to aim at. I was particularly lucky that I didn't have a failure ten minutes early when I was still over the mountains. As it was I had a choice of landing areas, although I don't think I could have done much better than your field.'

'Well, I'm very pleased that all has turned out well

for you. I drove out to your aircraft yesterday evening after the policeman called me about your landing and I couldn't see any damage. Do you think you'll be able to repair it easily?'

'To be honest, I don't yet know, although I do have one or two ideas. I'll have a better idea once I've been out to it and checked a few things. I've brought a set of tools along.'

'Perhaps I could make a suggestion. We could put your tools in my Landrover and then drive out to the field. I'll leave you there to do your work and then you can call me when you've finished. You do have a mobile phone with you?'

'That's very kind of you. Yes, I do have a mobile.'

'In any case I suggest you stay for lunch, whether or not you've finished the work. I can be preparing that while you're fixing your aeroplane.'

James attempted to suggest that she really had no need to go to such trouble but Jane waved away his protestation.

'Please don't mention it. This is the most exciting thing that's happened here for a long time. I might even write a piece on it for the local paper. Would you mind that?

'Well no, not really, provided you don't put in any nonsense about the courageous pilot bravely struggling to avoid crashing into houses. I can tell you that the pilot up front is usually the first to arrive at the scene of any accident and he is certainly not keen to crash into houses'.

'I promise not to do that,' she said with a smile.

Jane drove him out to the field and left him there to sort out the problem. He first checked the electrical connections but couldn't find any loose ones. He also had a set of spare fuses but having changed them over, and still not found a fault, he turned his attention to the fuel supply. As part of his pre-flight routine, he'd checked for water in the fuel. Nevertheless he drained off some more fuel and checked it, but there was no trace of water in it. Next he disconnected the fuel supply line and turned on the electrical pump. Since the fuel flowed freely he took off the carburettor and dismantled it. It looked all right but he would have to have it blown through in case there was a blockage in a jet. There was nothing more he could do at present and so he phoned Jane and then packed away his tools and the carburettor.

'We can eat on the terrace', suggested Jane, once they were back at the house. 'Would you like an aperitif? Gin? White wine? Rosé?

'A gin and tonic would be excellent, thank you.'

'Good choice. I'll join you in one.'

James followed Jane through French windows onto an extensive terrace tastefully adorned with high quality garden furniture. The terrace faced to the rear gardens, again extensively lawned and giving way eventually to a coppice and then to the mountains of the Lake District in the distance. He made himself comfortable while she rustled up the drinks.

'Is there much work left to do on your aeroplane?' she asked as she returned with two very large gin and tonics.

'Frankly I don't really know. If the problem is simply a blockage in the carburettor then I'll have it fixed tomorrow. If not, then I'll have to look deeper and perhaps even have the aircraft transported to Carlisle Airport, although I hope it won't come to that. In the meantime, does it present anything of a problem for you where it is at present?'

'Not in the slightest,' she replied and he noted, not for the first time, the deep blue of her eyes, her very white smile and her full, red lips. What on earth, he wondered, could a woman as attractive as this be doing living on her own? Perhaps her husband had died in the recent past.

They seemed to get on very well over lunch to the extent that James spoke about his failed marriage, his business, and his concern about what would happen to the business when they divorced. Jane spoke about her time with her husband, who had died five years previously, and about the sad relationship she'd entered into shortly after his death. Missing her husband and desperately lonely, she's succumbed to the smooth entreaties of a locally retired financier.

It wasn't his wealth that had attracted her as much as his man-of-the-world posture. Friends had advised her against him because of his past devious business affairs, which had obliged him to retire, because of his rude demeanour, and because he was married and living with his wife, a popular woman locally.

Fortunately Jane had eventually come to her senses and given him his marching orders but the affair had made an impact on her and she'd not since dabbled in affairs of the heart since. James listened intently to her story and decided he'd been right about the warmth of her personality. She was a genuinely lovely person and one with whom he was quickly beginning to feel very comfortable. However, time was passing and he had a problem to solve.

He explained that he hoped to return in the morning to continue with the rectification, thanked her for her hospitality and was about to take his leave of her at the front door, when a thought struck him.

'Would you allow me to reciprocate your hospitality by having dinner with me at my hotel? I'd be delighted if you would.'

'That's awfully kind of you. I suppose I could. My book reading club meeting for this evening has just been cancelled and so I don't have an engagement. But I hope you're not inviting me just because I gave you a bite to eat for lunch?'

'Certainly not!' exclaimed James. 'I've invited you because you'd be a charming companion.'

'In that case, kind sir, I happily accepted your invitation. At what time would you like me to arrive?'

'Would 7.30pm suit you?'

'Perfectly'.

With that agreed, James set off for the airport to have the aircraft carburettor cleaned. He returned to his hotel at 5pm, had a brief rest, followed by a shower and then changed for dinner.

He was waiting for her in the foyer when she arrived. She was wearing a wide brimmed black hat and a short black coat, which he helped her take off. Underneath she was wearing a deep blue velvet dress, offset by a discrete but expensive looking silver pendant which matched her small earrings. He couldn't claim to be an expert but they looked to him like diamonds.

'Shall we go to the bar first for an aperitif?' he suggested.

'I think that's a very good idea,' she replied. 'I would love a gin and tonic'.

Once settled in easy chairs she asked him how he'd got on at the airport and James explained he was fairly confident that the problem had been a blocked jet in the carburettor. A soaking in cleaning fluid and a blast through with an air pressure hose had probably solved the problem. However, he would know in the morning once he'd refitted the carburettor. After that they talked more about their past lives and continued their acquaintance over dinner. The candlelit dinner and good wine rendered the conversation somewhat more romantic than that about engine parts, important as they were to him at that time.

It was over coffee that Jane dropped a remark like a

small pebble in a pond, but one which was to presage gigantic changes in Charles' life.

'You're a pilot and an engineer, Charles. What do you think caused that awful crash in Spain?'

'I'm sorry. I suppose I've been so busy over the last thirty six hours I hadn't caught up with the news. Do you know any details?'

'Well, not really. I think the plane was trying to land at Barcelona but came down short of the runway. I think some people survived but I understand most were killed.'

Jane had James' full attention.

'When did this happen?'

'Yesterday.'

' My wife was flying to Barcelona yesterday.'

'Oh, James. I'm so sorry I didn't mean to shock you like that.'

'I'm sorry Jane but I'll have to go to my room and check.'

'I'll come with you'.

James knew that his wife had been flying from Stansted. In his room he found the piece of paper she'd given him with her flight number, time of flight and airline. He made a call to the airline which had opened a special number for the accident. He waited while a member of the ground staff looked through the passenger manifest.

'Yes, sir', said the stewardess. 'A Mrs Winchester was on the list and I'm afraid I must tell you that she did not survive the crash. Please accept our sincere condolences. We have been trying to trace you but the lady did not leave any next of kin details. Would you please let me have your details so that we can contact you again shortly but is there anything we can do for you immediately?'

Jane had been listening in shocked silence and

quickly gathered the outcome. She also heard him ask about a Mr Mark Johnson, describing him as a close friend in order to overcome any reluctance to disclose his name. In any case it seems that he had left his wife's name as next of kin and she had already been informed.

James put the phone down.

'You gathered the outcome of all that?'

'Yes I did, and I'm most awfully sorry. Is there anything I can do to help?' She stood up, came over to him and put her arms round him. 'I don't suppose you'll be able to sleep tonight. Why not come home with me and just talk. Would you like to do that?'

James was dreadfully shocked and looked it.

'We were getting divorced and we had not been happy together but she was my wife for eleven years and we did have some happy times together. I would not have wished anything like this on her.'

James could not hold back the tears that flowed freely down his cheeks and he made no attempt to hide them.

Back at her house, Jane poured them a large whisky each and then they talked into the early hours of the morning. Later she showed him to a guest bedroom where she helped him take off his shoes and then lay next to him, both fully clothed with their arms around each other.

When Jamees woke in the morning, he was alone. On a table next to the bed was a safety razor, shaving soap, liquid soap, a comb and towels. Twenty minutes later he made his way downstairs to find Jane sitting reading in the drawing room.

They greeted each other with a kiss on the cheek.

'You're going to be busy what with one thing and another but I think you should at least start the day on a full stomach. If you feel up to it I shall make you a cooked breakfast.'

'Thank you', said James. 'I would like that. And thank you also for your kindness last night. I very much appreciate it.'

'I think it did me good too,' she said. 'Since James died I've spent far too much time thinking about myself. In view of what's happened, what do you wish to do about your aeroplane?'

'I've been thinking about that. I first need to make a number of phone calls to make sure as many family members and friends as possible are aware of the accident and then I need to get back to Norwich to sort things out from there. I'll try to fit the carburettor later this morning. If that solves the problem I can fly to Carlisle Airport to refuel and then fly directly down to Norwich. If not I'll have to go down to Norwich by train, unless there's a commercial aircraft flight.'

'Well I think you should forget about your aeroplane and book the train right away. That way you'll have to come back', she added and she smiled as she said it.

'In that case you can be sure that I will come back.'

In fact James was able to fix the aircraft and so she came down to the field to see him off.

'Are you sure this field is all right for you to take off from?' she asked, genuinely concerned about the whole project. 'I got used to calling my husband James and I don't want to start all over with someone who has a different name.'

'Yes, it's quite long enough and the surface is excellent. I'll telephone you from my home in Norwich this evening'

'I'd be grateful if you'd telephone me from Norwich Airport after you've landed'.

James was glad of her warmth and of her concern and he looked forward to seeing her again in the near future. He took off into the blue….fully expecting to return to Jane and perhaps to start a new life. On the flight back he suddenly realised the business implications of Sophie's death. He wouldn't have wanted it this way but he was now the sole owner of Skyway Services Ltd.

EPISODE 10 – THE SANDS OF TIME – 2001

Historical Context

2001 *Foot-and-mouth disease wreaks havoc on rural Britain and Islamic terrorists crash aircraft on targets in New York and Washington; George Bush is signed in as President*

In fact James did return to see Jane a number of times but somehow the relationship didn't work out and their meetings became more and more infrequent. Yet James wasn't unhappy and he considered himself to be very fortunate. His business was thriving, he had a new exciting lady friend in Norfolk and he was doing what he wanted to do – flying and managing his aviation engineering business. In fact he sometimes thought his life was perfect, or at least almost perfect.

If there was a missing ingredient it was the lack of danger or excitement. The flying he did was very routine, apart from the Carlisle incident: checking out light aircraft after he'd serviced them or giving lessons to students. Occasionally he'd deliver spare parts and if he was lucky he'd get a commission to fly a part urgently required somewhere on the Continent but even that was interesting and pleasant rather than challenging or thrilling.

Over the years James had had several motorcycles and was now thinking of buying another one but behind the idea was a project. He'd been reading that at one time crossing the Sahara from north to south had been a common occurrence but that since the Algerian Civil War few people had attempted it.

The war had started in 1991 and had continued unabated until about 1997/98 but since then, although outbreaks of violence had continued, things seemed much quieter. Nevertheless there were reputed to be terrorists in northern cities and areas in the centre and the south still had some concentrations of terrorists. However, James seemed to be picking up a view, right or wrong, that a crossing was now a viable proposition. He kept turning over the embryo project in his mind and it might have stayed there but for a chance meeting with a couple of his student pilots in a hotel bar near Norwich.

The subject turned to motorcycling since one of them, Fred Aldridge, had just bought a new bike and ridden down France and around a good chunk of Italy. James aired his idea about the Sahara and Fred showed considerable interest but was disappointed when James suggested the whole trip could take two or three months.

'I'd love to come with you,' he said. 'I can't afford that much time but I know a chap who might also be interested,' and he wrote out a name and contact number. They then went on to discuss some of the logistics of the exercise but the talk was mainly speculative since they didn't have the necessary facts. It was evident that the project would require considerable detailed planning but even that there was still great scope for things to go wrong, which indeed they did.

In broad terms James' idea was to ride down to Dover from Norwich, catch a ferry to Calais, ride down France to Marseille, cross over to Tunis and then ride down through Algeria, Niger and end the trip in Benin in West Africa. From there he thought about catching a boat back to the UK.

Apart from information about terrorists, it would also obviously be necessary to locate water and fuel sources, to find out as much as possible about the condition of the roads, such as they were, and to learn about visa requirements. No doubt other needs would become apparent if and when the detailed planning actually started.

The following day he received a call from David Williams, the friend of Fred Aldridge, to say that he would indeed be interested to meet James to talk about the project. He seemed very enthusiastic and knowledgeable about motorcycling and motorcycle maintenance, which was a good start.

They met at Norwich Airport and James gave David a flight in a Cessna 175 before they went to the Baron of Beef pub in the City to start discussing the details. David was clearly enthusiastic about the idea but the more they discussed it the more the need for detailed planning became obvious. In broad terms James undertook to look at route planning, visas, ferries and any other aspect concerning navigation. David would look at motorcycles, maintenance, and equipment. They seemed to get on well and both looked forward to an exciting adventure.

One aspect of all this that concerned James was how to take off two months from his business. After Sophie's departure and death he'd taken on a very competent woman to replace her and so the administrative and financial aspects were fine. In his absence the mechanics could also cope and so the problem was on the flying side.

The mechanics could not test fly aircraft after remedial work and nor could they train students or maintain the parts delivery service. The business had been doing very well and because the demand seemed to justify it James had thought for some time about taking on a pilot. Now was the time to do it if the new pilot was to have time to settle in before he set off on his adventure.

In fact it was a year later, October 2001, before they were ready, having also taken into account the need to avoid midsummer temperatures and desert flash flooding. The Mayor of Norwich had organised a send off with local television, radio and a police escort to the outskirts of the City, and before long they were burning up the miles to Dover.

Each bike carried spare tyres, tools, water containers and a large reserve petrol tank strapped to each side. Between them they also had camping equipment and of course changes of clothing and personal toilet items. David had selected Honda Transalps and so they'd each bought one. The Transalp is described as a trail bike, meaning it is robust in construction and has a potential to travel off road, both essential characteristics. The disadvantages are that the bike is fairly heavy and has a relatively high centre of gravity.

Despite the weight they were carrying, James and David found no particular problem riding down to Dover, nor any riding down through France from Calais, but they were mindful that they had yet to ride the bikes with spare tanks full of fuel and water. They made a first overnight stop at St Omer where they had a splendid meal, drank two and a half pints of lager and turned in at 11.30pm.

In the morning they set off for Dijon in the rain but their spirits were raised by an early stop for a full English breakfast of egg, bacon and all the trimmings. It was a fairly challenging morning with further mist and rain but the weather improved after lunch and they were able to cruise down the auto route at a steady 75 to 80 mph. An auberge near Dijon provided a meal of eggs in red wine sauce followed by duck and cranberries, a selection of cheeses and an apricot tart.

The next day they arrived in good time at Istres, just short of Marseille, and found a quiet but welcoming inn. Here, after a splendid meal as the only clients, they passed the rest of the evening in the company of the congenial patron. The patron and David ended the evening in high spirits, literally and metaphorically, by drinking liberal quantities of red wine and performing what could loosely be called a Greek dance. At least they were twirling about to a Greek tune waving handkerchiefs in the air. The adventure had got off to a promising start.

A brief but exhilarating ride in the morning found them at Marseilles docks where they found the right quay and then waited for a couple of hours watching large numbers of Arabs arriving from Algeria and Tunisia. Some arrived as foot passengers but most arrived in overloaded cars, although the word 'overloaded' does not do justice to the ingenuity of the occupants, most of whom could barely be seen amidst the clothes, mattresses and domestic appliances that surrounded them. Even more remarkable were the goods stacked on the roofs in towers and precariously attached with bits of rope and string. One car sported a full three piece suite on its roof.

The trip across to Tunis was very agreeable and they disembarked the following morning, three hours later than scheduled, to start the main part of the adventure. So far all had been very easy but now the problems would start. First, however, James was intent upon seeing Carthage before leaving the Tunis area and so they set off in search of the ancient ruin.

It seemed ridiculous but in fact Carthage was not particularly well signposted and after several false starts, including a trip past the heavily guarded presidential palace, they pulled over to discuss what to do. At this point an Arab motorcyclist came up alongside and asked, in a strong American accent, if he could be of assistance. His name, in keeping with most of the Arabs they were subsequently to meet, was Mohammed and he not only led them the short distance to Carthage but insisted on paying their entrance fee when they suddenly realised that they had yet to obtain any local currency. He explained that he was a travel agent and that showing people around was his business.

Afterwards, Mohammed insisted on taking them to nearby Sidi Bout Said, an ancient Arab town overlooking a marina and the coastline, where he bought them each a cake rather like a doughnut without the jam. Over coffee he explained he had two degrees and a PhD from the States. He was clearly intelligent and very likeable and his story seemed entirely plausible and so when he asked if they needed a hotel for the night they were ready to accept his advice

In fact he led them to the Hotel Plaza, an extremely pleasant hotel overlooking the sea. It was not expensive and if Mohammed was getting a commission then so much the better. He deserved it and to show their appreciation of his kindness they suggested he return to the hotel later as their guest for dinner. However, Mohammed had another idea. Instead he would return to pick them up in his Landover and take them down town to an Arab restaurant.

They said au *revoir* to their newfound friend and then, still in their motorcycle kit, they sat by the pool eating a fish snack and drinking a couple of pints of beer. The trip surely couldn't continue on such a fortunate note. No indeed, it could not, although the evening turned out well enough.

Mohammed was back to pick up James and David before 8pm and, armed with 50 US dollars each, exchanged courtesy of the hotel, they set off for Le Chalet restaurant. Despite its name, the restaurant served a wide selection of Arab food and before long they were savouring a range of delightful appetizers. With Mohammed's guidance they went on to select some main course dishes, one of which seemed to be of particular interest to him. When it came it didn't look particularly attractive, comprising as it did an indifferent looking gravy with unidentifiable pieces of flotsam, but to please Mohammed they set about it with a faked enthusiasm. Mohammed, who didn't eat any of it himself, claimed it was a local octopus, which served only to raise James's concern since it clearly wasn't octopus and he wondered about the need for subterfuge.

He wondered even more when Mohammed suggested that he and David have their photographs taken with pieces of the concoction on their forks. Afterwards Mohammed was very amused to tell them that they had each just eaten a local delicacy, a bull's penis. James then understood why he'd found the meat somewhat gelatinous.

Over coffee Mohammed suddenly became very serious and insisted on talking about their intended ride across the Sahara. He listened to their plans and then chose his words carefully before speaking.

'I'm half Tunisian and half Algerian but I would not attempt what you're doing if you offered me a fortune. In fact I wouldn't even cross the frontier into Algeria. If you go, I do not think you will come out again.' He paused to let his words sink in and then continued. 'There are three major problems. Firstly there is the desert itself. Crossing it in a four wheel truck designed to cover difficult territory is hard enough even if you don't have a breakdown and you don't run out of fuel or water. On a motorcycle it's not impossible but it's very nearly impossible'.

'The second problem is that you're both riding motorcycles that the average person in Algeria would have to work a lifetime to buy and you are about to go off into the wilderness with two of them. Everyone is going to be looking at you with envious eyes and thinking what a difference to their lives those bikes would make and don't forget - there's not much law and order once you start heading south'.

'The third problem is the worst. Having your bikes stolen is one thing but meeting up with terrorists is another and believe me there are plenty of them in Algeria, particularly once you get further south. I implore you not to go'.

His words, and the sincerity with which he spoke them, had a sobering effect on the rest of the evening. James and David explained that having come so far they could not give up at the first hurdle and would have to give it a try. Before they'd left England they were vaguely aware of a continuing terrorist problem but it had seemed remote and all but finished. On their way down through France they'd begun to pick up a very different impression and now they were almost in Algeria they were getting the full version, and it didn't sound good.

When Mohammed saw they were intending to continue in the morning he brought out of his pocket what looked like two pills and put them on the table. 'Good God,' thought James. 'He's giving us a couple of suicide pills'. Afterwards David confessed he'd thought exactly the same thing. In fact Mohammed was giving them a couple of good luck charms. Then he took them back to their hotel and wished them well.

The following day was spent negotiating a dreadful road in a light drizzle from Tunis to Gafsa. There seemed to be endless road works which spread mud everywhere and the traffic was dense. Eventually, crawling along the high street in Gafsa and trying to avoid pedestrians, sheep and goats on a slippery and ill-made surface, they found a hotel at about 4.30 pm and booked a couple of rooms at reception with an affable chap who could have been French. He called upon a hotel porter, Taheh, to safeguard their motorcycles and carry their overnight bags.

The porter was worthy of note for several reasons. Firstly he looked like Odd Job from the James Bond film 'Goldfinger' in that he was physically square. That is to say he had a square body surmounted by a square head and he was immensely strong. He bounced each motorcycle, which was unbelievably heavy, up a short flight of steps and into a secure yard. Their large overnight bags were as small brief cases in his muscular hands.

He was also noteworthy in that he was a deaf mute, so that all communication was through sign language, and yet he not only readily understood what was required but also made known his own requirements. In a series of hilarious gestures and signs he communicated the fact that he had a woman with whom he would later be having sex and that this event would be much enhanced if they were to obtain a bottle of wine for him and his woman.

James and David were very happy to help enhance Mohammed's evening of romance but to their mind there was a potential problem. Apart from the fact that Taheh was a Muslim and therefore not supposed to drink alcohol, they had now entered the period of Ramadan.

Later over a dinner - comprising cheese omelette (minus the cheese), chips, goat chop, and a fruit tart – they discussed what to do about Taheh's request. They surmised that the penalty for the dispersion of wine by infidels to Muslims during Ramadan was probably dissection and use as camel fodder. During this conversation Taheh had positioned himself behind a pillar so that James and David could see him but the manager and bar staff couldn't. From this position he commenced miming the drinking of wine direct from a bottle, just to ensure that his new found English friends had not forgotten his request.

In the morning after breakfast they made up a parcel with paper obtained from the hotel and put it into a plastic bag. Outside Taheh had positioned their motorcycles and so, already fully kitted out, they handed Taheh two bottles of wine, wished him a successful evening and roared off down the road towards Nafta and the border with Algeria before the heavy hand of fate could reach them.

Passing the Tunisian border post at Hazoua did not present any difficulty but getting into Algeria was a little more of a problem having to deal with police, customs, money exchange and vehicle insurance. However a chance meeting with a Frenchman proved useful. He claimed that their intended route down through El-Meniaa, In Salah and Tamanghasset was unquestionably too dangerous because of heavy terrorist activity.

There was an escort Army patrol that went down there from time to time but to go alone would be suicide, or actually worse since one would not get to choose one's method of parting this earth. He strongly advised that it was better to choose an alternative route.

Now this was a bugger since they'd planned their route for a year and had relevant detail and maps, apart from the fact that they'd already booked a room in Tamanghasset. The only other route was through Hassi-Messaoud and In Amenas but on their long range map the connection cutting across to Tamanghasset looked tenuous and going via Tamanghasset was ultimately the only way. The revised route would involve a long haul of 705 kms with no fuel stops and 541 miles of pistes. They decided to reserve judgement and seek further information if possible.

Once through the customs they headed off for El-Oued, passing through a number of small villages on the way. One of these, according to what they'd read in advance, had the delightful reputation of welcoming strangers passing through with a hail of stones. As they approached all seemed quiet until quite suddenly a gang of youths appeared and started throwing bricks and stones at them, clearly anxious to sustain their folklore. Only one of their two bikes sustained a glancing blow as they weaved and dodged their way through. By now both bikes were carrying a full 5 litre fuel can on each side as well as spare water and all the other paraphernalia. With all that weight weaving and dodging on a broken and uneven surface proved challenging but all ended well and once out of firing range they were able to stop and laugh it off.

At El Oued they found the Hotel Louise, where water was reputed to be available from 7pm although in fact it was not turned on until 8.30pm. However, there was nothing further of note here and in the morning they set off on the road south towards Touggourt, where there was an incident. James was riding ahead of David and suddenly heard a shout from behind. He stopped immediately and turned round to see a tug of war between David and an Arab who was trying to steal a bag from his bike.

The problem was resolved when David swung a punch at the Arab who released his hold long enough for David to open the throttle and roar off, with James not far behind.

The Sahara Desert is a mix of scrubby villages, rocks, sand and sometimes breathtaking beauty. They were now in a region of pure sand on what looks on the map to be a good road but which in fact might have been a reasonable road at one time but was now a ribbon of bits of tarmac interrupted by bare sandy stretches and stone. In some ways this was worse than pure hardened sand known as 'a piste' since it was impossible to set a steady speed.

However their main concern now was to decide on

which of the two routes to take, since the road was about to fork.

The planned route, through El-Manias and In Salah down to Tamanghassert, had known terrorist groups, a point confirmed through conversations with the police and the Army. They also confirmed there was an Army patrol that escorted convoys south and they could wait for the next convoy. The other route offered worse riding conditions which might be so poor as to prevent subsequent access to Tamanghassert. Nor was there any certainty that they would not meet a terrorist group on this secondary route.

However, waiting for an Army patrol on the main route might well result in their visas expiring not only in Algeria but also in Niger, their next target. Rightly or wrongly they chose to take the secondary route and so branched left just short of Ouargla and set off for an overnight stop at Hassi-Messaoud.

Hassi-Massaoud owes its existence to oil and so it has a fairly cosmopolitan population but the foreign oil and business people live in secure compounds and rarely emerge other than to travel to and from the airport in armed convoys. James and David had no such support and arrived in town looking for a hotel. The finished up in the Petroleum Hotel, which seemed appropriate, and here they met two people of interest.

The first was an English teacher from Africa who bought them a drink and them took them shopping. The second was an Arab waiter at the hotel who, during dinner, made it clear that he wished to discuss a personal matter but was hesitant to broach the matter. James decided to draw it out of him and eventually reached the core of the problem. Mohammed (yes, yet another one!) was suffering from a broken heart. He had met a young American woman and been captivated by her to the extent that he was engaged in writing poetry to her.

Unfortunately the poetry was in Arabic and had to be translated into English. Being a fairly well educated Arab, the waiter spoke French but not English.

After dinner James met the waiter and teased out of him the meaning of his epic in French before making an attempt to translate it into English. This being Algeria, and therefore more strict about the observance of Ramadan, alcohol was not available in the bar but perhaps this was just as well or the translation might never have been finished. When he'd finished at midnight James put the evening down as one of the more bizarre evenings that he had ever spent but never did discover the success or otherwise of his efforts.

In the morning, with full fuel tanks and full reserve cans they set of south from Hassi-Messaoud and before long, not for the first time in Algeria, came to a road block set up by the Army as an anti-terrorist measure. The road block comprised log and barbed wire trestles but the most arresting aspect was the AK 47 rifles pointing in their direction as they came down the track.

With experience gained so far, they came to a gentle halt, casually took off their helmets and hung them on the handlebars, dismounted, put their bikes on their stands and advanced towards the rifles whilst simulating affable smiles. However this time there appeared to be no immediate relaxation of the guard, one of whom beckoned them into a shed whilst continuing to point his weapon at them.

Why, James wondered, were they being ordered into a shed at gunpoint? However, once inside the slight unease soon gave way to relief when he realised that the guards were simply using this as an office. Papers were displayed and accepted and cigarettes were offered. James and David had brought a quantity of cigarettes and ball point pens to offer as gifts along the way but this was clearly an occasion for the cigarettes. They chatted in French and then parted amiably and the bikes were once more flicking up sand and stones and dodging potholes and ruts in the track en route for Bel Guebbor. It was here that things went wrong.

Bel Guebbor appeared to be little more than a military outpost but could well have served as an overnight stop in the two-man tent they had yet to use. Unfortunately by the time they reached this fork in the road a vicious wind had developed making it impossible to pitch a tent. A soldier suggested that instead of keeping to the main track they could take a loop on another road which included a place called Bordj Omar Driss where they might find a place to spend the night. Later this road would join the original track. Having verified this on the large scale map, they unfortunately took his advice.

It soon became apparent that the track was in very poor shape, added to which, the driving wind had become very cold, making riding difficult. To make matters worse, the wind was blowing sand across the track obscuring it completely from time to time. It was now a question of carefully picking a way between holes, ruts and rocks but at the same time trying to keep up a speed that would see them in Bordj before nightfall. The idea of spending a night sitting in the open wind without shelter was not appealing.

James was leading and feeling very cold: so cold in fact that his arms were shaking and he was having difficulty controlling the bike, which would have been hard in ideal conditions with so much weight. They reached a little stretch where James thought the track was clear and so he opened the throttle a little before he suddenly realised that he was hitting some deep sand.

Perhaps he should have slowed down but instead, because the wind suddenly cleared some sand ahead and he saw a hard surface, he opened the throttle to coast through the sand under his wheels. He immediately realised his mistake as he lost control and the bike went from under him. After that he wasn't quite sure what happened until he became aware of David kneeling over him. Afterwards David told him that he'd seemed to be elsewhere for a few minutes and certainly his helmet had suffered a heavy blow on a rock. However, the main problem was that James couldn't stand up owing to a severe pain in his back.

David gave him a couple of pain killing tablets and then proceeded to demount all the bags, bottles and cans on James's bike. Stripped of everything, a bike required two fit met to lift it but with everything on there was no chance of doing it. When the pain killers had started to have some effect, David pulled James to his feet. Although James found this a very painful experience, the fact that it was possible seemed to suggest that he hadn't broken any bones.

The next problem was to lift the bike into an upright position. James was able to offer only a minimum of assistance but, as is commonly acknowledged, in an emergency people sometimes show superhuman capacities and that certainly seemed to be the case here. David somehow lifted the bike and they were able to put down the side stand.

Half an hour later, with the occasional break, David had rebuilt the mountain of accessories and the bike was ready to go. Neither David nor James had discussed the possibility that James might be unable to ride the bike since remaining where they were did not seem to be an option.

With considerable help from David, James gingerly swung a leg over his bike and found that he could at least sit there without experiencing an unacceptable level of pain. Adrenalin was no doubt also playing its part. So it was that they set off once more into the wind, still trying to get to Bordj.

Soon it was dusk and then night fell as though a curtain had been pulled over the world but although darkness added another complication, it also brought some relief as the wind speed decreased and less sand was blown across the track. Their headlights picked out just enough detail for them to carry on slowly. At least they were making progress once more even if they had to ride all night but they didn't have to because quite suddenly James saw something very unexpected and stopped his bike. David pulled up behind him, dismounted and walked up beside him.

'What the hell do you think that is?' asked James

'It's difficult to believe but it looks like an electric light.

'That's what I thought but what's it doing in this God forsaken place?'

Before they had time to speculate further, it seemed as though a figure crossed in front to the light, and then one or two more but they couldn't be sure because it was some distance away.

'How many do you think they are?' asked David.

'Your guess is as good as mine, but I would guess at least four.'

'They could be terrorists,' said David, really thinking aloud.

'They could. Actually I'm surprised they haven't seen or heard us. I suppose if they weren't looking on our direction they wouldn't have seen our dipped headlights and the Honda engines at slow speed are fairly quiet. Anyway, I think I'm going to have to approach them. With my back the way it is, I don't think I can continue much longer and if we stay here they'll almost certainly see us in the morning anyway. Wait here while I go and speak to them. If I don't return for you I suggest you turn back and get to hell out of here'.

James took off his helmet and gloves, hung them on his bike and set off to walk towards the light. Seeing someone arrive suddenly out of the desert night would surprise anyone, terrorist or not, and to see someone wearing a motorcycle helmet would only add to the unease. At least he could show a smiling face. Before reaching what was clearly some kind of encampment he called out from a distance so they were ready for his arrival.

Before he arrived he saw from the single outside light that there were several huts and by now seven men staring into the darkness in his direction. James was relieved not to see any sign of weapons. He walked towards the group and long before he reached them started offering a greeting in French in an effort to sound quite normal. They were clearly agitated and alarmed at his presence, which was hardly surprising. One of them started calling out 'Mohammed' and an eighth man came out of a hut to investigate the disturbance. He appeared to be the leader of the group.

James walked up to him and offered him his hand, which he took.

'I'm sorry if I surprised you but I'm motorcycling and have had a minor accident. I'm looking for somewhere to spend the night. My name is James'.

'My name is Mohammed but what are you doing here?'

James explained that he was trying to reach Tamanghasset but had fallen off his bike. In turn Mohammed explained that they were a group of men employed by an oil company in the area, at which point James added that he was not alone and that he would call his friend over.

Following introductions, Mohammed showed them to a hut which he offered to them for the night. There was nothing in it but at least it put them undercover.

James had heard of Arab hospitality offered to travellers and it seemed to be true. A little later Mohammed returned and invited them to one of their huts.

Inside all the men sat on carpets in a circle round a large bowl. James and David had clearly been invited to dinner.

'I don't think I feel hungry anymore', said David. 'What do think's in the bowl?'

'I have no idea,' replied James, 'but whatever it is we're going to eat it. We can't possibly turn down their hospitality. In any case it's probably only camel and since we've already each eaten a bull's penis on this trip I'm sure we can manage this.'

Room was made for them in the circle and they settled down in the group, who now seemed happy to accept their new companions. Hands were waved to encourage them to dip into the bowl. Fortunately both James and David were aware of the need to keep their left hands in their laps and to greet and eat only with their right hands, the left hand being kept for private functions.

The food in the bowl was rice and some kind of meat, which probably was camel, but it wasn't too bad and even David seemed suddenly to recover his appetite and join in the forage with some gusto. In fact they spent a pleasant hour chatting in French with James as always trying to keep David in the loop by translating. Since crossing over into France, with the single exception of the Englishman they'd met in Hassi-Massaoud, David had spoken only to James. It would be quite a relief for him to find someone else to speak with in English.

In the morning James had an unpleasant surprise. He couldn't move without considerable pain and so he lay on his back contemplating the immediate future and what options they had. When David awoke they discussed the problem and what they should best do. It wasn't an emergency and so there was no thought of calling for outside assistance, whatever that might be and so it was a question of either turning back or pressing on. Their large scale map, the one they had for this route, showed aircraft symbols at Hassi-Messaoud, which they'd already passed through, and at In Amenas, which lay ahead. Clearly there were airfields at both places but they did not know what aircraft or whose aircraft. For all James and David knew, they could be private airfields and aircraft, perhaps belonging to an oil company. Either way it meant James would have to continue riding.

They decided to press on for two reasons: firstly, In Amenas was closer than Hassi-Messaoud and secondly they were not yet prepared to give up. The Sahara is an extremely inhospitable environment and physical fitness is essential. However, there was a possibility that James's back would improve with a little time. The decision made, James took a couple of heavy duty pain killers and shortly afterwards David pulled him to his feet and helped him dress before they went out to say thank you and farewell to Mohammed and his colleagues.

James found getting on to his motorcycle very difficult and painful but once on, and the painkillers having taken full effect, he was able to ride, and so they set off at 8am. Unfortunately, they found that the route ahead was inaccessible and so had to retrace the final 50kms of the previous day's ride, passing the scene of their accident *en route*.

Once on the main track, which they realised they should have taken in the first place, they were able to make good progress but it was a long day's ride with only the occasional camel pack to relieve the view of sand. One pack broke into a gallop at the sound of their engines, leaving the herdsman cursing at James and

David as he chased after his animals. James felt guilty about this but thought getting out of earshot as quickly as possible was the only sensible action to take. At 5.30pm they rode into In Amenas.

As they made their way slowly down the main street, James felt this place was probably the Arab equivalent of a one-horse town of the mid west USA in the late nineteenth century gold rush days, except that it didn't have a decent hotel and a saloon bar and probably lacked a sheriff. At first their hopes rose when they saw a sign to the Grand Hotel but there was nothing grand about the reality.

The reception area immediately gave the game away. The desk was literally rotting away beneath the blistered paint that had been applied many years previously and the whole room seemed to be falling back into the desert on which it had originally been built.

The manager met them with some enthusiasm and showed them to their room. In fact the room was an outside shed on the edge of the desert and the inside was every bit as bad as the outside. It boasted two single beds and, as the manager was pleased to point out, a wardrobe.

Nor was his enthusiasm in any way dampened when, on pulling open the creaking door, all three of them looked down on four collapsed shelves surmounted by a pile of rubbish. Quite how anything could be put into it was unclear. The toilet had not been cleaned for many years and in any case didn't work and so a trowel and a short night walk into the desert seemed the only acceptable option. When the manager asked if they would be eating in the restaurant they thanked him but said they would be providing for themselves.

Later they cooked some of their supplies over a primus stove on the bare boards of the shed and otherwise occupied themselves for the evening and most of the night with the wildlife that seemed to be attracted by the heat and light, and perhaps the smell of the food. The wildlife comprised a range of weird insects and creatures that found their way into the room around the ill-fitting door. Most of these things were unknown to them and seemed quite alien to planet earth.

However their existence in the shed was short lived since James and David, with nothing else to do, dispatched them with the aid of a pair of spare shoes. Their motorcycle outfits, usually used to protect them from the elements and from the occasional fall, offered good protection now against the invaders and so they chose not to undress for the night. In any case James would have found it too difficult.

In the morning James's condition had worsened. He could hardly move with the pain, he had a severe headache, he felt extremely cold and he seemed unable to quench his thirst. Riding a motorcycle had become impossible and it seemed sensible to seek medical attention if any were available. To their surprise the manager said there was a hospital in town, which seemed unlikely, but they set off anyway to find it.

It did not seem to be a friendly town. All the women they saw in the street wore burkas and most of the men wore stern expressions on faces that looked as though they'd been chiseled out of the nearby rock. No doubt life here was hard, and it showed. James had to walk very slowly but they made progress and eventually arrived at their destination which, although it turned out not to be a hospital but a small clinic, was nevertheless welcome.

A man in a white coat explained there was no one there who could help and that they should come back later. When they did they found a very helpful lady doctor who listened to James' explanation of what had happened and then x-rayed James' back. The fact that the clinic possessed an x-ray machine was yet another surprise.

Afterwards a technician asked James to leave the room and invited David in while James sat outside. Ten minutes later, wondering what the technician was doing with David, James went back into the consulting room to find he was examining David's head and David was unable to explain that he hadn't banged his head. Clearly communication had not been entirely successful and so after further words the technician examined James's head instead. The results were that although James had suffered a blow to the head which was causing his headaches, that was unlikely to be a lasting problem.

However, he had torn ligaments in his back which would not be back to normal for several weeks and in the meantime would require physiotherapy. James bought some pills from the clinic to relieve the pain.

Under the circumstances the outlook for further progress looked very poor. Owing to the threat of terrorism they had been obliged to take an unplanned route and were not even sure there was access to Tamanghasset. James could not at present get on his motorcycle, let alone ride it.

Finally, they were now behind schedule and even if they managed in a few days to reach the border with Niger to the south, their visas to that country would have run out and they would be denied access and have to face the prospect of retracing their route up the entire length of Algeria. Unfortunately, the sands of time were running out and so, thinking of the symbol of an aircraft on the map, they decided to explore the possibility of a flight out of In Amenas.

The hotel manager said there was an airfield not far away and an office in town that handled flights. It seemed unlikely in this remote place but he seemed to know what he was talking about even if he knew nothing about running a hotel. And indeed he did. They found the office and were told they could catch a flight to Algiers in five days' time. Even more incredibly, the office clerk said that their motorcycles could be loaded on the same flight. Quite how this would be achieved, they couldn't imagine but it was an excellent prospect compared with their assumption of having to leave them in the Sahara.

James and David still had in mind that they could cancel the flights and continue the trip if James's back improved considerably and if there was still sufficient time before their visas expired. Unfortunately James's condition did not improve sufficiently and their visas to Algeria, Niger and Benin were on the point of expiring when they decided there was no option but to abort the whole trip.

On the day of departure they called a taxi so that James, still unable to ride his bike, could accompany their luggage to the airport. David followed the taxi on his bike, parked it at the airport and then returned to the hotel in the taxi so that he could ride James's bike back to the airport. All should have gone well but James became concerned when David had not returned after what seemed a very long time.

In fact David, who found he didn't have enough money to pay the taxi, had decided to go to a bank with the taxi driver but had had no luck in obtaining money. They had then set off back to the airport in convoy but on the way back the taxi driver had taken a wrong turning and they never saw him again.

At the airfield they were pleased to note the arrival of their aircraft, a Boeing 737 of Air Algeria, but they encountered a problem over their motorcycles. They could be loaded but only with empty fuel tanks, a fact that was made known to them only about half an hour before the flight, and at present both tanks were fairly full. They therefore set about siphoning fuel out of their tanks and into their reserve five litre tanks but getting mouthfuls of petrol that burnt their mouths and throats was not a good start to the trip.

However they succeeded and then tried to give away the fuel in the spare tanks but no one would accept it and so they finally resorted to pouring it into the desert. Shortly afterwards, as they climbed away and headed for a first stop at Hassi-Messahoud, they were looking down on the very inhospitable lunar landscape they had so recently ridden over.

Having landed at Algiers, they booked into a hotel at the Houari Boumedienne Airport. The following day, having already reserved seats in In Amenas on a flight from Algiers to Heathrow in a few days' time, they set about getting their motorcycles dispatched to the UK.

The official in In Amenas wouldn't book the bikes through to London but instead had given them a price and told them they would have to pay cash in Algiers. This was clearly a fiddle which the clerk in Algiers was quite happy to go along with except that he now doubled the price. Five hours later, having jumped through a number of bureaucratic hoops and paid the original sum, they left the freight department and tried to decide how to spend the next few days holed up in the airport hotel.

The first thing they decided was that, despite the element of risk, they were not going to spend all their time in an airport hotel and so they stepped outside to find a taxi. There was a range of vehicles but one that caught their eye was a green and yellow rusty contraption that looked as though it was being held together by string but remarkably was not emitting steam, or at least not at that moment.

They booked it, not simply because it was the cheapest vehicle on the rank, but because of its unbelievable appearance which appealed to their sense of humour. They also quickly found that the owner and driver of this machine was a treasure.

Of course it came as no surprise when he introduced himself as Mohammed but his introduction extended to his house, his family, and his sex life with his wife, which was more surprising. However the highlight of his repartee was his knowledge of British public figures, which included the Queen, Margaret Thatcher, the Queen Mother, Churchill, Tony Blair and Robin Hood, and his insane ability to mimic them. His English was limited and yet he was able to get across immediately their main characteristics in comic strip fashion. James and David decided that he was their man for the rest of their stay in Algiers.

However, not all was plain sailing although the first day went well enough. Mohammed took them on a tour of Algiers, which included the docks, the seafront, the main shopping area, the Casbah and the drug centre. Mohammed dropped them off for a while in the centre but while wandering round the backstreets they attracted the attention of a group of youths who questioned who they were and what they were doing. They seemed friendly enough when they learned of the motorcycling venture but caused James and David to think that staying in the main populated areas might be more sensible.

On the second day Mohammed's car broke down at traffic lights in the town and James and David had to get out and push to restart it, although James was not really able to be of much help. This seemed entirely in keeping with the whole surreal escapade and so caused much hilarity. However, there was a serious side to this as Mohammed explained. His battery was defunct and if he couldn't replace it, he couldn't earn a living and if he couldn't earn a living his wife would without doubt curtail his marital rites. It was that serious. Clearly, since Mohammed lacked the resources to buy a battery, James and David would have to come to the rescue, which of course they did and for the rest of their stay in Algiers Mohammed was their driver and entertainer.

James and David finally got back to the UK, followed three weeks later by their motorcycles, which had been damaged by staff at In Amenas who apparently had dropped them on their sides and loaded them on pallets. David therefore arranged for them to be collected and repaired by a garage close to Heathrow before James and David could ride them back to Norfolk, but at least this gave several weeks grace for James's back to improve sufficiently for him to make the trip.

In fact he'd torn ligaments which took several months to repair, with the aid of a chiropractor. Of course they were both sad that they had not achieved their aim in riding all the way down to West Africa but they had had an exciting and worthwhile adventure. Also, in the final analysis, the decision to cut the trip short was not really one they'd had to make since it had become impossible for them to continue.

A post script to the adventure came later in the form of two press reports. The first, a month after they had returned, was about a convoy travelling south to Tamanghasset along James's and David's original route, under the protection of an Algerian Army patrol. The convoy and the patrol had been completely wiped out by terrorists. Mixed with genuine sadness at the plight of those killed was a slight sense of satisfaction that they had made a wise decision in changing their route.

At least that was how they felt until they read a second report a couple of weeks later. This report explained that a group of thirty people travelling close to In Amenas had disappeared. It is thought they were taken by terrorists but that was never confirmed and the group was never seen again. Perhaps James's injury had been a blessing in disguise.

EPISODE 11 – A VERY FRENCH TRADITION
(2002 – 2004)

Historical Context

__2002__ U.S. and Russia reach landmark arms agreement to cut both countries' nuclear arsenals
__2003__ North Korea withdraws from treaty on the non-proliferation of nuclear weapons and U.S. and Britain launch war against Iraq
__2004__ North Atlantic Treaty Organization (NATO) formally admits 7 new countries: Bulgaria, Estonia, Latvia, Lithuania, Romania, Slovakia, and Slovenia and Israeli prime minister Sharon announces plan to unilaterally withdraw from Gaza Strip

James Winchester continued to work hard from 2002 to 2003 and Skyway Services continued to flourish but he was increasingly becoming aware of the passage of time. It was now 2004 and he was 65 years old. He was not yet ready to retire but on the other hand he was no longer prepared to work all hours of the day. He employed two engineers, two pilots and an administrator/accountant and he did not wish to expand the business further.

He was taking more breaks and a few years ago he'd bought a chalet in the Pyrenees for skiing in the winter and mountain walking in the summer. As usual in the summer, he'd driven down to the cottage for two weeks but as part of that had booked into a hotel in northern Spain for four nights.

It had been a very pleasant four days but tomorrow he would return to his cottage in the Pyrenees for another four days before driving up the length of France to catch a ferry to England. James sipped his beer and watched the sun sliding gently into the Mediterranean.

There were still people on the beach just across the promenade from where he sat on the terrace of the Monterey Hotel on the Costa Brava but the direct heat of the sun had now gone. Instead he felt himself immersed in a warm clamminess that was quite to his liking and such a contrast to the cool average temperature in England. It was also in contrast to the cold sharpness of his beer, of which he now took another sip.

He'd enjoyed the short break and had used the time to explore the area along the coast as far as Cadequez. He'd also been to the Salvador Dali Museum in Figueres and driven down the coast to Barcelona. Yet there was something very significantly missing from his holiday and that was contact with others. Having been once unhappily married, he'd spent most of his adult life as a bachelor and so was quite accustomed to loneliness. Yet he was essentially a social animal and enjoyed many good friendships. Here in Spain he'd met and talked with only one English couple but everyone else he'd met had been either Spanish or German and unfortunately he spoke neither language.

It was therefore with particular interest that he tuned into a conversation in French which was being conducted by two ladies at the table next to his. Although his French had many imperfections, he could understand them for the most part and they were talking about their mother, who lived in Paris. He glanced at them out of the corner of his eye and realised that he'd seen them in the sea earlier in the afternoon and thought that might give him an acceptable entry into their conversation.

'Pardon mesdames, mais c'était vous que j'ai vu dans la mer cet après-midi ?'

He wasn't quite sure that his somewhat inept opening line would be well received but he couldn't think of anything to ask other than if it was them he'd seen in the sea during the afternoon. However, he needn't have worried since they seemed only too pleased to speak.

He wasn't proud of his French but it was rather better than their English and so they spoke in French. He quickly learned that they were two sisters and that one of them, Colette, lived in Paris, whereas the other, Louise, lived in Switzerland. He explained that he'd spent four days at the hotel but that he was due to leave in the morning. They had been there for two weeks but Colette was catching the overnight sleeper to Paris that night and Louise was leaving in the morning for her home in the Valais Valley.

They laughed that they'd been staying at the same hotel but had met only on the last evening. James also learned that Colette was single and Louise married, although no further mention was made of the husband. Colette was petite, almond eyed and very Parisian in a friendly but formal manner. She was wearing a simple but very chic evening dress, embellished by an intricate black and white pendant. Louise had also been born in Paris and had lived there for many years but had been in Switzerland for the past ten years. She was more flamboyant and excitable than her sister and she wore a red summer dress which seemed to match her temperament.

A little later the ladies suggested that they all dine together at their table in the hotel restaurant. Their table turned out to be his as well but they hadn't met over the previous four days simply because they'd eaten at different times. Over dinner, since the ladies didn't have cars, James suggested taking Colette to the station in Figures in his car and of course Louise also came to see her sister safely away on the overnight sleeper to Paris.

On the way back Louise suggested a night cap and so they sat out under the stars and had a cocktail. In the background was the sultry music of a quartet on the terrace. In other circumstances it could have been the start of a romantic affair but James was conscious of the fact that she was married, although he didn't know that she was separated and wouldn't find out for some long time. In the event he said goodbye and went to bed with thoughts of his drive into the Pyrenees the following day.

He thought of the French sisters occasionally over the following months but he had no contact with them until the following May, when he received an email from Louise asking him if he intended going that summer to the Monterey and, if so, when. In fact James had intended as usual to go to his cottage in the Pyrenees and since the Monterey was only another four hours further on, he could easily find time to spend a few days in northern Spain; in any case a beach holiday made a pleasant contrast with the mountains.

The ladies would be at the hotel for two weeks in July and he would go there for a week. The only difference this time was that they would be joined by Marie, a friend who lived in the south of France, but for James the idea of spending a week with three ladies was not unattractive.

And so it was that one Saturday in July he strolled out onto the terrace of the Hotel Monterey and spotted the three ladies in animated conversation, such that they didn't spot him until he had walked right up to their table.

'Oh, la la. C'est James,' exclaimed Louise, the most excitable of the three. She rushed round, gave him a warm hug and of course the obligatory kiss on each cheek. Colette, more reticent than Louise but nevertheless smiling broadly, seemed very pleased to see him and also gave him a hug and a kiss. He was then introduced to Marie and they shook hands.

The week passed quickly and very enjoyably. They breakfasted together, had lunch in the hotel and dined together, either in the hotel or down in the centre of the old town of Roses. During the day they drove around the area, visiting places of interest such Cadaquez village, one of the well-known haunts of Salvador Dali, Figueres to see the Dali Museum and even down to Girona and Barcelona for a day out. In the evenings after dinner they strolled along the sea, stopping from time to time at different hotels for a drink and a dance. James danced with all three of the ladies in turn and consequently had a good deal of exercise each evening.

Throughout this time there was much friendship but no romance. From James's point of view, Louise was out of the question because she was married and Marie already had a boyfriend in her home town. He found Colette attractive but she was very reserved and did not give any signals that she wanted a deeper relationship. And so the week passed.

On the final Saturday morning, they said their farewells on the hotel steps and James drove back to his cottage in the Pyrenees. It had been a most enjoyable week but now he had to turn his mind to some DIY the cottage needed and to chopping down a few trees which were threatening to engulf the sloping grass in front of the house. He liked DIY and tree felling because they were very practical activities in contrast to his normal work and he'd become quite adept at felling even largish trees thanks to the advice he'd received from a woodsman who lived just below. James's cottage was in a forest at a height above sea level of 3,500ft, some 500ft over a village in the mountains.

Often in the mornings he would walk out onto the little patio in front and look down on a sea of clouds, with just the spire of the church rising through like the mast of a sunken vessel. Above, the sun would rise into a clear blue sky.

Maintaining the house and the sloping ground in front was fairly hard physically but he enjoyed the exercise, particularly in that environment. He also enjoyed seeing or sometimes just being aware of the surrounding wildlife. Once, when he and a friend had been at the cottage for a week's skiing and there'd been an overnight fall of snow, the friend had rushed in excitedly while he'd been making breakfast and dragged him outside.

'Come and look at this. What do you think caused these?'

He'd pointed to some large footprints which were impressed in the snow all round the cottage. They were much too large to be those of a dog, deer or wild boar or any of the other animals that were frequently around those parts. David was no expert but to him they'd seemed like the traces of a bear. On the other hand he knew that although there were still bear in the mountains and that a local village, Aulus-les-Bains, had once been the centre of thriving bear trade, there were now very few left. He'd said nothing but the following summer when he'd returned there were post cards for sale in the local bar because, as the patron explained, a couple of bears had been around some of the higher lying cottages.

On this occasion though, James saw no exciting animals, although from the scratch marks on the grass it was clear that wild boar had been around most nights. It was nevertheless with something of a heavy heart that he locked up the house and headed for St Girons and then took the autoroute around Toulouse on his way back to England.

In fact he wasn't far past Toulouse when his mobile phone pinged to tell him he'd received a text message, which he looked at when he next stopped for a coffee further north.

To his surprise he found it was from Louise, asking him what he was doing the next month, August, and whether he would consider visiting her and Colette in Switzerland. He replied, thanking her for the suggestion and promising to give it serious consideration, but by the time he arrived home in England, he'd decided to take up the offer.

He booked a flight from City Airport, London, to Geneva, the added interest being that he'd never before flown from this small airport in east London with its relatively short runway projecting out into the Thames. The take-off wasn't perhaps as dramatic as that at the old Kai Tak airport at Hong Kong, but nevertheless it did afford an excellent view of the City of London. It was a beautifully clear day as they crossed the Channel and flew south over Paris, and even from 36,000ft he could clearly see the roads radiating out from the principal junctions. Before long they reached the Alps and then made their descent into Geneva Airport.

Not surprisingly the Airport reflected Swiss cleanliness and efficiency and before long he was leaving precisely on time on a train from below the airport for a wonderful two hour train journey around Lac Leman, through Lausanne and Montreux and up the Valais Valley to Sion. It was the most beautiful train journey he'd ever undertaken and he would have been content had it lasted longer. It was therefore after what seemed a short two hours that he stepped off onto the platform at Sion, but not without some anticipation of further pleasure to come – and there they were – Colette and Louise. After a bout of warm hugs and kisses, Louise explained that she had booked the hire car as James had asked and that they could now pick it up from the town.

As James drove the car to Louise's village, there were many excited exchanges of information about recent activities on all sides before Louise dropped a minor bombshell, or at least that's how it seemed to James. She suddenly explained that their mother had accompanied Colette to Switzerland and was staying in the flat. Consequently there was no room for James to sleep there. However it was not a problem since Louise had booked him into a very pleasant pension in her village and she was sure that he would be very agreeably surprised. Yet it wasn't that that surprised him. What did surprise him was her next throwaway line that he would be spending the night there with Colette.

In all the time he had spent on holiday with the two sisters, and more recently with Marie, there had been no suggestion of romance and they had simply enjoyed their time together as friends. Now a romance was being thrust upon him and he needed to adjust to the idea.

First, however, he wondered what Colette herself thought about this arrangement. Although clearly she must have given her assent to it, it was possible that Louise, much the more extrovert of the two, had pressurised her into it. As he was driving, he could only listen to Colette's response and not look her in the eye but she sounded genuinely enthusiastic about the idea, allowing for her normally reticent manner.

Louise explained that mother was making dinner for all of them at the flat but suggested it would be a good idea for the three of them to stop at the pension on their way. James could see the flat and he and Colette could leave their cases there. Colette it seemed had already packed hers and put it in his car, which he hadn't noticed. Life was full of surprises.

It was a beautifully maintained and decorated pension, showing great attention to detail, reflected in its lavish furnishings, its paintings and its major domo who greeted them in charming style without a trace of condescension or obsequiousness. M. Leroy was dressed in a startling white shirt, a deep red waistcoat and matching bow tie and he spoke impeccable English and French, and no doubt German too but James was in no position to assess that.

He escorted them up to a bedroom which amply fulfilled the promise of the rest of the establishment, with its rich drapes, charming pictures and four-poster bed. The two sisters, or at least Louise, had clearly put some thought into the somewhat unusual arrangement that was unfolding. No words had passed between Colette and James since her clipped acknowledgement in the car that she concurred with the situation. James suddenly realised how the parties in an arranged marriage might feel but at least he wasn't making a long term commitment.

M. Le Leroy had ceased to exist in the room, although his actual withdrawal had passed unobserved by all three of them. However, his reappearance several minutes later was certainly noted since he arrived flourishing a tray bearing two glasses of champagne for the happy couple. Of course James insisted that Louise and Colette each had a glass and suggested that he himself would take the opportunity of having a shower following his journey. Access to the capacious shower room was gained through two half doors somewhat reminiscent of cowboy western saloon bar doors.

Once inside he quickly stripped to his underwear and was on the point of removing that when he realised he had left his bag of toiletries in his suitcase in the bedroom. After a quick expletive and a moment's hesitation he decided there was no point in redressing since only the previous month he'd spent a good part of a week with the sisters in a pair of bathing trunks little different from the black underwear he was now sporting. Consequently he would simply re-enter the bedroom as he was.

In retrospect James saw the scene which ensued as very much akin to scenes from Brian Rix farces so popular in a previous decade. Also in retrospect, the scene seemed to evolve in slow motion and he imaged it as it would have appeared to the audience in a West End theatre. He entered stage left, purposefully and ostensibly with a calm which he didn't entirely feel, wearing his black underpants. The ladies, ensconced on the bed and sipping their champagne, shrieked at his arrival and gave vent to a series of 'Oh-la-las'.

Louise, in a clearly prepared pantomime, reached into her bag, withdrew a handful of artificial rose petals and threw them into the air, most of them floating gently down onto the bed. This then was the scene that met M. Leroy as he entered stage right bearing a third glass of champagne, clearly not to be phased that his male guest was preparing to spend an evening with two ladies rather than with the one he'd envisaged. However, even he could not have anticipated that his guest would have been preparing so quickly for action that he was already stripped down to his underwear.

The last rose petal settled on the bed, James stopped in mid stride, M. Leroy hesitated momentarily, and the ladies ceased oh-la-la-ing with their mouths still open and their eyes open wider still so as not to miss a single moment of the pantomime. It was of course M. Leroy who restarted the action, moving effortlessly forward, proffering the glass and, at least as far as James could tell, not reflecting any sense of surprise on his implacable features. James, determined not to be outdone in the sang froid stakes, took the glass and thanked him, albeit in a perhaps slightly strangled voice, at which point M. Leroy withdrew gracefully. James wasn't sure whether he caught the slightest glimpse of a smirk as the door closed.

After a quick shower, James drove the sisters up to

Louise's village to meet maman, who'd been preparing dinner in Louise's flat. He wasn't quite sure what to expect or indeed how she would receive him. He also wondered if she'd been party to the arrangement no doubt master-minded by Louise. In fact she was dressed in black and looked very severe, more a member of the French ancien regime than a chic and modern Parisian.

Nevertheless, James would break the ice with his bonhomie which seldom failed to establish a warm and friendly atmosphere.

' Bonsoir, Alphonsine. Je m'appelle James'.

She looked at him without a smile and said, in cool and measured tones, that he would kindly refer to her as Madame Legrand and she would refer to him as Monsieur Winchester, at which point James felt his tried and tested ability to establish an amiable rapport had met its match.

Conversation proved difficult during the meal, despite Louise's gallant attempts to add a little levity. A recurring theme was the excellence of Madame Legrand's pork stew, which in all honesty James had some difficulty in eating but Colette, despite remaining as quiet as usual, seemed perfectly at ease. Occasionally she smiled at James, who hitherto had given little thought to the night ahead but who now began to think about it.

He looked at her as she delicately picked her way through pieces of pork, potato and carrot and wondered if she would be quite so demure and reticent in the four poster bed that awaited them. However, he was abruptly brought back to the present by Madame Legrand who was asking him a question but since he hadn't heard the beginning of it he had to ask her to repeat it.

She was asking him why he'd chosen Colette and not Louise, which was quite a surprise since he hadn't been aware that he'd had a choice of either of them.

Consequently he expressed the first thought that came into his head, namely that Louise was married and Colette was single. This wasn't too far from the truth because that had been his initial reaction when he'd first met the two sisters. Afterwards however, he realised that it was the very demureness and reticence of Colette that attracted him.

Madame Legrand registered no surprise, but then she did not seem readily to express any emotions beyond a faint distaste of rather lesser beings such as himself. So the evening passed, not unpleasantly but rather formally, and it was time for James and Colette to leave.

Fortunately the farewells were not too protracted and before long the two of them were on their way to the pension in the village. It was only now that James began to feel just a little uncomfortable. Reticence was not normally one of his characteristics but then normally a romance would have had some kind of introduction or lead up. As things stood he'd never even kissed Colette, other than a friendly French peck on the cheek, and yet now the two of them were destined for the same bed.

Once passed M. Leroy and into the room, James of course offered to let Colette use the bathroom first while he read a book. After twenty minutes she appeared looking very demure in a light blue silk dressing gown, wearing he knew not what underneath. He quickly grabbed his dressing gown and wash bag and went into the bathroom. When he emerged the room was in darkness and so he slipped off his dressing gown and got into bed, expecting to find her there and yet there was no sign of her. Admittedly it was a large bed and Colette was petite but she really did seem to have disappeared.

'Where are you', he asked. 'Are you in here?'

'I'm here', came the response, and with that she suddenly popped up from the depths of the bed with a laugh and fell into his arms. And so the ice was broken

246

and a night of love ensued.

The morning brought a more sober reflection as he lay in bed with Colette asleep beside him. The idea of spending the next few days with her was delightful but the parallel concept of spending much of that time with her mother was less so and therefore he needed to devise an escape route that would allow him to savour the one without the other.

It was then that he struck on the very attractive idea of going to northern Italy. The Simplon Pass was at the top of the Valais valley and from there it was a drop down via the town of Domodossola to Stresa on Lake Maggiore and then Lake Como, and even Lake Garda if time allowed. To his relief, Colette was enthusiastic about the idea and when they both went up later to Louise's flat maman presented no difficulty and so it was, later that day, that they took the beautiful route up to the Simplon Pass and over into Italy.

It was a long time since James had been to the Lakes and he'd almost forgotten just how beautiful they are. Moreover he'd never been to Stresa on Lake Maggiore, where they made their first stop, and he was delighted with the place. He very much liked the new and old towns of Stresa and was overjoyed with the small islands of Isola Bella, Pescatori and Madre and the ferries that made travel to them so easy. They found a small hotel and explored the area over two days before moving on to Lake Como where they found an even more pleasant hotel overlooking the lake.

On the first morning at Como, Colette got out of bed to stand on the balcony and look out across the Lake. James lay propped up in bed looking at Colette whose slim outline was revealed through her diaphanous nightdress by the sharp early morning light. Behind her small figure the first seaplanes of the day were taxying to take off from the deep blue water. As a pilot taking in the whole scene, James suddenly felt that his life had edged a little closer to Paradise.

All told they spent four days around the lakes before taking the route back to Switzerland and Louise's flat. James and Colette stayed at M. Leroy's pension for two more nights and James felt so happy and so well enough disposed to Mm Legrand that he took her and her two daughters for a drive around the area, including an interesting ride over an unmade road to the ski resort of Zermatt. On his last evening, maman again made dinner, during which she turned to James and very graciously thanked him for taking Colette to Italy for what had clearly been an enjoyable trip.

'The pleasure was all mine,' said James.

'Of that I have little doubt,' she replied archly, but James thought he sensed an uncharacteristic twinkle in her eye. The following morning he parted on good terms from all three and on particularly good terms of course from Colette. They agreed that he would visit her in Paris in the near future.

Afterwards he reflected how strange it had been, that he'd spent two holidays with Colette without the slightest suggestion of romance and then quite suddenly he was involved in a relationship that had obviously been arranged. What was also rather strange was the fact that even now, because of her reserved nature, he felt he knew her very little about her.

He knew she was a senior administrator for a large insurance company, that she had a very sharp eye for detail, that she had quite a keen sense of humour, and that she could be passionate. He also knew that she had a liking for the arts, music and painting in particular. Yet he felt there was much more below the serene surface that he could only so far conjecture about.

He wasn't in love with her but she interested and excited him and he would follow up the suggestion about visiting her in Paris. So it was that several weeks later he found himself boarding the Eurostar for Paris at Waterloo Station, before the service was transferred to St Pancras.

This was his first journey by Eurostar and he was impressed not so much by the speed as by the quietness and smoothness of the trip. After a snack, a glass of wine, a chat with a fellow traveller and the passage of some two hours and forty minutes, he was walking down the platform at the Gare du Nord in Paris and waiting there to greet him was his demure little lady friend in a pretty felt hat and elegant black dress, a style she seemed to favour and one that was very chic. She greeted him with a warm kiss and a hug and for the first time he felt completely comfortable with her.

Colette may have been a rather timid lady in his estimation so far, but in the Parisian traffic she was a tiger and before long they had reached her apartment in to the east of the City, just within the périphérique, on the other side of which lies the Bois de Vincennes. There, over coffee, she explained the arrangements she had made for him to see Paris over the next few days. James had been to Paris before but had never had such a competent and knowledgeable guide, but then she was a born and bred Parisian and she knew her way around.

Of course all the usual visits were on the itinerary: the Eiffel Tower, the Arc de Triomphe, Montmartre, la Place de la Concord, the Tuileries Gardens, the Louvre, the Musée d'Orsay, The Rodin Museum and so on, and James was fascinated and bewitched by it all. He also thoroughly enjoyed the atmosphere of the cafes and bars around the Latin Quarter and St-Germain, including of course the Brasserie Lipp, Les Deux Margots and the Café de Flore. They went to many of the famous sites, including one or two he hadn't anticipated, such as the one recommended to them in Montmartre.

They'd spent a pleasant hour or two looking at the work of the artists, having coffee and generally soaking in the atmosphere when Colette, almost as an afterthought, suggested they should visit the Office de Tourisme just to see if anything in that area had escaped her planning. An affable but somewhat matronly lady was in attendance and helpfully suggested a few things including the Musée d'Érotisme. If he was mildly surprised at this suggestion he was even more surprised by the alacrity with which Colette took up the idea. This was indeed Paris and before long all three of them were consulting a colourful brochure which the lady had produced. Perhaps she thought she could help add a little spice to the lives of her two visitors.

The Musée, which was subsequently featured in the Sunday Times Supplement, is situated down in the Pigalle area not far from the Folies Bergère. It's a tall building on several stories and not in any way overtly salacious, either inside or out, which made it all the more approachable. James was not a prude but he did not consider himself to belong to the dirty mackintosh brigade and to his relief there was no sign of a dirty mackintosh inside the building.

What they did find was a number of exhibitions, some of them permanent, such as those on contemporary art, bordellos and popular art, and others of a temporary nature. Imagery was presented in the form of statuettes, photographs, paintings and drawings and the subject matter dealt not surprisingly with the human anatomy, copulation and various contraptions supposedly used to enhance carnal pleasure.

In a way it was all rather unexceptional – unexceptional that is until James climbed the final flight of stairs to the top floor. As his head rose above the level of the floor he became aware of a somewhat dubious looking male statue, clad only in a leather thong and a rather sinister mask and carrying a whip in one hand.

'Look at this strange thing,' exclaimed James in French, laughing and turning to Colette who was climbing the stairs behind him. 'It's quite bizarre'.

What followed was even more bizarre. The statue stepped towards James and asked him if he wished him to start his act. James could not imagine and did not wish to try to imagine what the man's act might be. Instead he told him that he would happily pay him not to start his act, took Colette by the arm and immediately steered her down the stairs.

'Well, that was a close call', said James, very happy to be outside in the fresh air.

'Oh, I don't know,' replied Colette with a knowing little smile. 'His act might have been quite interesting'. There was more to this demure little Parisian than met the eye.

The whole week was interesting, stimulating and entertaining. It was also quite expensive since Colette, while providing much information and organising a range of visits, made no contribution to the costs incurred. James made a second visit to Paris and exactly the same pattern emerged.

It was while he was thinking about a third visit that he received from Colette a menu from an expensive restaurant in Paris with her choice of dinner. James was by no means a parsimonious person but not for the first time he wondered if he was being asked to buy dinner or shares in the restaurant. Consequently he did not immediately respond but instead discussed the matter with Toby Mitchell, a friend who was a Francophile who'd spent many years in Paris as a diplomat.

'Well, what's the problem old chap? he replied. She's your mistress and you pay the bills. You can't blame her; she's simply following a very French tradition.

James turned this over in his mind and decided that of course Toby was right. Isabelle had organised the stay in the pension in Switzerland on this basis, their mother had accepted the arrangement on this basis, and Louise herself had seen herself in that role from the beginning. The only person who hadn't seen the relationship in that light was James himself. He'd had a rather more romantic concept of his relationship and was perhaps a little disappointed in his own naivety. The acquisition of a mistress was of course a very French tradition but it didn't quite suit James's concept of a romantic attachment. Consequently he wrote a polite note to Colette gently putting an end to their liaison.

EPISODE 12 - LAST TANGO IN BUENOS AIRES (2006)

Historical Context

__2005__ London hit by Islamic terrorist bombings, killing 52 and wounding about 700. It is Britain's worst attack since World War II; the Irish Republican Army announces it is officially ending its violent campaign for a united Ireland and will instead pursue its goals politically; Angela Merkel becomes the country's first female chancellor.
__2006__ In defiance of the U.N. Security Council, Iran president Mahmoud Ahmadinejad announces that Iran has successfully enriched uranium; North Korea test fires missiles over the Sea of Japan; India test-launches a missile with a range of 1,800 miles; Hezbollah, a Lebanese militant group, fires rockets into Israel

James felt he had his affairs under control. It was twenty years since he'd retired from the RAF and he'd expanded his aviation business considerably in that time. More importantly it could more or less run without him, although he continued to fly and do some engineering because he enjoyed it. However, his real function now was to make the strategic decisions and he didn't have to be present all the time to do that. However, he still didn't have very many breaks from work and he had it in mind to take one now.

He was thinking along those lines when he received an email from cousin Elizabeth in Buenos Aires to say that her mother was very ill with cancer. When he was a child his Aunt Bunny had been his favourite relative outside his own immediate family and he'd been unhappy to see her and Uncle George emigrate to

Argentina when he'd been offered an important banking job there forty years previously. George, who'd apparently been something of a philanderer in his day, had died five years ago and Aunt Bunny had subsequently been enjoying life as a merry widow ever since, until her recent illness. In her letter, Elizabeth had written that if James thought about coming out, accommodation would not be a problem. James read into this offer that Aunt Bunny was very ill and that if he didn't go he might not see her again.

Visiting a dying relative had not been the kind of break James had had in mind but he wanted to see his Aunt and he'd never been to South America before and so he decided to go and perhaps to have a look round while he was there. He read a little about the country, confirmed with Elizabeth that he would visit for two weeks, although not all of it in Buenos Aires, and booked his flights from Heathrow with British Airways.

Two weeks later he settled down in his seat in a Boeing 747 for the 13 ½ hour flight armed with two books, a magazine and a newspaper. He didn't mind long distance flights as long as he had enough leg room. There were no letters to write, no telephones to answer, no meetings to attend and no deadlines to worry about. He could drink a little, eat, read, watch a film or simply sleep but first he thought about Aunt Bunny and Cousin Elizabeth.

He'd no reason to believe that Aunt Bunny had been unfaithful to Uncle George but he did have the impression that she'd been a lively girl before and since her marriage. She'd always had very strong principals about some things such as liberty, honesty and fairness but had always seemed unconstrained by protestant strictures about sex. Not for her the cold severity of the northern European indoctrination. Although born and bred in Shropshire, she had more of a Mediterranean temperament, warm and sunny most of the time but always with the possibility of the odd thunderstorm.

He remembered her as a warm, compassionate and passionate person who was generous to a fault. He'd met her and George several times over the years when they'd been on trips back to the UK and although he'd seen her getting older, her nature never seemed to change. However, he was prepared to find a change now that she was ninety and in ill health. It would be unfair to expect otherwise.

Elizabeth he didn't really know. She'd been eight when she and her parents had left the UK for Argentina and eighteen when he'd last seen her on one of her infrequent trips back to England. She was now forty eight years old, twenty years younger than he was, and he had no idea what she was like or what she did for a living. He hoped she took after her mother rather than her father, who'd always struck him as being a little pedantic.

James enjoyed the flight but had had enough of it by the time they touched down at Ministro Pistarini International Airport, Buenos Aires. Elizabeth had said she would be waiting for him in the arrival lounge wearing a yellow dress, which seemed a good choice of colour. He couldn't imagine there'd be too many other women wearing the same colour and there weren't.

As he exited the door from the customs area and came into the arrival lounge she was waiting for him, and he was very pleasantly surprised. She stood out immediately from the other people waiting to greet their friends or loved ones or business associates. It wasn't simply the yellow dress but also the tanned skin, the blond hair, the broad smile and the gleaming white teeth. She looked a picture of health and fitness. She seemed to recognise him immediately and came up to him with arms outstretched to greet him.

'Good Morning Cousin James. I hope you had a good flight. It's lovely to see you again after all this time.'

She gave him a warm hug and he smelled the musk of her perfume and felt the soft contours of her body against his. She had developed into a mature and very attractive woman and his visit to South America had already taken on a new dimension.

Elizabeth had her own house outside Buenos Aires but she drove him to her mother's apartment close to the city centre. In any case she'd been staying there most of the time since her mother's illness had manifested itself. On the way he learned that she worked in finance in the city and was something of a wheeler dealer in shares. She was personable, clearly intelligent and very likeable. She was also unmarried but he didn't discover any more about her on the short trip to Recoleta, a downtown residential neighbourhood. However he did learn that Aunt Bunny had good days and bad days with her cancer and that today seemed to be one of her good days.

In fact he was surprised when he met her because she appeared to be in excellent shape and it was difficult to believe she was seriously ill. She was also as he'd remembered her: warm, lively and adorable and that's how she still seemed, despite her age. Elizabeth had clearly inherited her mother's temperament.

Aunt Bunny was very pleased to see him and expressed her gratitude that he had flown out to see her. He declined an offer of a meal, having eaten fairly copiously across the Atlantic, accepted a cup of tea, and was pleased when Aunt Bunny suggested he should take a nap after his trip. It was 2pm when he woke up to find the two ladies had just finished lunch. He gratefully accepted a salad and an offer from Elizabeth to take him down town. She had some shopping to do but also suggested he might like to have a quick look at the city.

On the way she explained that Buenos Aires was the most visited city in South America, ahead of Rio de Janeiro, and the second most visited city of Latin America, after Mexico City. She told him that it's known for its European-style architecture and rich cultural life and, in terms of its population, is considered to be one of the most diverse cities in Latin America. She was obviously proud of her city and anxious to show it off to him.

Later she was to return to pick up her mother for dinner but in the meantime, having quickly done her shopping, she took him down to La Boca, a popular destination for tourists visiting Buenos Aires, with its colourful houses and pedestrian street, the Caminito, where tango artists perform and tango-related memorabilia is sold. Several of the tango girls tried to entice him into their bars but Elizabeth kept a firm hold on him.

'This is an interesting place to visit during the day,' she told him, 'but I suggest you don't come down at night. A young man like you could come to harm. In any case you'd probably lose your wallet'.

They sat at a table in the street and watched the people passing by as they drank a beer. Here and there in the street were tango girls who posed with tourists in dramatic dance poses for photographs. Back home a man could claim to have danced the tango in the street with an attractive Argentinean girl. The place was exotic, colourful and lively and struck an instant chord with James and the way he was feeling. He was on holiday and this was an encouraging start.

Later, they picked up Aunt Bunny and found a delightful restaurant down town where you could pick out your own pieces of meat and fish and have them cooked to your liking. Banks of cold savoury foods and sweets ensured all tastes were catered for. James had already decided to pay for the meal as a way of responding to the hospitality he was receiving but he was delighted at the price. In recent years the exchange rate of the Argentine peso had fallen dramatically against most major currencies which made life difficult for most Argentineans and very cheap for visitors.

Over dinner the ladies asked James where he planned to visit during his stay and he explained that before leaving the UK he had bought air tickets for brief trips to Iguazu and Bariloche. Aunt Bunny thought it an excellent idea that he should look round Argentina while he was there and said he'd chosen wonderful places to visit. Iguazu was the name of the river separating Argentina from Brazil and it was renowned for its waterfalls. Bariloche was an old Swiss, German and Austrian settlement near the western border close to Chile. Aunt Bunny was sure he would find both fascinating.

When Elizabeth excused herself to go to the washroom, Aunt Bunny added that it was a pity he couldn't take her daughter with him. Elizabeth had recently broken off a liaison and needed a break with a 'nice' man. Apparently the boyfriend hadn't been a nice man. James had no time to think about the suggestion, let alone make a response, when Elizabeth returned.

'I was just telling James it's a pity you can't go with him on his trips. A break would do you good'.

'Yes, I'm sure it would, but unfortunately I really can't get away from work at present or I would accept. That is, if he's offering'. She smiled sweetly at James.

The following evening, Elizabeth and James went downtown together, had dinner and then went on to a tango club. Of course it was Elizabeth's idea since she was a very competent tango dancer and James had no idea how to do it but she was a good teacher and he was a quick learner, particularly after a couple of whiskies.

He picked up a few basic steps and a few twirls and after a nervous start really began to enjoy the erotic movements and the pulsating rhythm of the music. He also enjoyed being with Elizabeth who was gorgeous, exciting and enticing.

It was midnight when they left club and headed off in Elizabeth's car. The trip to her mother's apartment couldn't be more than fifteen minutes and so after twenty minutes James was surprised they had not arrived. After another five minutes they passed through automatic wrought iron gates into the drive of a very attractive house.

'Is this your home?' asked James.

'Yes. While I'm living with mother I like to check on it from time to time.'

'Do you normally do your checks at this time of night/'

'No, but I thought we could have a nightcap and I could check on the house at the same time.'

'What a sensible idea,' said James approvingly, his mind wandering on to other possibilities.

The house was chic and ultra-modern and the fittings, fittings and furniture were in excellent taste, which didn't surprise him. She was a chic and cultured person herself.

He sat down on a white leather settee in front of a realistic gas fire while Elizabeth poured him a whisky and dry ginger.

'Take your shoes off and make yourself comfortable'.

While she poured herself a martini and put on a little soothing music and turned down the lights, he did as she suggested and felt his feet sank into the deeply piled cream carpet.

'Thank you for a really pleasant evening, Elizabeth. I really enjoyed it.'

'Well it hasn't quite ended yet.'

'No, of course not,' he said rather lamely. 'Your good health.'

She sat down beside him.

'I've enjoyed the evening very much as well,' she said. 'I haven't been out with a man since I finished an affair six months ago but I think I'm returning to normal.'

'I'm pleased to hear it. Was it difficult to finish the affair?'

'Yes it was. I was very fond of him but we simply weren't suited for the long term'.

'And that's what you're looking for, a partner for the long term?'

'At my age, yes, but in the meantime I also need some warmth and passion from time to time so why don't you kiss me?'

'I didn't think first cousins were supposed to do that sort of thing,' he added smiling.

'It's not wise for first cousins to get married and have children but I wasn't thinking of either this evening.'

He kissed her tenderly on the forehead and then on her lips which were moist, open and inviting.

'I think we should discuss this further in the bedroom,' she said.

In the bedroom there didn't seem to be much need for discussion, at least initially. She was wonderfully warm, passionate, inventive and ultimately tender and it was only later that they discussed the whys and wherefores of their lives: what they'd done in the past and what they hoped for in the future. Then they decided that in the immediate future they'd better head back to mother's apartment or there'd be embarrassment all round. Mother might well assume what they'd been up to but at least they could put up a pretence that they'd been dancing until 2.30am.

In fact over breakfast in the morning Aunt Bunny expressed her hope that they'd had an enjoyable evening, looking knowingly at James and he thought he detected a slight smile around the corners of her mouth.

'You certainly look well this morning my Dear,' she said, turning to Elizabeth.

'Yes, thank you Mother; going out with James did me a world of good.'

'I'm so pleased. You've not been yourself since you ended your relationship with Simon. Now you're much like your old self.'

They all knew what had taken place and they all seemed delighted with the outcome. It was a far cry from the reaction of the vicar of Alderley Edge and his wife all those years ago when he'd sampled the delights of their daughter. Now he experienced the rosy glow of having been of service to a fellow human being. What a lovely way to help another, he mused to himself over a boiled egg.

He spent the next morning around the apartment helping Aunt Bunny since Elizabeth was at work and the afternoon in the City, or the Paris of South America as it was sometimes known. The following morning he was down at the Aeroparque Jorge Newbery airport to catch a two hour thirty minute flight to Bariloche where he'd made a reservation for a couple of nights.

His tourist book told him that Bariloche, situated in foothills of the Andes on the southern shores of Nahuel Huapi Lake close to the border with Chile, had had a Swiss settlement in the nineteenth century, which accounted for the preponderance of typically Swiss style chalets and the manufacture of chocolate in the area.

There had also been a large influx of Germans over a number of years but what the guide book didn't mention, and what he'd learned from the Internet, was the deliberate policy of President Peron to actively attract Nazi SS officers to Argentine, as a result of which many finished their days in Bariloche. These included Adolf Eichmann, Josef Mengele, Aribert Heim, Erich Priebke, Eduard Roschmann and "Bubi" Ludolf von Alvensleben. There was even a story that Hitler and Eva von Braun had not died in his Berlin bunker but had escaped to Bariloche and lived out their days there.

One version has it that they escaped from Berlin in 1945 and hid at Hacienda San Ramon, six miles east of Bariloche, until the early 1960s, although another version says they lived on the estate of Inalco. This was all very interesting as background information but what he found on arrival was a very pleasant and pretty little town by a beautiful lake. He decided to spend the rest of the day in the immediate vicinity and to take an excursion the following day. He was looking forward to the excursion but would have been even more excited had he known what lay in store.

The following morning he boarded a coach outside the hotel along with a group of other tourists and they set off for a pleasant ride to one of the surrounding lakes. There they boarded a boat before cruising down a large and beautiful lake surrounded by snow-capped mountains, the whole scene reminiscent of the Alps. He was struck by the calmness of the water that gave rise to reflected mountains almost as perfect as the real mountains above them. He also thought that the fleeing Nazis must have felt quite at home here.

Eventually the boat pulled into a little landing stage behind which was a charming restaurant in log cabin style where lunch was to be served. The restaurant was tastefully decorated inside and he selected a table in the centre of the room. The waiter brought him a bottle of water; he ordered a small bottle of red wine and was studying the menu when someone spoke to him.

'Excuse me, Sir,' but my mother asks if you would like to join us'.

He looked up and saw that he was being addressed by an attractive young woman of about thirty five. He guessed she was Argentinean but she spoke English almost without trace of an accent. He looked across the room and saw an even more attractive woman smiling at him from another table.

'Thank you; that's very kind of you. Yes, I'd certainly like to join you.'

He followed the daughter to her table where the mother extended her hand and laughed.

'You must think me very forward but we saw you sitting alone and thought you might prefer to have a little company. Please sit down. My name's Sophia, Sophia Torres, and this is my daughter Lara'

'James. James Winchester but how did you know I was English?' asked James, first shaking hands with the mother and then the daughter.'

'Well it would be true to say because you look English, but I actually overheard you speaking to someone on the boat. We're Argentinean and we live in Buenos Aires'

'And you both speak remarkably good English.'

'Thank you. You're here on holiday I assume?'

James explained about his aunt and then went on to add a little about his current life.

'You didn't mention if you're married, James,' said Sophia.

'No, I'm not married. How about you?'

'I'm a widow and have been for the last twenty four years'.

'That's remarkable,' commented James, thinking aloud.

'Is it?'

'Well, I simply mean that it's surprising that

someone so attractive should be single for so long.' James was concerned about seeming ingratiating but had been forced into an explanation.

'Thank you for the complement but I loved my husband very much and I've never found anyone to replace him.'

They chatted further over lunch about their lives and interests but James learned nothing more about the husband. Afterwards they boarded the boat together and set off for the next destination, where they were shown a very old tree and then climbed a large number of steps to gain a good vantage point with a splendid view. The atmosphere was very happy and there was much laughter as they took photographs of each other.

Sophia and Lara had one camera between them and before long the battery was flat and so James used his camera to take all the remaining photographs. Of course this meant exchanging email addresses so that he could send on the pictures to the two ladies. They were returning to Buenos Aires in the morning and so they decided to meet for dinner in Bariloche that evening.

Before the day was over James had developed a strong liking for Sophia. She'd confessed to being sixty five years old but could easily have passed for someone in her early fifties. She had raven black hair, a dazzling smile and a figure to die for but there was a depth to her that he found particularly fascinating. She was intelligent, cultured, sophisticated and she reminded him of his first love in Venice; in fact she was not dissimilar and she was the brightest prospect he'd found since those early days. He decided he needed to see her again in Buenos Aires and so suggested dinner there when he'd returned. She agreed and gave him her telephone number.

In the morning, he saw them off at the airport and spent the rest of the day on a second, shorter excursion but his mind was more on Sophia than on tourism. The following day he caught a flight back to the capital, told Elizabeth and Aunt Bunny all about his break in Bariloche and rang Sophia to arrange dinner for two days' later. Elizabeth was pleased for him that he'd found someone nearer his own age and wished him well.

Aunt Bunny had had a bad spell while James had been away but was now much recovered and looking forward to going out and, since it was Saturday and Elizabeth was not at work, the ladies suggested they should all go out for lunch at the Gato Blanco restaurant. James had assumed the restaurant was somewhere towards the centre of Buenos Aires, but he was wrong. They walked from the flat in Belgrano to a railway station and caught a train in the opposite direction to Tigre on the delta further up the River Plate.

Whether the Plate is a river or not is open to question since it's really a marginal sea or inlet from the sea at the confluence of the Uruguay and Parana Rivers from where it flows eastward into the South Atlantic Ocean. At its widest point it's about 87 miles. The restaurant is somewhere in the delta about a fifty minute boat trip from Tigre. Although James prided himself on his navigation skills, 'somewhere in the delta' was the closest he could come to after the meandering boat trip, but the restaurant was a very pleasant surprise.

It was situated on the edge of the water and beautifully appointed with large areas of seating both inside and outside. As it was a hot day, they chose to sit outside and James ordered a bottle of champagne. With the Argentinean peso so low against the pound sterling it wasn't very expensive but he'd have bought it anyway. He was very upset about Aunt Bunny's condition and wanted to do what little he could to give her a modicum of pleasure.

Perhaps he should have felt a little awkward about

Elizabeth but she seemed to be in high spirits and not all distressed that he seemed to be on the point of finding another woman. In any case, she'd made it clear she was not looking for a long term relationship with him and so he put any potential misgivings to one side and enjoyed her company. Considering Aunt Bunny's condition and her prognosis, it was a very happy interlude and one that all three would remember with pleasure and that James would also remember for his admiration of Aunt Bunny's positive attitude and enduring courage.

James was due to take his second excursion in three days' time, the day after he had arranged to have dinner with Sophia and he suddenly had an idea. Why not invite her to join him on his trip to Iguazu Falls? Although it was short notice she might be able to find the time. First he rang Aerolineas Argentinas to make sure there was still a place on the flights and then the Hotel Cataratas to ensure there was another room available. He succeeded in both and then rang Sophia; to his delight she accepted the invitation.

The night before they left for Iguazu, they had dinner in Buenos Aires at a restaurant with music. After each course Sophia wanted to dance and for the most part they danced the tango. James confessed that it was Elizabeth who'd taught him the few steps he knew but didn't go into detail about his relation with her. In any case that had been a one-off incident and was now finished. Sophia was impressed that he'd picked up the dance so quickly and set about teaching him rather more complicated routines.

It was a glorious evening. Sophia looked devastatingly attractive in a royal blue dress, which set off her jet black hair, her deep blue eyes and her rich, red lips. She moved with an ease, grace and sensuousness that did full justice to the seductiveness of the dance and the rhythm of the music, gliding, turning, arching her back and from time to time pausing momentarily and striking an exotic pose. At such times she stared him straight in the eye with a look that seemed to bore into his sole.

This was not simply a woman but also an embodiment of all that was glorious, enticing, intelligent, and desirable about the female of the species – and he wanted her with an almost uncontrollable passion. Unfortunately this was neither the place nor the time, and the time was 1am. They left the restaurant and James escorted Sophia back to her house and then took the taxi on to his Aunt's apartment. They had a flight to catch at 10am.

Iguazu Falls are situated on the river Iguazu which divides Brazil from Argentina at the latter's most northern extremity. On the flight up there, they passed Uruguay on their right hand side and then overflew the inland north east Argentinean promontory with Uruguay giving way to Brazil on their right and Paraguay on their left. For most of the two hour trip the terrain below was typically dry but quite suddenly the vegetation changed to equatorial forest. Shortly afterwards they landed.

There was a Hotel Cataratas bus at the airport and after a short trip they arrived. When they were shown to their rooms, James was once again struck by the strength of the pound sterling against the Argentinean peso. For what seemed a very modest sum they'd acquired two enormous bedrooms in a five star hotel and from their windows looking to the rear, they could see a delightful garden and an alluring swimming pool. Their three day stay looked very promising.

After a quick shower, they met in the bar for a gin and tonic and then sat down for lunch.

'Would you like to go to the Falls this afternoon or wait until the morning?' James asked.

'Well this is my country you know and I've been

before. So why don't you decide? But if you want my opinion, I suggest we take an easy afternoon by the pool, look at the Falls in morning from our side and then from the Brazilian side in the afternoon. There would still be another day to take a second look if you fancy it. The weather looks good for both days.'

'That sounds like an excellent plan and in any case how could I go against the suggestion of such a captivating woman?'

'My mother always told me to be careful of men who flattered so easily.'

'And did you always follow her advice?'

'Well, that's for me to know and you to wonder.'

After lunch James was reading a book on a sun bed by the pool when she emerged from the hotel wearing a wide brimmed straw hat, sun glasses and a red one-piece swimming costume. She could have been a Hollywood film star and a number of male heads turned to admire the view.

She dropped her hat and glasses on a sun bed next to him and suggested a swim, to which he readily agreed. It was very hot under the full glare of the afternoon sun and he was perspiring freely.

Sophia dived in first making hardly a splash as she cut cleanly into the water. James followed, making a slightly less clean entry but continuing under water until he'd completed a length.

'Do you like swimming?' she asked.

'Very much, although of course I'm not as good at it as I used to be when I was younger and swam regularly'. He was thinking of the time in Cyprus when he'd gained the gold award for personal survival without any preparation.

They laughed, chatted and swam gently about, thoroughly enjoying the occasion and each other's company but after almost an hour decided to try a little more sunbathing. James read his book while Sophia, who hadn't brought a book with her, closed her eyes and appeared to doze.

Perhaps she did for a little while but then she gently put her hand across to touch and hold his arm. He put his book down and held her hand in his. They seemed so well suited that it was an entirely natural thing to do. They both felt very close.

'I feel as if I've known you for a long time,' she said eventually.

'I feel the same way too,' he added with complete conviction. He'd had a number of close liaisons over the years but the only other time he'd felt quite as strongly for another woman was when he'd met Libena in Venice.

'Let's go up to my room,' said Sophia.

'Are you offering to show me your etchings?' asked James.

'No, but I hope I can offer you something of interest.'

They went up to Sophia's room still in their swim suits and immediately she'd closed the door she put her arms round him and kissed him gently on the lips.

'I like to take a shower after the pool. Why don't we take one together? There's ample room'.

She slipped off her swimsuit in the bathroom, which was really a wet room with a shower at one end, smiled at him unashamedly and walked into the shower area. He took off his trunks and joined her. As the water splashed over them, he took her in his arms and kissed her wet lips passionately, her breasts pressing strongly against him and his rising need probing between her thighs.

'Patience, James, patience,' she murmured in his ear.

'It's no good talking to me,' said James, 'You need

to talk to him'.

'Oh, I see. He has a mind of his own I suppose.'

'Yes he does and we certainly don't always see eye to eye. At school I often had to walk about the corridors with a copy of the Times to cover his inappropriate behaviour.'

'And does this fellow have a name of his own as well as a mind.'

'His name is Oscar.'

'Well Oscar,' she said, taking hold of him firmly. 'I've got plans for you.' She then took James by the hand and led him into the bedroom where they spent the rest of the afternoon and early evening making love. At first there was an intense urgency as they came together and he plunged into her repeatedly until they lay beside each other to recover. Then their love making was more tender and protracted until once more their passion reached an intensity that exploded and shook them to the core.

At last with passion spent and now calm, relaxed and deeply contented, they felt the need for a drink and dinner and so showered, dressed and went down to the bar. Now their relationship was different. They were in love and felt as one with each other. There was tenderness, sensitivity and an unspoken understanding between them that had not existed before. There seemed less need to fill every gap with words because they could read with other's thoughts and feelings without a constant need to speak. When they did speak it was to some purpose. Later that night they went to sleep in each other's arms and they did not make love again until the early hours of the morning when James felt Sophia gently caressing Oscar, who had already awoken and prepared himself for action.

In the morning after breakfast they caught a taxi to the Falls on the Iguazu river. Sophia had been a number of times before but James was stunned and delighted at what he saw. The Falls covered a huge area and comprised a number of branches that split from the main river before cascading off the edge of a very high cliff.

To reach the most impressive part of the Falls, the Devil's Gorge, they traversed a walkway that took them across part of the river until they were able to look directly down a thundering cascade of white spume that filled their ears with its roar and dampened their faces and clothes with the mist thrown up into the air. It was a majestic sight and a reminder of the heart stopping power of nature.

In the afternoon they went across to the Brazilian side of the Falls where a path wound through a forested area and where coati, small animals of the raccoon family, repeatedly crossed in front of them. Suddenly the path reached the edge of the cliff and once more they were treated to a spectacular view. Again they were almost lost for words and most of the time simply watched in stunned silence. It was a day they would never forget, partly because of what they seen but also partly because it was the start of a compelling love affair. Unfortunately it was also almost the end of the affair.

That evening, after dinner in the hotel, they danced to the music of South America provided by a quartet and of course, amongst other dances, they moved, gyrated and swayed to the tango. They were both exhilarated and ecstatically happy and felt certain they would spend the rest of their lives together. The feeling continued throughout the following day and the day after, when they caught a flight back to Buenos Aires.

James had not forgotten his original intention in coming to Argentina and so was anxious to get back to see Aunt Bunny as soon as possible. Having dropped off Sophia at her house, he ordered the taxi back to Aunt

Bunny's apartment in the Belgrano area of the city. When Elizabeth opened the door he knew all was not well. She was almost in tears as she ushered him into the living room.

'I'm afraid mother's taken a turn for the worse while you've been away. I had to take her to hospital for an overnight stay. She's back now but she's heavily sedated and the specialist says there's nothing more they can do in the hospital and that the end is fairly near. I hope you've had an interesting time with your new friend but I'm glad you're back in time.'

Sophia had suggested that he stay at her house during his remaining three days in Argentina but James now decided he must stay with Elizabeth and her mother to be close at hand in case of emergency. The following afternoon Aunt Bunny seemed to rally a little, to the extent that James felt able to accept a dinner invitation from Sophia. Sophia was keen not only to see him but also to show him properly round her house.

It wasn't clear how they would arrange to spend their time together in the future but James had already hinted that he was now, at the age of 68, finally ready for retirement. Whether that would be in England or in Argentina, or indeed elsewhere, they had yet to discuss. He didn't think he would have too much difficulty in selling his business and then he would be a completely free agent.

Sophia had prepared a wonderful candlelit dinner for them both and afterwards they sat listening to music and discussing their future together. It was unsaid but assumed by both that they would make love before James would leave to return to Aunt Bunny's. At about 10pm James went to the toilet and on his way down the corridor noticed an open door with the light on inside the room. It appeared to be a library or office but what particularly caught his attention was a large framed photograph of an officer in Argentine Air Force uniform. He wouldn't normally have been so rude but the picture intrigued him. Of course Sophia had told him she was a widow and that her husband had been in the military but more than that he didn't know.

On returning to the living room he told Sophia that he'd noticed the photograph from the corridor and asked if that had been her husband. She explained that he'd been on duty as a pilot at Port Stanley, during the Malvinas Conflict as she called it, when the airfield had been subjected to an attack by RAF fighters. Her husband had attempted to run to his aircraft to get airborne but had been killed on the ground.

'I'm terribly sorry to hear that,' he said, not adding that he himself had taken part in the war. 'What was the date?'

'He was killed on 11 May 1982', she said. 'It was two days before our wedding anniversary'.

James felt a terrible chill run down his spine. The date was indelibly imprinted on his own mind because that was the date when, with two other Harriers, he'd carried out a ground attack on Port Stanley Airfield. He'd been part of the attack that had killed Sophia's husband and had quite possibly been the direct cause himself of his death. He felt dreadful and unable to grasp immediately the full significance of this new turn of events.

'Are you all right, James?' she asked. 'You look quite pale. I loved my husband very much you know, but it was all a long time ago and life must go on.'

'Yes, of course,' mumbled James, desperately thinking of some excuse to avoid telling her the truth. 'I didn't want to say anything earlier as you'd prepared such a lovely meal but I felt a little strange earlier today. It might be a virus or something I ate earlier.'

'Well you silly boy. You should have said

273

something. How do you feel now?'

'I'm awfully sorry but I don't feel too sharp. I'm sorry to spoil the rest of the evening but I really think I should go back to Aunt Bunny's. We can talk in the morning.'

'Of course you must and I'll drive you back but do you think you could manage one dance before we leave?'

'Yes of course,' he replied and so they danced the tango. It was his last dance in Buenos Aires.

During the night he wondered what he should do but constantly came back to the thought that no matter what his feelings for Sophia he could not continue his relationship with her. Should he tell Sophia the truth or should he come up with some other explanation? His mind was in turmoil.

The immediate problem was deferred by the occasion of another. Elizabeth came into his room in tears to say that she thought her mother had just died. Together they checked for her pulse and for any sign of breathing but there was no indication of life and Aunt Bunny was already feeling cold. Her spirit had clearly departed. They called for a doctor who confirmed that Aunt Bunny had died.

James stayed in Buenos Aires to help Elizabeth with the funeral arrangements and during this time he saw Sophia from time to time. At first Sophia assumed that James was still unwell and then she turned to Aunt Bunny's death as a reason for James's preoccupation. Eventually she came to the realisation that his ardour for her had cooled. She told him that she very much regretted his change of heart since she'd thought they were looking forward to a wonderful life together but there was no use in pretending and she wished him well. Perhaps they could write to each in the future.

On the flight back to the UK James wondered if

he'd done the right thing. Perhaps he should have told Sophia the truth and perhaps he would write and tell her when he'd cleared this mind. The only certainty for him was that he could not continue the relationship under the circumstances whatever Sophia might think or say. In fact months later he did write and tell her the truth, partly to clear his own conscience but also to let Sophia know that she was still the most desirable woman he knew but by then she'd already met someone else.

EPISODE 13 - GOING DUTCH (2007 - 2008)

Historical Context

<u>2007</u> Romania and Bulgaria join the European Union, bringing the number of member nations to 27; Russian president Vladimir Putin announces that the country will suspend its participation in the Conventional Forces in Europe Treaty, a cold-war era agreement that limits the deployment of heavy weaponry; Gordon Brown replaces Tony Blair as the prime minister of Great Britain (June 27); The African National Congress chooses Jacob Zuma as its leader

James Winchester was a lucky chap and he had the decency to acknowledge his good fortune. His business had been a great success but it no longer needed him and he was preparing to sell it and invest the proceeds.

He had another, perhaps less important although nevertheless interesting reason to think himself lucky. In 2006 he'd met a glider pilot in Norfolk who'd asked him if he'd be interested in a gliding holiday in South Africa. Apparently he knew a few glider pilots there and in particular the leader of the group, Richard Venter, who lived in Durban and owned a couple of gliders. The plan was that the group would meet at Richard's place and then drive the 875 kilometres, to pass to the north of Lesotho via Ladysmith and Bloemfontein, and arrive at Gariep in the Karoo. Here they would glide for a couple of weeks at an airfield which opened for only three months each year. Because of the heat, the airfield was famed for its powerful thermals.

James had emailed Richard to ask if it was all right for him to join the group and had received a very encouraging reply which had sparked off a regular correspondence. Over the months which followed his plan for a two week trip had expanded to five weeks, at least three of which would allow James to make a tour of some of the more interesting parts of South Africa. Richard had kindly offered to lend him one of his two cars.

Just before the Christmas of 2007 James caught a flight from Heathrow to Johannesburg and then a connection to Durban, where Richard met him and took him to his house on the outskirts. They stayed there for a couple of days, during which time James had a good look round Durban and met the rest of the team, and then set off for the ten hour drive to Gariep.

The two weeks gliding at Gariep in the Karoo was excellent and after that James had set off south to start a tour of the country in Richard's BMW. He'd driven straight down route N1 to Beaufort West to spend the night in an old hunting lodge, and in doing so had stepped back a century into something which could have been from the film 'Out of Africa'. From there he'd spent ten days travelling to Cape Town, Stellenbosch, the Garden Route, the Transkei, and Durban. Now, having called in for a couple of days to see Richard who was back home, he'd travelled further north and was just entering the small town of St Lucia in the Greater St Lucia Wetland Park on the Indian Ocean.

The tourist office directed him to an excellent bed and breakfast run by an elderly Afrikaans couple and before long he'd showered, changed and was walking down the high street in search of an evening meal. The street was a collection of mainly white and pretty one-storey buildings liberally interspersed with restaurants and bars. As night was beginning to fall the one important thing to remember, a point reinforced by Rika, his landlady, was not to take an evening stroll off the high street and down towards the Umfolozi River. The river was teeming with crocodiles and hippos which had an unpleasant nocturnal tendency of coming out onto dry land from time to time. She'd told him a story of a newly-married couple who'd not heeded the warnings and had decided to swim just near the edge one evening. Tragically she'd been taken by a crocodile. Civilisation and raw nature lived cheek by jowl in a place such as this.

The high street was teeming with life, much of it in tee shirts and jeans, but with a smattering of more elderly gentile people, the ladies in pretty cotton dresses and the men often sporting white straw hats and summer jackets. James found December in South Africa too hot for a jacket and wore a short sleeved shirt and slacks.

He concentrated on his primary concern, to find a cool beer in a shaded area, and a thatched bar surrounded by tables and chairs under leafy trees offered promise. The first beer barely touched the sides of his throat and it wasn't until he'd started the second that he became aware of two women at an adjoining table. He was surprised it had taken him so long to notice them since throughout his gliding period, and subsequent travelling, the one comfort he'd lacked had been feminine company.

One of them was blonde and fairly amply built and the other slim and tall with dark brown hair. He tuned in to their conversation and reckoned they were Dutch, which almost certainly meant they could speak more than adequate English. He had no understanding of Dutch but he did hear the name Hluhluwe-Umfolozi, which was the name of a game reserve he intended to visit the day after tomorrow. Since he understood nothing else they said he thought he would try to strike up a conversation, if only for a little companionship.

'Forgive me for interrupting, ladies, but did I hear you mention the Umfolozi game reserve?'

The blonde girl smiled a sweet smile and replied, 'Hi! Yes, we were just discussing our plan to drive there the day after tomorrow. Do you know it?

'No, but I've been well briefed by a friend, and by coincidence I'm driving there myself the day after tomorrow'.

'Well that's great', said the dark haired girl. 'Perhaps you could tell us a little about it. Why don't you join us'?

James moved over to their table and introduced himself. They did likewise and he discovered that the blonde was called Salvia and the brunette, Gabrielle, and that they both came from Amsterdam. This was helpful since he'd been there and was able to discuss a little about the city and particularly about the art galleries. He also told them as much as he'd learned about the game reserve.

He found both girls attractive. They were very different in appearance in that Salvia was on the heavy side, but gloriously upholstered, whereas Gabrielle was like a lean and hungry racehorse champing at the bit, but both had an excellent sense of humour and a lively 'joie de vivre'.

They were all drinking beer but switched to red wine with the meal and the conversation flowed easily. However, like James, Salvia and Gabrielle had had a long day's drive and by 10.30 pm they decided to go back to their respective B&Bs and meet up in the morning to take a river trip and to visit the wetlands. James went to sleep that night wondering how far the new friendships might develop. He felt very contented and looked forward to the morning.

When he arrived, they were already at the river landing stage and greeted him warmly, each giving him a hug and a peck on the cheek. They paid their fares and took up their seats near the prow of the boat. As the boat pulled away the Captain, an amiable chap originally from London called Steve, started his commentary. He had a well-rehearsed patter which he interrupted from time to time to comment on wildlife of special note as it appeared and there was plenty of note, particularly the crocodiles and hippopotamuses. The latter were clearly discernible in families whilst the crocodiles occasionally broke the surface with a swirl or dragged themselves onto the bank.

James found the trip very interesting but his attention was frequently distracted by the presence of the girls who appeared to enjoy flirting with him. He sat between them and occasionally they both put a hand on his knee. On one occasion Gabrielle put an arm round his neck and put her face so close to his that he was almost tempted to kiss her. It might have been his imagination but Salvia seemed frequently to position herself in such a manner as to afford him a clear view down her cleavage. They also made it known that they did not have any boyfriends. Was he imagining all this? Had he been away from feminine company for too long or were they really being a little more than friendly?

This happy little excursion eventually came to an end as they docked back at St Lucia and then made their way into town for a sandwich before heading north for a drive round the wetlands. Since James had elected to take his vehicle and drive there was little scope for physical contact, although the conversation was quite frequently suggestive. The river had provided a wealth of interesting fauna, including an eland and a sea eagle. By comparison, the wetlands were disappointing and they saw little; perhaps they were simply unlucky, which is sometimes the case on such expeditions. After arriving back in St Lucia, they parted, agreeing to meet during early evening for a drink and a meal.

Back at his B&B, Rika, his Afrikaans landlady,

made James a welcome coffee and he settled down to read a little more of his current book, a history of the Zulu Wars. After the game reserve, he intended visiting the scene of the British Army's defeat at Islandlwana in 1879 and the subsequent defence of Rourke's Drift. In fact he'd read only a couple of pages when his mind began to wander back to Salvia and Gabrielle and to his thoughts about them.

He liked both of them, even though they were very different, and he found difficulty in deciding on his preference, not that he thought he was going to be offered any sort of choice but speculating and hoping did no harm. They both appeared to enjoy his company and had made no effort to seek out other male company since he'd met them the day before. Perhaps they simply regarded him as some kind of protection in a foreign land that was not without its dangers. The latter seemed a much more likely possibility and so he put his over-active imagination to rest.

That evening they found a different restaurant, drank the same beer and talked about the trip in the morning to Hill Top. Afterwards they found a cosy little bar and drank some more beer, James sitting between Salvia and Gabrielle. At one point, after he'd told a funny story, Gabrielle turned and kissed him. His spirits rose and he began to think that there was more than a faint chance that things would turn out well.

The next day they drove in convoy to the game reserve via Mtubatuba, an all-black township. They stopped briefly but didn't feel welcome, which was hardly a surprise considering the general poverty of the town. Eventually they reached their destination. The entrance to the reserve was about 17km from the accommodation but the drive was interesting, with frequent reminders about the importance of not leaving the car. On the way they saw zebra, giraffe and monkeys but the girls were particularly taken by a family of rhinoceros that parked itself about 30 yards in front of their cars and looked at them inquisitively, if not a little threateningly. In the lead car James felt extremely impotent with the realisation that either of the adults could have crushed his little car, with him in it, simply by leaning on it. After about fifteen minutes the male decided that the interlopers were unworthy of further attention and he imperiously led his family off down a slope.

They reached the central accommodation area, which was indeed on top of a hill with commanding views of the surrounding hills in all directions. In the spacious reception area they were warmly greeted, registered and given the keys to their sleeping accommodation, which comprised thatched rondevals. These were round and reminiscent of Zulu huts but there the similarity ended since the rondevals were furnished to a comfortably high standard with all the conveniences of modern hotel rooms.

They were situated about 50 yards from the reception and restaurant area and James was pleased to note that he and the girls had been allocated rondevals next to each other. They unpacked their cases in their respective rondavels, showered and then returned to the bar and restaurant area by reception for a coffee.

Large windows afforded an excellent external view of the hillsides and without leaving the restaurant they could watch several giraffe and buffalo grazing in the warm afternoon sun. However, at this point James was more concerned with the internal view afforded by Salvia and Gabrielle. Salvia had almost squeezed herself into a shirt and a pair of shorts but an attractive and rather large expanse of pink flesh remained uncovered. Gabrielle's tee shirt revealed disconcertingly prominent nipples. However, James was not alone in admiring the internal view. They were joined by a handsome man in his mid-forties wearing safari clothes who introduced himself as one of the rangers anxious to ensure that all was well with the guests. James noticed that his anxiety had not extended as far as another table occupied by a couple of men who looked new and rather lost.

'Would you like me to explain the safari tours available?' asked ranger Peter Brown, to which the two girls readily assented and James reluctantly agreed. Essentially there was a dawn tour and a night tour and it was advisable to book both in order to see a good range of animals. However, it was also possible to go out in one's own car. Peter Brown then went on to expand his theme.

'The Hluhluwe Umfolozi Park is the only park under formal conservation in KwaZulu Natal where the 'big five' occur, these being the lion, elephant, leopard, buffalo and rhinoceros. Set in the heart of Zululand, this is the oldest game reserve in Africa, along with nearby St Lucia Reserve, where Zulu kings such as Dingiswayo and Shaka hunted and put in place the first conservation laws. The Reserve was established in 1895.

James's reservation about Peter began to dissipate. He was, after all, quite a pleasant chap and the information he provided was both relevant and useful. So much so in fact that he prompted Peter to say a little about the Zulu War battles of Isandlwana and Rourke's Drift, which had taken place not far from where they were. Peter also provided more information about the Boer War battles in Kwa-Zulu Natal.

On Peter's advice the three decided to book the night safari after dinner and another early morning one, and perhaps to do one of their own later during the three days they were to be there. After that they left to walk to their accommodation. On the way Salvia said,

'Don't you think the set up a little strange?'

'In what way?' asked James.

'Well, here we are walking along outside without any protection from the wildlife, which could be anywhere around here. I mean there are lions, leopards and God knows what around here.'

'Perhaps they don't come near here because of the people,' ventured Gabrielle.

'Well, the monkeys do because we were warned to close our windows. And when we come back from dinner it's going to be quite dark down this path.'

'Then I'll make sure I'm with you,' said James, 'since they're obviously going to prefer to eat you two before me.'

'Perhaps it's just as well we have James to protect us then,' said Gabrielle, putting her arm round his waist, and James felt very happy. Nor had they appeared to harbour the slightest interest in Peter Brown.

Having showered and changed they met outside their rondevals to walk back to the restaurant for dinner. It was dark, the air was heavy with humidity, and the cicadas were creating a cacophony of sound. James's earlier bravado during daylight was now tinged with a frisson of excitement. Perhaps Salvia had been right in voicing her anxiety. The only view they had was of the path, illuminated by rather dim lights, but on either side was complete blackness. There could be any number of creatures watching their progress towards the restaurant and it was with some unspoken relief that the three of them reached the sanctuary of the brightly lit reception area, bar and restaurant.

It was only then that James noticed how the girls were dressed. Salvia was wearing a very chic blue dress that contrasted well with her blonde hair. It also gave welcome prominence to her ample figure. Gabrielle was wearing a slinky black dress which clung tightly to her lean figure. Both looked absolutely stunning.

The choice of food was delicious and interesting. For the less adventurous there was a range of familiar foods, including steak, pork and fish. For those who welcomed a challenge there was ostrich and crocodile. They accompanied the meal with some excellent South African wines from the Stellenbosch area north east of Cape Town. It was an altogether enjoyable evening with the added anticipation of a night safari to follow.

It was a warm and balmy night as they set off in the safari truck for a planned trip of one and a half hours but Peter had warned them that it could get cooler later on and so they all had long trousers and sweaters. James was happily squashed between Salvia and Gabrielle as the truck headed off down a narrow road away from the domestic accommodation. The trucks lights picked out the road head well enough but not the surrounding areas. However, the driver had a couple of swivel search lights available for watching the animals later on. The driver, Henk, was at pains to explain that he would do his best to find animals by visiting favourite spots but that there was always a strong element of luck involved in a successful safari.

But Lady Luck was clearly with them. After only about ten minutes, Henk brought the truck to a gentle stop, switched on a searchlight and whispered 'Leopard!' Sure enough, loping silently through a group of trees was the ghost-like image of a leopard, white and silvery in the piercing light from the truck. It moved gracefully and effortlessly, clearly tracking its unfortunate prey. James was impressed and the girls were beside themselves with excitement, gripping his arms tightly until all trace of the leopard had disappeared.

With senses sharpened by the experience, all the tourists on the truck peered with acute anticipation into the darkness ahead, wondering what sights lay in store.

James shared their interest and even though his anticipation of possible delights to come occasionally took a rather different direction, he was nevertheless keen to see what animals might be abroad in the surrounding darkness.

Suddenly the truck stopped. Henk appeared to have seen, heard or sensed something. There was silence in the truck as everyone peered into the night until, after several minutes when James was just beginning to think that Henk might have been mistaken, a great crashing of branches announced the arrival of a huge bull elephant immediately in front of them on the track. It was no more than thirty feet away and it was immense. James thought to himself that the word 'awesome' is one that is frequently overused; on this occasion it seemed entirely appropriate.

This was not an example of an immovable object meeting an irresistible force since neither appeared to define the truck with all its occupants, which seemed to shrink in size against this grey monster. The elephant and the truck remained stationery, the elephant gazing down at the truck with what appeared to James to be a disdainful if not malevolent eye. James felt the two girls holding on to him tightly and at other times would have welcomed the physical contact but at this particular moment he experienced a level of concern which tended to dampen his ardour. The path did not seem wide enough for the animal and the truck to pass each other and the animal did not seem inclined to move back into the trees.

If James momentarily felt himself to be bereft of a plan of action, the driver did not. Henk blasted the horn and drove at the elephant, which seemed to James to be an absurdly dangerous tactic. The elephant gave an exasperated snort and surprisingly allowed itself to be edged into the trees to make way for the truck. As the truck passed by, the elephant was so close that James could have reached out and touched it, but he refrained from doing so. Most of the tourists in the truck breathed a sigh of relief and a number gave nervous laughs. Salvia and Gabrielle, no doubt fired with adrenalin, gave James a hug which he had hardly deserved since he had felt as apprehensive as they had.

The remainder of the trip was interesting but certainly not as gripping and they came back to Hill Top at midnight. Perhaps under normal circumstances they'd have been ready for sleep but with adrenalin still in their systems, they felt the need for a nightcap. Since the bar was closed they returned to James's rondeval where he was able to provide the girls with a glass of wine and himself with a beer. They sat around and discussed the trip until there was little more to say about it and then went on to elaborate their plans for the remainder of their time in South Africa once they left the game reserve in forty eight hours' time. Salvia and Gabrielle were intending to head down to Cape Town, whereas James was intent on driving on to the Drakensburg Mountains.

By 1am all three of them felt it was time to sleep and the girls left for their accommodation next door. James crawled thankfully into bed, all thoughts of seduction long since expelled from his thoughts, and fell immediately to sleep.

He was awoken by a shout, followed by a stifled scream and without hesitation he leapt out of bed. The noise seemed to come from the girls' rondeval and in any case the next nearest accommodation was some distance away. He arrived at their door in his pyjamas and slippers and was about to knock on the door when a further scream prompted him to try the door immediately. Not surprisingly it was locked.

'Salvia! Gabrielle! What's the problem?' he

shouted.

'For God's sake help us', shouted Gabrielle. 'There's a snake in our room and it's enormous'.

'Can you open the door?' asked James.

'No!' cried Salvia. 'It's between us and the door, but please do something quickly. It looks very dangerous and we're terrified'.

The obvious answer it occurred to James was to rush up to the centre and seek professional help but it would take time to get there, to wake someone and for them to get down here. But the situation demanded immediate action and so he would have to do something himself. But what? He was unarmed and didn't know what to expect on the other side of the door, other than some kind of large snake. Simultaneously the dreadful thought struck him that they were in the middle of black mamba country.

'Oh shit! Not that, dear God, anything but that'.

He had read about the black mamba before coming out to South Africa and seen photographs. He remembered reading that it is the longest venomous snake in Africa, growing in length up to anything from 8 to 14 feet in length. It is reputed to be the fastest snake in the world, capable of moving from 10 to 12 mph, and very aggressive if cornered. He particularly remembered reading that a bite from a black mamba is almost always fatal, and death follows very quickly. The elephant now seemed a friendly alternative.

'Hold on,' he shouted. 'I'll be back very quickly.' Clearly he couldn't crash into the room without any kind of weapon and so he dashed back to his own rondeval and looked around for something to use. A sub-machine gun would have met the purpose but failing that he grabbed a broom and the lid of a dust bin which was just outside. Back at the girl's rondeval he noticed a length of tree trunk being used as a flower bed edging and decided to use that as a battering ram to get through the locked door.

It was heavy but with the rush of adrenalin in his veins he could have lifted and thrown a telegraph pole. The door didn't look too stout. He swung the log back and then literally threw it at the door, which gave way with a resounding crash. James immediately picked up the broom and the dustbin lid, the latter as a shield, and stepped in through the doorway.

With incredible luck the log had not only crashed through the door but also temporarily trapped the snake, which now turned its head to face the new arrival. It was huge and James had a brief moment to see that it was a green grey colour and that as it opened its mouth it was black inside. It was indeed a black mamba. With the dustbin lid held high as some kind of protection, he swung the broom handle at it, catching it just below its head. It was not enough to do it any serious damage but enough to deter it for a moment, particularly as it was still hampered by the log across its body. This gave James time to get in a second blow and this time, with a better aim, he caught it squarely on its head. It lay on the floor temporarily stunned and James didn't hesitate. He clubbed it time and time again, at least ten times, until its head was a squashed red mess and the brute was clearly dead.

It was only then that he looked at the girls. They were standing on top of a double bed holding on to each other and still looking very white and terrified, but clearly unharmed.

'Come round to my place,' said James, 'until we've got this mess sorted out.'

The girls edged very gingerly past the snake and with relief walked the short distance to James's rondeval, where they burst into tears and gave him a delicious hug and a kiss and he gave them each a whisky and water.

'The windows are closed and I'll close the door behind me,' he said, 'but I must go up to the Centre and report this right away. I shan't be long and you'll be perfectly all right.'

'Thanks James', said Gabrielle. 'We'll be perfectly fine now. Why don't you have a whisky yourself? You look as though you need it.' He did and then left for the central block which housed the office and restaurant.

In fact there was a receptionist at the desk on night duty and he wondered if after all he should have run up there in the first place and got him to find a ranger. On the other hand it would still have taken time and perhaps too much time before one of the girls, or perhaps both, had been attacked and quite probably killed. The desk manager was quick to appreciate the situation and to call out a duty ranger, who was on the spot in ten minutes.

James outlined the incident briefly and they both went back to rondevals. The girls were both now more relaxed, thanks to the whisky, but still showing signs of their unpleasant experience. James and the ranger, a young man called Garth, went next door to examine the carcass of the mamba.

'You were extremely lucky to do what you did without getting bitten,' said Garth. 'I certainly wouldn't like to try that. Our advice to our clients is always to call in a ranger but I can appreciate you needed to act quickly. I should think your friends are very grateful,' he added, and James thought he caught just the hint of a smile.

'I'll bring a truck down right away and get rid of this brute. I'll also call in a cleaner and get the mess cleaned up so your friends can go back to bed.' A quantity of blood had seeped onto the floor from the battered head of the snake. It was only now that James felt a shiver of fright about the whole event. Until that moment he'd been on a high with adrenalin coursing through his veins. Garth's parting remark was to the effect that, contrary to the Game Reserve's advice, the girls had left open a window, which is how the snake had gained access.

Garth went back up to the Centre and James returned to his rondeval to explain to the girls what was happening. It was 2.30am but no-one was ready for sleep and so they drank beer while the girls discussed every aspect of the events of the evening: what might have happened: what did happen: how brave James had been: how they would probably have died but for his intervention. James said little, feeling a little embarrassed at the girls' adulation of his heroics, and yet at the same time pleased that had not let them or himself down. He'd never before seen himself as a hero and was more than a little surprised at what he'd done but he'd really done it in the heat of the moment without much time for thought.

A little later the ranger knocked on the door to say that the girls' rondeval was ready and so they could go to bed. There would be an internal investigation and all of them would be required to make statements in the morning. It was also possible that the local police might conduct their own investigation.

The girls seemed reluctant to leave and eventually confessed their concern. James tried to assure them that there couldn't possibly be a reoccurrence since the windows and door would be firmly closed but that wasn't enough reassurance for them. Their suggestion was that he should sleep in their rondeval, which contained a spare single bed. From his point of view, events had taken an unexpected and rather strange turn. He was actually going to sleep in the same room as both of them but in his own bed, which was not quite what he'd been hoping for. He could not help but remember a saying he'd once heard. 'Cheer up. Things could be worse, and so he cheered up and things got worse.'...as they did.

At least, he thought to himself as he pulled the sheets round him in his single bed, you're very tired and so you shouldn't have any difficulty in falling off to sleep, and indeed he didn't. The problem was that he woke up at some time during the night to an initially strange sound, which turned out to be heavy breathing, although not that of a person verging on snoring in their sleep. This was an altogether more urgent sound of breathing which was now accompanied by periodic groans. His growing fear was confirmed by a few whispered words, 'Shhh...James might hear', followed by, 'Don't worry, after what he's been through he won't wake up until morning.'

There followed more subdued groaning followed by sighs of satisfaction.

'Oh no,' thought James. 'Oh bloody hell, no!' The girls were making love in their double bed. They were in fact lesbians, and with that his dreams of the past 48 hours fell tragically to earth like beautiful white ring doves caught inadvertently in a spray of buckshot.

EPILOGUE – 2008

Historical Context
2008 Cuban president Fidel Castro permanently steps down after 49 years in power; Democratic senator Barack Obama wins the presidential election against Sen. John McCain.

Shortly after returning to the UK James had a meeting with his staff to explain his wish to sell the business and retire. He had not been looking forward to telling them because of the uncertainty it would create for them but he needn't have worried. While they were kind enough to say they would be very sad to see him go, they also saw it as a great opportunity for themselves. They had anticipated that at some time he would want to retire and had already had discussions among themselves. Their decision had been that when the time came they would pool their resources, add a mortgage, and offer to buy him out.

This came as a very happy release to James who was only too pleased to accept their offer. He might have gained more on the open market but he wasn't greedy and he could see how much they wanted to become co-owners of the business. They had a grand dinner to celebrate his departure and James was free to take whatever route he wished for the remainder of his life.

He'd enjoyed his cottage in the Pyrenees but thought that it was now time to sell it and buy a more permanent residence in France. He did this but retained his house in England as a bolt hole should he ever need it. Within six months he was living in south west France and enjoying his retirement in a new setting. Initially he had no ties but then, inevitably really, he met a French lady and she moved in with him. As far as anyone knows they are still living there together.

AUTHOR

Michael Brookes was born in Manchester and later, following a grammar school education, studied English and history at Liverpool University. Called up for National Service in 1959, he took a three year short service commission in the Royal Air Force which he later converted to a permanent commission, finally retiring in 1986. He then worked as deputy director of a regional local government body for sixteen years, during which time he took a master's degree in business studies, and was subsequently self-employed for six years as a private consultant. He now plays badminton and golf, writes, paints watercolours, is learning to play the saxophone and spends much of his time in France.

Printed in Poland
by Amazon Fulfillment
Poland Sp. z o.o., Wrocław